Masquerade

& Other Stories

Marija Elektra Rodriguez

HUNTRESS INK

DEDICATION

This book is dedicated to my family.
To Rogelio, who indulges my passion for
horror and life in general.
To Kata, Giovanni, and Angelo, thank you for
all your love and support.
To Vero, I'm forever grateful to my milkmaid.
To Elurra, you are the sparkle in our eyes.

CONTENTS

CONTENTS

CONTENTS

ACKNOWLEDGMENTS

Thank you to Chris and Dorothy for taking a punt on me. I hope it paid off.

Jackie, who has been my editor on this literary journey, I'm grateful for your guidance and gentle hand.

To all the darklings at SM Lit, you keep the Gothic genre alive in all of its various incarnations. The world needs more outlets like this.

Thank you to Rogelio and Elurra, who tolerate my midnight escapades to storyland and provide inspiration for so many of my tales. Love you both.

1 IN LOVE WITH DROWNING

touched a fingertip to the water's surface. Fluid rings fluttered from the contact, a ripple in the giant looking glass of the lagoon. I had injected the water with a pulse, and I felt it reciprocate, breathe salt into my lungs. I knew that I was finally home.

He floated toward me from beneath the surface, his sapphire eyes blending with the lagoon. Indolent eyes, taking me back to those sweaty nights of my adolescence, when sex was our only poison, strong enough to dilate the pupils and dissolve memories.

From underwater, he whispered to me. His soundless lips moved in a slow, sinuous pulsation, in perfect cadence with the ripples from my fingertip.

"Eva."

Then the water flattened and he was gone.

Agrigento, 2010

"Eva?"

I felt Alvaro's hands on my bare back, nails raking at the knots in my shoulders. I was lying against the cool limestone barrier of the lagoon, and his nutmeg fingers felt delicious as they danced over my agitated body.

"I heard it was an ancient wishing well," he said, gesturing absently toward the water hole. "There must be an underground water source running right through this valley of pagan temples." Awe washed over his features as he inhaled the scenery.

I'd forgotten what it was like to look at Espiritu Santo with virgin eyes. The way the water played tricks on your mind, inviting you in, but not letting you leave.

"You're right, but it's forbidden to wish for certain things. It's forbidden to wish for the dead to return," I whispered. I turned the old story over in my mind. It was an ancient wishing well of sorts, but the villagers had neglected to tell him the dark history behind the site.

"There was a sacrificial pit built over the lagoon in the Archaic Period. The Greeks would send virgins to collect the tears of the dying in little perfume vials, and then sprinkle those tears into the water as an offering to chthonic gods." I breathed the words out, barely audible, as though I were locked inside a hallucination.

The sun caught the water at that moment and brought me out of my lethargy. It shone against the lagoon's cobalt face, bathing us in amber and peach. I could almost see the *parthenoi*, in that luminous brilliance, as they dripped the tears of the dying into the water. The same sun shone on me as it had on them, and this made me want to see if there was any truth to the old myths.

"Is the name Latin?" he questioned, his hands probing deeper into my flesh. His French was cut with a Tunisian-Arabic accent, his voice like velvet, decadent and smooth.

"Bourbon," I replied, "they captured Agrigento in the eighteenth century."

"It's so...ethereal." He paused, carefully selecting his words. "You never told me why you left Agrigento all those years ago, why you haven't been back until now."

As we sat in the endless silence of that moment, the ruins of the Doric temple began to cast shadows over the lagoon. Black fingers gradually crept across the water's surface with the setting of the sun. The lagoon felt out of place in the arid valley, surrounded by the dusty earth of Agrigento and the honeycomb necropolis of its ancient inhabitants.

"No, I never did tell you why I left." My voice was filled with calculated indifference.

And I don't intend to, I thought.

I pulled on the knot of my bikini top. The fabric gently fell away. Slowly, I turned onto my back and offered him my breasts.

Alvaro, his fingers clumsy with anticipation, began to kiss at my body as though he were a starving dog, a faint, brutish sound escaping his throat. I couldn't understand why we were together, why he stayed with me. I was bones wrapped in grief.

"Alvaro," I whispered into his ear, lingering on his name so that it came out more like a breath than a word.

"Mmm?" he hummed from somewhere near my neck.

"I forgot the contraception. Will you run back to the hotel and get it?"

"We don't need it," he quickly replied, and continued to work his way down my décolletage.

"Alvaro," I continued, softening my voice and stiffening my body, forcing him to abandon his indulgence, "I don't want a child. We've talked about this already."

He exhaled heavily, frustrated, and rolled his body away from mine. A hand passed through his hair, and it seemed to get lost in his black tangle of curls.

"No." He paused, bitter overtones invading his voice. "You just don't want a child with me."

Another endless silence followed. The day seemed filled with them. I didn't feel like fighting with him again.

I had scratched that wound many times before. Perhaps he was correct, but I just let his words hang and didn't offer him any comfort.

He stood up, shook the dusty earth from his legs, and walked away.

Marseille, 2002

I rested my tired arms against the wrought iron railing of my balcony. It was just large enough to fit a tiny table and two chairs. And a handful of flowers stolen from a churchyard. Perfect.

Through the haze of summer rain, a peach-colored sun burned across the bay, bathing Marseille in golden dust. It gave the bare flesh of my arms a sepia hue, as though the entire city were drenched in honey.

The drops of rain fell like ice cubes on my skin. My hair stuck to my back and the tops of my breasts in long black streaks. But I didn't care. Everything was new and fresh, making me dizzy with possibility.

It was a liminal time; I stood between the start of euphoria and the end of restraint.

The emotions in my blood were as foreign to me as I was to Marseille. I was sixteen, a runaway, and living on my own for the first time in my life.

This is what it means to be alive, I thought.

I absently rubbed the scar on my right palm, a nervous habit from my former life. As I stood in the rain, I inhaled the smells of the city, a cacophony of scent. The shower seemed to toss them all together. The salt from the bay mixed with the asphalt of the street and the rust on my terrace.

A gargoyle protruded from a niche in my wall, a claw extended to scratch at the vacant air. It was decaying beauty, covered in moss and darkened with age. I was utterly alone, and it felt like paradise.

"You love the rain too?"

Startled, I jerked my head around, the wet hair veiling my vision.

I noticed his eyes first, an intense shade of sapphire contrasting brilliantly with his burnt-cinnamon skin. They were such a vivid color, causing me to feel self-conscious about my lack of clothing and disheveled appearance. I pulled the hair away from my eyes and tucked it behind my neck, partly to keep my hands occupied.

I said nothing. After an uncomfortable silence, he spoke again.

"I'm so sorry. I didn't mean to…" He was standing on the balcony next to mine, an apologetic look on his face. He extended a hand over to me, a warm smile playing on his lips.

"I'm your neighbor, Edmund," he continued with inviting eyes. Our balconies were less than half a meter apart, so he could easily reach me. Conscious of the way my wet clothes clung to my body, I had crushed my fingers against my chest. I hesitated briefly and then leaned over, extending my hand to meet his. There was a horrible scratching sound. Loud and sharp. The grinding of metal against metal. I felt my head tip forward and the railing give way beneath me.

I shrieked. It was six stories straight down to the pavement, and half my body was dangling across the railing.

My heart hammered in my chest, air caught in my throat. I envisioned my cracked head on the footpath below, gelatinous tissue seeping out of my ears and nose.

In the confusion, Edmund grabbed hold of me roughly. Our eyes met briefly, and he looked as scared as I felt. Then the apprehension dissolved and relief played out on his features.

"You okay?" The words slipped through the grin on his lips. He looked close to thirty, but when he smiled in that way, he could have been a teenager.

I laughed uneasily, but with relief. The iron barrier had dropped sharply and crashed against the tiles, the bolt tangled in an elaborate wrought iron rose. It was still attached to the wall—barely—and jutted out at an awkward angle.

"Yeah, I'm…normal." I had meant to say that I was fine. My French was sparse, and I still stumbled for the words, reaching for my native Italian. He cut me off, his voice clinical and calm.

"Don't lower your arm."

I stared at him blankly, not understanding his instruction.

My hand was resting on my temple, pulling back a streak of hair that had fallen across my eyes. My thick, gypsy black hair, the only thing I had inherited from my dead mother.

Edmund took a step back and then jumped across the railing of his balcony and landed on mine, knocking the table as he did so. He grabbed my right wrist with both his hands and squeezed it tightly.

"You're going to be fine. You're going to be okay."

I stared into his whirlpool eyes, not understanding. I hadn't realized how heavily it was raining. My skin felt soaked, my head disoriented, as though I were drunk.

I glanced at his hands clutching my wrist. They were covered in blood, as was my arm. My eyes traveled to my white shirt. It had turned crimson.

The queen of hearts painting all her white roses red.

I had torn my forearm open, ripped across the vein vertically from wrist to elbow. It was surreal; I didn't feel any pain. I just watched dumbly as my wrist vomited blood onto Edmund.

Then instinct flicked on and I felt the alarm rise in my chest. I turned to enter my apartment and slipped on the viscous fluid. The terra-cotta tiles were covered in my red honey.

Intense dizziness washed over me in that instant. I was about to black out. The blood was all over my thighs and feet. My head was hammering with the beating of my heart, my eyelids dragging up and down against my vision.

Edmund was speaking, but I couldn't understand him. His voice was soundless, faraway, locked behind those brilliant eyes.

Then all of Marseille went black.

Agrigento, 2010

I sat on the limestone stairs for hours after Alvaro left.

In the reflection of the water, I could see my entire life. The acid youth of beatings and prostitution in Agrigento. The feverish captivity as a stowaway aboard the *Sancta Sophia* as it cut the waves to Marseille.

And Edmund. Most of all, I could see Edmund again.

I didn't mean to cry, didn't mean to break the superstition. Who even believed in such things anymore? I felt the wetness on my cheeks and thought that it might be rain. My tears caught the Mediterranean sun and were briefly illuminated, shining like the eyes of a forgotten god. They dripped into the sapphire water and disappeared, absorbed into the looking glass.

It's forbidden, I thought. But my mind had breathed the words my lips could not.

I wish we were together again.

Marseille, 2002

"You're talking in your sleep."

I heard wind chimes in the background. Some indistinct birdsong from my youth, with soft, high notes that cascaded into a dark opus.

My mouth was dry and my throat ached. I wanted hot milk and honeyed bread—and a shot of bourbon to ease the thudding in my mind. I forced my eyes to open, my long eyelashes blurring my vision like streaks of tar.

"Drink this." Something warm flooded my mouth. I was ecstatic, for an instant, as the painful dryness of my tongue was comforted by the fluid. Spiced wine. Lemon and cinnamon boiled with agar. I felt it deep within my abdomen, mellow and piquant, seeping into my blood like poison.

"You split your vein open, then hit your head. You lost a bit of blood. But you're okay. Lucky for you, I'm a doctor." His pale-blue shirt was on the couch beside me, smeared with my blood. I enjoyed the look of his body; his spicy skin matched the wine. I wondered what he tasted like.

"Where am I?" It was almost my apartment, but not quite. The mirror image.

"This is my place. See that door?" He gestured toward a wall with an ornate tapestry hanging from it, the fabric depicting Psyche and Eros in an embrace. I could make out a doorframe beneath the tassels of the carpet. "It connects our apartments. This used to be a hotel, Le Méridien."

"That explains the gargoyles."

He laughed and his smile was warm. He moved to sit on the floor beside the couch where I lay, his face close to mine. I could smell him then, the salt from his skin mixed with the copper from my blood.

"You live alone, don't you? You're so young. Too young to be on your own." This was the voice of a doctor, with empathy and concern. I felt ashamed. My first instinct had been to try to bed him, as though I were some kind of stray animal. He was not like the village men I was so accustomed to. And I was no longer a child of the streets. I no longer needed to sell my affections and fight off beatings.

"I'm twenty-five," I lied. My voice sounded false, even to my own ears.

"Sixteen," he countered. He was correct. Dead-on.

"That's not what my lease says." I had saved and stolen enough money to rent the small apartment on the *rue du passage* for a month. The landlord hadn't asked any questions, and I hadn't offered him any answers. Cash was the only language of delinquency.

"What's that tattoo on your hand?" His eyes followed my arm and came to rest on my right palm.

The symbol of three blades of wheat in the shape of a *trinacria* had been burned into my flesh.

"I can't tell you that." My voice was unsteady, catching in my throat.

I had never talked about my mark with anyone. I hadn't needed to in Sicily. Everyone understood what it meant.

Edmund stiffened. "I'm not going to interrogate you. Your business is your own. But I'm going to take that carpet down and leave the door unlocked. Whenever you need someone…" He paused, staring into me with his eyes like fire. I had to look away. The moment felt intensely intimate, and it made me uncomfortable.

"If you need someone," he continued, "you just open that door. I'll be right here." He touched my forearm with his finger. The action was so subtle, almost tentative. I barely felt his skin on mine. I didn't know what to say, so I just pursed my lips and nodded.

"It's not a tattoo," I whispered. "It's a burn. I was branded. Like they do to animals." He let my words hang, not forcing me to elaborate.

"What do I call you?" he finally asked. I was silent for a moment. I had long ago decided that I would have a new name to match my new identity. But now it felt wrong.

"Eva," I whispered, deciding not to invent a fiction. "You can call me Eva."

Agrigento, 2010

"The spirits of the dead are attracted to that chasm."

A gnarled finger pointed to the sapphire lagoon. Alvaro became distracted by the serrated fingernail that invaded his vision. A streak of tar was so deeply imprinted on the woman's flesh that he could almost taste the ash on her hands, the faint scent of smoke and sweat mingling on her skin. Her shoulder blades jutted out of her black dress like amputated wings.

He grew agitated. She was ignoring his questions.

"This is where Orpheus bargained for Eurydice," she continued. "He ripped the earth apart to follow her into Hades." She paused to make a tearing motion with her hands, the words rattling in her mouth through decaying gums and hollowed teeth. "Then the waters of the underworld welled up to connect the living with the dead." She spoke the words with utter conviction, absorbed in the story that flowed from her mouth.

Alvaro was skeptical. He kept waiting for her to thrust out her hand and demand payment for the tale. But the old widow only looked at him with wild, vacant eyes, her irises dilated and half-crazed.

"I'll start again," he began, forcing patience into his tone, the kind of voice a parent would use with a disobedient child. "Her name's Eva. She grew up in a village somewhere near here, but left when she was sixteen. We just arrived from Marseille a week ago. She's gone missing. The last place I saw her was right there"—he pointed to the water—"yesterday, sunning herself on that limestone step."

"It's the limestone that makes the water turn sapphire. The same limestone they used for the temples." Her voice had become pensive, almost dreamy.

Exhaling heavily, Alvaro turned to walk away.

They are all useless, he thought, *these Sicilian villagers with their codes of silence.*

He would have to get the French authorities involved if Eva didn't turn up in the next few hours.

"Missing, eh?" The widow drew out her words. They sounded guttural, and she expelled the French from her throat, drowning it in her Sicilian accent. He stopped and turned to face her as she continued. She was speaking vaguely, to no one in particular, as though Alvaro were absent and she was talking to the water itself.

"She wished for him, didn't she? Someone dead." The loose mouth was wrapping around her protruding teeth. There was something grotesque in the widow's face. Her skin looked like it had been caught in a barbed wire snare.

"You got her, eh? A nice, pretty little live one."

Alvaro became anxious at her words. They were odd, and yet they scratched at something in his memory.

It's forbidden to wish for the dead to return.

Eva had said something similar before she went missing, something odd, out of place for her.

He stared out into the lagoon, and it suddenly appeared sinister to him, as though it were animated, living, breathing, and concealing desires.

His anxiety became paralyzing, and he silently prayed that she was still alive.

Marseille, 2004

"Edmund, I'm back!" I called, pushing the door open with my shoulder, the handle catching on my wedding ring. "I would have called, but I lost my phone in Barcelona."

I fumbled with my luggage and dropped it in the hallway. The door between our apartments never closed now, not even when I went away for a week.

A pungent odor slammed into me as I walked across the lounge room, causing me to gag.

I presumed it was the garbage disposal. It had broken months ago, and Edmund had promised to fix it before I returned.

"Edmund!" I called again, but there was no answer.

I flicked through the pile of mail and then collapsed onto the bed. I hadn't slept on the train and was exhausted. Kicking off my boots, I peeled away my stockings, my skin feeling damp.

I wanted to sleep, but the smell was too distracting. He must have liberated some rotten meat or fish.

Where is he? I thought. It was late. I had expected to find him reading on the balcony or watching a film noir. I needed an indulgence. I'd been gone for a week, and my libido was in overdrive. I decided to wait for him in the bathtub, with chocolate and wine—if we had any left.

My naked feet padded across the polished wooden floor, and I was conscious of the sound my skin made as it came into contact with the mahogany.

Something was off. Our apartment was never this quiet.

That smell.

It was getting intense. There was something odd to it, like rot and bitter almonds.

I followed the stench to the kitchen, thinking there was a mummified rodent trapped somewhere.

But I never got that far.

Edmund was hanging from a wooden beam, his body at an odd angle.

I saw the thick rope around his neck. His head rested to the side, just as it had many times against my breast.

Someone was screaming, swearing.

It took me a moment to realize that it was me. My voice sounded distorted, almost bestial.

I was by his side, trying to get him down. I couldn't do it. He wouldn't move. Just dangled like a limp animal caught in a trap.

The floor was a mess, blood and pieces of flesh everywhere.

I slipped and landed hard on my side. I saw intestines around my feet, like the white fat of a butchered pig.

I stood and pulled at his arm. It felt different. Wrong. Too stiff and cold.

I pulled again, harder, and the bones in his neck made a horrible crunching sound.

He fell to the floor, the blood spilling from the wound in his abdomen.

He had been split open, from throat to groin. Strung up like a slaughtered animal.

Then I saw it on the floor. In blood. The three long, intertwined lines. The *trinacria*. The old village symbol, matching the brand on my palm.

I let his head slump to the side. I slid down beside him. Curled up in his blood. Defeated. There was no point.

He was long since dead.

Agrigento, 2010

The sun vanished below the horizon, and I was still sitting alone with my fingertips in Espiritu Santo.

Edmund was with me then. He was an aural hallucination, haunting me with his silent words and voiceless lips. He was in the touch of the water against my skin. The limestone smell of the lagoon as the wind danced across it. The taste of the salt on my lips.

He had left something under my skin, like a fragment of glass. I was forever picking at the wound.

I stared out into the water, black as the night sky. It wrapped me in ice-cold comfort and turned me into dust. I saw him again, floating just under the midnight surface.

I kissed the water, stroked its glacial face. And I fell in love with drowning.

This story appears in *Make a Wish*, edited by George Wilhite.

2 THE REMAINS OF BEAUTY

hey will sacrifice you in the springtime, when the grain is scattered." My mother's voice was fragile, soft, and feminine. It quavered between pity and grief. She ran her ivory hand down my long chestnut hair, her fingers coming to rest at my elbow.

She looked over me with glazed jade eyes, a glassy film across her irises. But she didn't let the tears stain her cheeks.

"Be strong, Névia. Remember Iphigenia. Your blood will make the earth fertile again."

Her features were imbued with misery, her lower lip fluttering with emotion.

We stood at the outskirts of our village, in the center of a cherry orchard. I remembered how it had looked in my youth, with the treetops kissing above our heads, filtering the sunlight into an ethereal shade of amber. But now the trees were black and malnourished, stretching their skeletal hands to the sky as though to beg for food.

My mother tied baby's breath in my hair and kissed me lightly on the lips, her lipstick like a bloodstain on my mouth.

That was winter.

———•‹•·)◆(·•›•———

This is spring.

I hear music around me. Deep, incandescent notes that flash before my eyes like lightning. It's happening again—my senses are bleeding into each other. The mournful aria is dragging me out of my slumber. It tastes like copper on my tongue.

I blink, but my vision is hazy, like I'm looking through water. They must have sedated me with the spiced wine. A barbiturate cocktail is dancing through my blood.

The rope is tight around my neck and limbs. It feels coarse, scratchy, against my skin. The altar is cold under my back. It's like lying on ice.

There's some silk across my abdomen, but my legs and arms are bare. I'm adorned in gold and rubies. They feel heavy against my chest, and I think the necklace is tangled with my hair. I know the jewelry well; it's haunted my dreams since I was a child. They say it's cursed. Well, of course it is—they always use the same necklace for the sacrifice. It's the only one that won't be damaged in the fire.

I have to look attractive if I am to be burned for the gods. And when it's all over, there will be nothing left of me, of my pretty little face. Just ash. The remains of beauty.

The ritual is starting.

The priestess walks toward me. I can taste her in the air. The soft scent of lavender is tickling my abdomen. There is something piquant about her fragrance, as though the anger is eating her alive on the inside, but she has veiled herself in indifference. I think she loves my brother, but he pays her no attention. She left a few scratches on my skin when she bathed me for the ritual—enacting her retribution, I suppose. Not that it matters. Soon I'll be dust.

People are dancing all around me, but I can't make out their faces. It's just a blur of noises, limbs, and torsos that translate into a cacophony in my mind. I know a crowd has gathered to watch, to indulge the beast within.

They could have picked another virgin, but I had no father to defend me. My mother always said Apollo was her lover. But I think it was the Phoenician trader who gave her all her jewels.

The music is changing—the notes taste different. It's intense, building like a wave and then crashing on my tongue.

The priestess has lit a fire. I hear the crackle of the wood and leaves like drops of violet in my vision.

The dancers carry baskets, and inside one a blade is hidden. They usually cover it with grains of barley, but there is no food to spare anymore.

The priestess cuts a few strands of my hair and throws them into the flames. They sizzle and melt in an instant, as though they were always ash. It's the initial sacrifice. The one to awaken the gods.

Iphigenia didn't flinch when she was on the altar. They had tricked her, lured her to her sacrifice with a fiction. Her father told her it was her wedding day—she was promised to

Achilles, the finest of the Greeks. But they murdered her instead.

They didn't need to bait me to my death. I was never really meant for this world. I should be happy I'm leaving it, but I'm a little sad to go. The melancholy is like a hot breath on my cheek. Or maybe that's the priestess. She's standing so close now. She's getting ready to cut me, to put the knife in my chest.

Time to close my eyes.

—◆◦◦◗◆◖◦◦◗◆—

What's happening? Someone is screaming from the crowd.

"She's poisoned!" It's my brother. I just hope he doesn't tell everyone what he—

Gasps and cries are rising from the audience. They're in some kind of frenzy, their feet pounding on the dry earth like a pack of wild beasts chasing their prey. It sounds like someone has fainted—my mother, perhaps. But I fear that she knew our secret all along.

There is a long silence. I think he's leading them to the cherry orchard. That can only mean one thing—he really does want to spare me. But at what cost?

I hear footsteps again, but it's only one

person. That lavender scent once more, but this time I smell her anger like red streaks of lightning across my vision. It's coming to the surface; she can't beat it down anymore.

I feel something lightly placed upon my abdomen. It's damp and gritty, like it's covered in dirt. There's an odd smell in the air, as though the corpse of a small animal had been left to rot in the springtime sun.

It couldn't be, could it? Surely they wouldn't dig it up.

"Is this yours?" I can't see what the priestess is talking about; my neck is still tied down. I try to lift my head, but it does no good. Her face has invaded my vision. Her pupils are wild and crazed, like two black tadpoles swimming behind long lashes. The sweat is glistening on her olive skin, and it shines with a subtle incandescence.

Now she's clutching it, holding it up for me to see. I force my eyes shut. I never wanted to look at it—that *thing*—again. That pulpy mess. That tangle of hair.

The circular mass of limbs and eyes that should have been my child.

But nature has a way of punishing parents. Especially when they share a bloodline.

"You disgust me!" Her spit is hot and foamy on my face.

I faintly hear other footsteps now. Light and fast. But they are so far away.

Too late.

The priestess steps back, her eyes furious with revulsion.

She raises her hand again. The blade catches the sun as she swings it toward me.

And—magnificence.

The pain is stunning. Like the inside of a star. It builds into a crescendo of gold and crimson. It's like nothing I've ever tasted before. Cherries and roses, with cinnamon and mastic. The perfume of death is a symphony of scents—soft and earthy with spicy accents that cascade into sweetness. It's the first blossom of a flower after the long winter or the homely smell of a warm-blooded creature after a season of slumber.

It's spring.

This story appears in *Spring Fever*, edited by Dorothy Davies.

3 THROUGH A GLASS DARKLY

he gypsies have a tradition, in the village where my mother is from, that when people die, the mirrors in their home must be covered. This prevents the soul from being trapped within the reflection.

I never cared much for superstition.

Not until Eve died.

------◆━‹•⊷◊⊶•›━◆------

I could hear echoes of Eve throughout the house. Eve painting my lips with garish makeup before a performance at our school fete. Eve on the swing outside, smoking her perfumed cigarettes with her Catholic school gloves on, concealing the small tattoo of a bird that Rocco had given her. Eve teaching me to cook a real French fondue on my sixteenth birthday, sipping kirsch from the bottle just hours before she died.

"Are you coming inside, Amryn, or are you going to stand out there like a stranger?" Mom's voice cut through my memories. She stood on the front porch, her hands on her hips, a wide smile accentuating the dimples on her cheeks. She had aged a little since I'd seen her last. There were a few more gray hairs at her temple, and the lines around her mouth were just a little deeper. Her curly black hair was tied in a loose bun that showed off her elongated neck and delicate profile. Perhaps she was looking for another husband.

"I missed you, Mama."

I choked back the emotion in my throat— I hadn't been home in more than three years. I'd completed my undergraduate degree abroad, studying French and Italian at the Università di Bologna. It had been Eve's dream to travel through Europe and study languages in an ancient institution. And I was living it for her, because she could not.

I collapsed into my mother's arms, and she hugged me tightly to her chest. Her hands squeezed my shoulders, and then she grabbed me by the waist. I laughed as she pinched my sides.

"You've lost weight! Your ribs are like pitchforks!" she exclaimed with concern, holding me at arm's length and scrutinizing my appearance. I could see her mentally calculating how much food she would need to cook to make me plump. Before I left for Italy, she had advised me that European men like a bit of meat on their women.

Pursing her lips, she leaned closer to whisper in my ear.

"Put some lipstick on—you have a visitor." Her dark eyes sparkled, and she grinned mischievously.

Here we go, I thought, *another potential husband.*

"You're back!" A male voice resonated from within my home. Rocco walked casually out of the drawing room and joined us on the porch, one hand tucked into the pockets of his jeans, the other running through his dirty-gold hair. He had grown it longer since I'd last seen him, and his skin was tanned, probably from working outside. His green eyes glistened as he looked me up and down, catching me off guard; I don't think he'd ever looked at me that way before. It made me feel self-conscious, and for the first time in ages, I was concerned about my appearance.

He pulled me in for an awkward hug, and I felt my cheeks flush as he squeezed me a little tighter than I had anticipated.

"I haven't seen you since—"

"Yeah, it's been ages—over three years," I cut him off. I hadn't seen him since Eve's funeral, and I didn't want to resurrect the memory.

"I'll leave you two alone." My mother grinned and winked at me as she turned to enter the house, dragging my suitcase behind her. Her lack of discretion made me feel embarrassed. I'd known Rocco for most of my life; we were neighbors and had always been friends. He'd been Eve's boyfriend all through high school, and I was the nondescript addition to their relationship.

"Let's sit on the swing," he suggested, dragging me by my hand. I felt a tingle in my stomach at the way his fingers intertwined with my own. He had held my hand many times before, but never like this, and I felt a lump of guilt rise in my throat. Everything seemed so different and yet so familiar. It was almost indescribable, the subtle, organic change that washed over everything in my absence. I felt like an interloper in my own home, like I didn't really belong there anymore.

I let my fingers curl around his, and I followed him to my backyard, to the decaying love swing that was tucked away in the corner of my mother's garden behind her rosebushes and olive trees.

We didn't speak as we walked down the overgrown pathway. I knew I should say something, break the long silence, but I was disoriented by my mother's unkempt orchard.

Something was wrong with the way the sunlight bathed over us; it seemed to turn a haunted shade of sepia as it filtered through the olive leaves.

The air was much too cold for June, and I shivered violently, the breath before my eyes thickening like a plume of smoke.

I squeezed Rocco's hand a little tighter.

Was he not sensing this?

A familiar smell was also invading the air, something out of place in the garden, growing more intense as we approached the swing. I couldn't quite recognize the scent; it was like jasmine mixed with myrrh.

He sat on the swing and pulled me close to his side. The corrugated iron creaked under our weight, and we both laughed at the sound. It was cathartic—I couldn't remember the last time I had laughed so freely.

"This swing needs a bit of work. I could fix it over the summer," he offered, running a calloused finger down the rusted iron frame. I had a vague memory from my youth of the antique love seat being white. Eve used to scratch the paint off with her fingernails and see spectral faces in the patterns.

"This is the lady trapped in your mirror," she had whispered to me once, her eyes large with concern, pointing to an indistinct shape on the corrugated iron frame. "She looks just like me—like us."

But I could never see what she saw. My world was slightly different from Eve's, as though her eyes were washed with a filter of sadness—a constant melancholy that drove her to decorate her flesh with fine razor cuts. I existed in a place that was much plainer, simpler. Perhaps that's why Rocco had loved her and not me.

"That would be nice," I replied absently, still shivering from the walk.

"Are you cold? I thought Europe had the coldest winter on record last year—you should be immune." He pulled me to his side, his arm wrapped around my shoulders like a comforting blanket. He smelled delicious, the faint scent of cologne blended with the saltiness of his skin.

I felt his hand linger around my waist, his fingers playing with the tips of my long hair, just as I had seen him many times before play with Eve's black tresses. His breath was hot against my cheek, elevated, almost a soft pant, as if he were nervous.

What happened next was a mosaic of sensations. His lips pressed against my own, catching me off guard, and I felt a ripple of electricity shoot through my limbs.

His hand ran up my spine and paused at the nape of my neck, his fingers curling around my hair in playful scratches.

I didn't have time to think; my body simply reacted, eager for the encounter.

The thoughts of guilt—of Eve—were suffocated by the physical sensations. I felt his tongue massage my mouth, and I parted my lips to allow him entry.

His need was overwhelming, almost instinctual, as though we had a long history of intimacy.

I felt cold fingers on my knee, and they slowly ran across my thigh, under my skirt. Adrenaline pounded through my blood as he pulled my panties to one side.

"Eve," he mumbled, his lips tangled in my neck.

The familiar scent of spiced jasmine was suddenly overwhelming. It invaded my lungs, sucking the oxygen out of me. I struggled not to gag.

He's mine! The voice slapped at my mind like a whip.

I pulled away from him sharply, my nails digging into his chest. He looked bewildered, but not disturbed or scared, as I was. He hadn't heard a thing.

"I have to go," I mumbled abruptly, stumbling off the swing as I hurried toward the house.

I could hear Rocco calling after me, his voice penitent and confused, but I ignored him and the sound faded to a distant whisper. His cries were a haunting echo of the name that was not my own.

"Eve! Eve! Eve!"

———◆‹•·›◆‹•·›◆———

Alone in my room, I sat in my antechamber and stared into the ornate mirror before me.

My mother had brought the mirror with her from the old country, an exquisite artifact created by a distant ancestor. It was the only possession to accompany her on the forty-day sea voyage as she left behind the poverty and disease of postwar Europe.

The room smelled of the fresh apples that my mother had left for me on my dresser— stunning crimson apples from her small orchard in our yard.

I inhaled their scent deeply and traced my fingers across the thick, elaborate frame of the mirror. It was carved from some kind of black stone that I couldn't identify, etched with such detail that the engravings shone silver when the light caught them.

I had always thought the frame was baroque, but as I examined it in detail, I realized that it was much older. The carvings contained a series of rose vines painted with tiny thorns that were entwined with one another. There was no beginning to the pattern and no end.

The glass was not as ancient as the frame; we had to replace it after the accident, after Eve died. It didn't seem to fit with the rest of the mirror, as though there were two worlds colliding in a single space. A remnant of the past fused with the present.

I searched in my dresser drawer for a lighter. The small white candles were still embedded in the mirror's frame, and I wanted to ignite them as my ancestresses had done before me. I dimmed the lights until the room was almost black and lit the candles one by one. A honeycomb glow pulsed from the frame, causing its silver veins to throb in time with the light. It was as if the mirror were becoming animated, beating with life as the shadowed specter of my reflection stared back at me from a pool of dark liquid.

"Through a glass darkly," I muttered sotto voce, the girl trapped in the frame imitating my words with precision.

Eve and I had sat in front of this mirror many times during our youth. In the soft glow of the candles, we looked identical, living mirrors of each other. She would brush my hair and plait a braid from my temple, her long white fingers moving through my tresses as though she were playing a melody on a stringed instrument. She had tucked baby's breath into my braid and told me that I was beautiful.

"We're sisters," she had whispered, her rosebud mouth so similar to my own. But I could see the subtle distinctions, the differences that made Eve beautiful and me plain. Her eyes were emerald and iridescent, where mine were flat and brown. My complexion was much too fair when I sat next to Eve, almost pallid. Her peaches-and-cream skin was glossy and tinged with a rose hue across her cheekbones. I was the peasant, she the princess.

"We're not," I had replied despondently, "but I wish we were."

"I'll tell you a secret," she countered eagerly, her bright eyes flashing in her reflection despite the dimness of the room. "I heard my mama crying to her sister last night, when they thought I was asleep. We share a father. That's why we look so alike—we are sisters by blood."

My small hands flew to my mouth, the gasp escaping my lips before I could contain it.

"Liar!" I had shrieked, my voice a mixture of anger and excitement.

"It's true!" she protested vehemently, and I saw by the conviction in her features that she was not inventing a lie.

I was silent for a long while, my lower lip trapped between my teeth. It dawned on me then that I had always known, or at least always suspected.

Neither Eve nor I had ever met our father. Mine had been a marine and was killed overseas before I was born, and Eve's had died in a car accident around the same time. Lies our mothers had told us.

Now, as I gazed into the mirror alone with my memories, I felt guilt gnaw at my abdomen. Eve was my sister, my best friend. I had tainted her memory by letting Rocco kiss me, touch me—even if he had acted out of grief and longing for her. I was no better than my mother, claiming another's love as my own.

Exasperated, my fingers stumbled in the dim lighting for an apple. I was famished—I hadn't eaten since I'd left Europe the day before.

I brought the fruit to my lips and took a generous bite, the apple crumbling in my hand as I did so.

Sourness invaded my mouth. The apple was soft and pulpy and seemed to move across my tongue of its own accord.

There it was again, the scent of spiced jasmine.

I dropped the fruit onto my dresser and spat the contents of my mouth onto the floor.

Maggots were vomiting out of the decayed apple, fat and waxy, crawling from the rotten core, endlessly replicating themselves. I felt a moist slither work its way down my chin, and I shrieked with horror, my hand slapping violently at my face. In the confusion, I heard a loud smash, and when I looked up, the glass of the mirror was splintered in two. I must have hit it with my fist—there was blood covering my hand and snaking down my forearm. I hadn't felt a thing.

That's when I saw her. In the dimly lit, cracked shard of glass. She was staring at me like she had been there all along, by my side, the silent witness to my actions.

Sister, she implored, her liquid green eyes glassy and vacant.

There was something sirenesque about her voice, the way it surrounded me in warmth, dissolving the cold that had invaded my bones ever since I had returned home.

She was my mirror image, the stunning transformation of my plain, unexceptional self through the lens of the looking glass. Her delicate mouth, so much like my own, was now a blood red gash that pulsed with her words.

We could be together forever. Her raven hair hung about her face like an onyx veil, and the dim flickers of the candles blotted her eyes with darkness. I was transfixed—I couldn't tear my eyes from her.

"Evangeline," I whispered, her name passing over my lips like a specter. I reached my fingers to her face, and she reciprocated, mimicking my movements with exactness.

Her eyes glanced down toward my dresser, communicating to me without words.

You know what to do. You've seen me do it before. Like I did on your sixteenth birthday.

A shard of glass had fallen out of the frame. It was triangular and sharp, the tip as pointed as a blade.

I glanced at my wrist and saw a small cut was forming—a jagged abrasion slowly tearing my skin apart.

I could feel something sharp underneath it, a rough spindle trying to dig its way through my flesh. The sensation tore at my mind—I had to get it out. I would gnaw off my own hand to make it stop.

Like a crazed animal, I picked at the wound with my thumb and forefinger; small, bestial cries rose in my throat as I did so. I could feel it, just under my vein. I just had to reach in a little deeper…

My fingers locked on the object, and I ripped it from my arm. Relief flooded over me as the hideous scratching abated.

I brought the object closer to my eyes to examine it. It was small—about the size of the tip of my thumb—and it shone in the inconstant candlelight. The miniature face of

Eve stared at me from behind hooded eyelids and black lashes.

It was a piece of mirror, trapped under my skin.

The relief was fleeting. The horrible scratching sensation started again. This time it was spreading quickly—running up my arms and invading my spine.

I could hear someone screaming hysterically, and in my confusion, I failed to recognize my own voice. My nails tore at my arms, at my legs, at my chest. The shards of mirror were infecting my blood, cutting me open from the inside out.

And there was Eve, trapped in the mirror, a mocking smile distorting her mouth—staring darkly at me through the glass.

The wound is already open—you just have to let it bleed.

"You only turn sixteen once!"

Eve cracked open the bottle of kirsch and poured a small amount into the fondue. She had melted three types of imported cheese in a large pot, and it smelled amazing.

Sipping on the cherry liqueur, she moved her hips evocatively to the music that pervaded my kitchen. She handed me the bottle and gestured for me to drink.

I held the kirsch to my nose and sipped tentatively on the bottle.

It burned as it washed down my throat, and I coughed and sputtered awkwardly. I felt my tongue quiver and I wanted to throw up. Eve giggled.

"You're such a virgin, Amryn!"

"Maybe," I mumbled under my breath, wiping my mouth on the sleeve of my pajamas. "When is everyone else getting here?" Eve had organized the slumber party for my sixteenth, and I had to beg her not to turn it into a full-blown drunken orgy. She had agreed to keep it low-key—just our closest girlfriends—but only because it was my birthday.

"Any second now," she replied, pouring the fondue into a large ceramic bowl and arranging dipping snacks on a plate.

As if on cue, the doorbell rang.

Eve giggled with delight and rushed to open the door.

Somehow she managed to look sexy in her shapeless flannel pajamas, the sleep shirt hugging her rounded breasts and hips while showing off her tanned legs. I felt frumpy in my baggy top and shorts.

"Hi, guys," Eve cooed as she embraced our three closest friends—Yvette, Veronica, and Raquel.

There was a flurry of chatter, and the house seemed filled with people even though there were only five of us.

"Happy birthday!" Veronica and Raquel greeted me with warm hugs. My cheeks flushed with heat at all the attention. Yvette was oddly quiet and did not greet me directly, but she had been distant for the past week, so I didn't think much of it. I smiled warmly at her, and she reciprocated with a mechanical facial expression, her lips contorting into a shallow smile but her violet eyes remaining cold. She reminded me of a reptile.

It was a moonless night outside, and the wind moaned as it wrapped itself around my house. I eagerly shut the front door and hugged my sides, the icy air tickling my skin like pinpricks.

"Let's head up to Am's bedroom," Eve suggested, the fondue balanced on one hip and the plate of snacks on the other. "I've got a surprise for you."

My bedroom had been rearranged so that we could all comfortably lie on the floor surrounded by pillows and blankets. There were a dozen bottles of fruit-flavored liqueur, and Veronica began mixing cranberry cocktails for us.

"I got these from Rocco, especially for tonight." Eve popped open a small bottle of eye drops, and I noticed Yvette visibly stiffen at the sound of Rocco's name. I wondered what was going on with her, but my thoughts were quickly overtaken by Eve's gift.

"Oh, Eve," I whispered, my voice nervous and slightly excited. The other girls crowded around to inspect the contents of the optical vial.

There were five small pills inside the bottle.

"What is it?" Raquel questioned, pushing her glasses a little farther up the bridge of her nose.

"Just something to help us relax," Eve replied, a confident grin spreading across her lips. I had never tried drugs and rarely got drunk. I usually threw up before things got too exciting. Eve had once mentioned to me how much she liked to get high and have sex, and I had seen the wounds on Rocco's back from her enthusiasm.

"I don't want to do it," Raquel protested. "I have a chemistry final next week."

"It's not that strong," Eve insisted, forcing a pill into Raquel's hand. "It will sharpen your senses, and besides"—she let one of her dazzling smiles do all the convincing—"it only lasts for a few hours. You'll wake up tomorrow more refreshed and alert than you've ever felt." Eve had that kind of effect on others; she could make them feel they were immortal, the only ones who mattered in her world.

"Trust me." She flashed me a conspiratorial gaze, and I knew she was lying. But I didn't care; I really didn't need any convincing. I was ready for a break from reality, something to cut through the fabric of my small, claustrophobic life.

I gingerly took a pill from Eve's hand and popped it into my mouth, washing it down with one of Veronica's cranberry cocktails. It left a bitter taste on my tongue and a faint trail of acid down my throat.

The next few hours were a blur, and when they were over, Eve would be dead, lying in a bloodied mess on my bathroom floor with a shard of mirror splintering her wrist. But for now, she was alive, and the party was just beginning.

At first I felt nothing. Veronica was sprawled across my bed, her head hanging toward the floor and a languid arm stroking my carpet as though it were a giant beast. Raquel was tangled with her, giggling as I had never heard her before. We were playing truth or dare, and it was Eve's turn.

"I dare Veronica and Raquel to kiss." She flashed me the conspiratorial grin again, her eyes alight behind her long, dark lashes. "And nothing too innocent. I want entertainment." I started to feel my flesh crawl slightly, and a plunging feeling invaded my stomach. The pills were beginning to seep into my blood.

Veronica began to protest, but Raquel was on top of her with little encouragement. I heard Yvette gasp and Eve giggle as Raquel put her entire body into the kiss, her fists curling into little balls around Veronica's naked shoulders. Raquel's mop of chestnut hair veiled their faces, and when she was done, she threw her head back and howled like a triumphant wolf, her hands pinning Veronica beneath her like prey. Veronica wiped at her face and grimaced, squirming to free herself.

Timid, bookish Raquel was a succubus in my bed, her eyes glassy and wide with dilated black pupils.

"Truth or dare, Amryn?" It was Yvette's turn to ask the question. My head felt a little hazy, and I threw back a mouthful of passion fruit wine. I still had that sinking feeling in my stomach.

"After that"—I gestured vaguely at my bed, at Veronica and Raquel with their tangled limbs and hysterical giggles—"I'll go with truth."

Something hardened in Yvette's expression. Her violet eyes looked almost arctic in the dim lighting, and her lips were drawn into a tight line.

"Why did you fuck Eve's boyfriend?"

The giggling and laughter stopped abruptly. Veronica wiped the saliva off her chin with the back of her hand and glanced from me to Eve. Raquel had the same wide-eyed expression on her face, but she seemed detached from her body, her legs and hips continuing to twitch inadvertently.

Yvette's eyes burned into me, and I could tell by the way her chin was contorted that she was biting down hard on her inner lip.

The entire room was silent, waiting for my response. I stared dumbly at Yvette and then at the ground.

Eve was perfectly still. She sat next to me, her hands wrapped about her legs. I tried to mumble a response, but it came out incoherently. Eventually, she spoke.

"Is it true?" she asked softly. Her emerald eyes were not accusing, but I couldn't meet her gaze. Instead, my throat quivered, and some kind of meek, detestable sound crawled out of me.

"Don't try and bullshit your way out of it, Amryn!" Yvette spat, her wide lips quivering with the force of her acrimonious words. "Steven tells me everything, and Rocco got drunk after last week's game and told half the soccer team about the birthmark on your ass!"

Steven was Yvette's flame-of-the-week, and he and Rocco were close. She had backed me into a corner, and the drugs had finally washed over my mind. I opened my mouth to speak, to explain myself, but the words were paralyzed, trapped behind my tongue. My lips just kept moving, stretching in a soundless rhythm. I bit down on my jaw and forced my teeth to clench together.

A tear rolled down Eve's cheek, and it shattered me to see it. She stood silently, walked into my antechamber, and locked the door behind her.

I eventually regained control of my voice.

"You don't know what you're talking about," I spat at Yvette as I hastily stood to follow Eve. My cheeks flushed with heat, and the tears were streaming from my eyes. Veronica and Raquel exchanged worried looks and watched in silence.

I heard Yvette swear and call me a slut. She had had sex with more people than I could name, and I had only ever done it once. That one time with Rocco.

It had been so horrible that I wanted to burn the encounter out of my memory.

I jiggled the handle to my antechamber, but Eve had locked it from the inside. I tapped lightly on the door, but there was no response. I could hear her sobbing gently.

"Eve," I began, sinking against the door, "it's not what you think." There was no response from the other side.

"It was a long time ago, before you two were serious." I knocked gently again, but it was no use. "I'm sorry," I whispered into the wood. I didn't know what else to say. I heard her feet move against the tiled floor and the soft thud of her hand against the door.

"You know I've loved him since we were little. He's the only one I've been with." Her voice was choked, barely recognizable. "You're as bad as our father!"

"Please open the door," I begged, barely containing my sobs. I just needed to tell her face-to-face what had happened, to make her understand. I had loved him just as she did, but he didn't want me—he had never wanted me. He never looked at me the way he did her, and when he held my hand or touched me, it was as though I were a child or a sibling. She had gone to Europe with her mother two summers earlier, and he had missed her terribly. She was gone for almost three months, which had seemed an eternity back then.

He'd gotten drunk one night, and the entire time he was inside me, he kept murmuring her name.

I knew it was wrong and the guilt had been paralyzing, but I just lay there—wanting to live as Eve did, wanting to *be* Eve for a short while. When it was finally over, I no longer loved him. My sense of self-disgust was overwhelming, and it obliterated all other emotions. I had purged myself of wanting him.

Her shadow moved away from beneath the door, her feet dragging across the tiles. I should have said it all to her, blurted it out, but instead, I just let the tears snake down my cheeks.

There was a scream followed by a loud smash. Eve's sobbing had grown silent.

"Eve! Eve!" I shrieked into the door, shaking the handle violently. It didn't budge.

I pounded my fists into the wood, and I saw Veronica's slim arms at my side, echoing my actions. Raquel was hysterical, her hands ineffectually scratching at the wall, calling for Eve. Yvette pulled us away. She raised her leg and brought it down hard against the door. Part of the frame cracked slightly. She raised her leg again, a guttural sound escaping her throat as she did so.

She beat the door repeatedly, and it seemed as though the moment were trapped in infinity.

Eve was silent on the other side.

I grew agitated; it felt as if insects were crawling across my skin. Sobbing, tearing at my hair. I didn't quite understand what my body was doing as my legs began to rush at the door and I collided heavily with the wood. The top half of my body fell through the frame, and I lay sprawled in my antechamber, my face scratching against the tiles and my lips soaking in something thick and wet.

Behind me, I heard muffled screams. Someone was wailing hysterically.

I raised my eyes slowly, the viscous fluid smothering my mouth and dripping down to my breasts.

And there was Eve, bathed in blood, covered in fragments of my broken mirror. A large triangular shard protruded from her wrist, and in it, I could see the reflection of her eyes.

Her beautiful, iridescent eyes vacantly stared back at me, her emerald irises turned to glass.

This story appears in *Mirror Mirror*, edited by Dorothy Davies.

4 CHILDREN OF THE DARK

For Ariadne, who shall never see the light again

 gaze upon her porcelain skin as she disrobes in front of the Murano mirror. She is just as I had been centuries earlier, unblemished, untouched by a man. Her hair is raven and her lips are plump, and as I whisper her name, she shudders, as though I had breathed upon her nape.

"Ariadne."

The name is a specter across my lips. And I know now that she is mine.

Forever.

"Circe instructed Odysseus in the chthonic rites to raise the dead, the shades of the underworld." She utters the words into the inky night, her feet dangling through the metal railings of the bridge. It's the edge of the earth—or the edge of civilization, at least—and she dips her limbs into the emptiness without fear.

"They were the first vampires, drinking the blood of sacrificial sheep to reanimate their forms." She speaks to her partner, an inconsequential boy of sixteen, and I have the urge to kill him right now, to drain his body of blood, to tear the heart from his chest, just to have her all to myself.

She holds a small bowl into the void and lets it slip through her fingers. A black liquid spills into the night, and the bowl seems to float on its way down to the river, a shimmer of gold against the blackness. The smell of blood cuts the air, and instantly, I'm all instincts, all about the kill.

There's a series of small splashes as the blood hits the river below, but she won't hear that. Her senses are too weak, too human. It sends a jolt through my body, and I want to dive into the river after the precious fluid. But I'm here for her. She's the one I want tonight.

"Where do you read this shit, Ari?" The boy speaks, and it makes me want to crush his throat just to stop the sound. He has the face of a fifth-century barbarian, the kind that sacked Rome, with brutish hands and ruddy skin. I've seen him fumble with her before, his thick fingers groping at her flesh, and it pleases me to know I can take his life in an instant.

"My mother taught me the ritual when I was young." *Before she died.* It's what she doesn't say that distracts me. I can sense the emotion burning in her body. It's like a pheromone, a primal signal. She's raw and aching, and she wants the boy to connect with her, to share her pain. But he has other things on his mind.

"Interesting," he mutters. *Family of freaks*, he thinks, and he grates his teeth across each other to hide his disgust. *No one will miss her when she's gone.*

She hangs her hand across the rail, into the blackness. She wants the ritual to work, for something to happen. But the shades of the dead aren't in Hades anymore. Like me, they are children of the dark. We are part of her world—the rattle of the wind or that flash of light in the corner of her eye. She just doesn't know it yet.

"Did you ever wish you could just disappear? Dissolve into the night?" Her voice has a dreamy quality about it, raw and breathy. Just as mine used to be, when I was alive.

"Every day," he replies, the facetious little roach. He pulls a silken handkerchief from his pocket and unwraps a knife. The blade is long and triangular, with elaborate engravings. He plays with the tip, turning it against his finger, not hard enough to break the flesh, but enough to stir my appetite.

"I got this for you. For when you…"

There is something dark in his eyes, and I recognize that brutal instinct coursing through his body. It's the mark of a predator.

"…cut yourself."

"I don't do that anymore," she says quickly, shame and helplessness washing over her features.

He lifts the fold of her skirt to reveal her thigh, a streak of alabaster against the night. Touching the blade to her knee, he runs it slowly across her skin all the way to her sex. Her heart picks up pace, and she presses her lips together, fear and excitement mingling in her blood.

She needs to stop the brute before he goes too far. Soon his urges will take over and there'll be no turning back.

He leans forward and kisses her ear, placing his hand on the back of her neck. It's a dominating move, but she doesn't realize it.

"Let me cut you," he whispers, his eyes hazy and glazed over with anticipation.

She shudders, realizing something is wrong.

But it's too late.

He plunges the blade into her thigh, just kissing the artery. Her blood is crimson and rich, spilling down her leg. It's like a drug to me, and the instincts take over.

She screams and scratches at his face. A fat chunk of his skin scrapes off under her nails, and he howls like a wounded beast. His anger is hot and pulsating, spilling into the air like pollution.

His hand tightens around her neck, and he slams her face into the metal railing. She goes down with a groan, but she's not unconscious yet.

He picks up her limp body and holds her close to his chest.

"You're nothing but a slut, a cheap bitch no one will miss." There's a hatred in his eyes that wasn't there a second ago. He's in his killing zone now, and she's his first. I can smell the disgust seeping from his blood; he's confusing her with another woman, molding her into someone else, someone who hurt him as a child. Someone who haunts him still.

He lifts her over the railing and drops her into the night. She's like the blood, floating to the river below. Her body is weightless, and she leaves a trail of crimson against the night.

She hits the river with a violent splash.

That's when I kick into action.

I'm behind him, so close that he could touch me if he had any idea. He's still watching after her, his heart on fire. He is fear and exhilaration in a bag of flesh.

A small cry comes from his lips, and his hands tear at his hair. He can't believe he's gone through with it, after fantasizing about murder for so long.

He finally turns around and sees me.

This is going to be fun.

There's a stifled cry stuck in his throat and a look of horror on his face that tickles me. I'd laugh in his face if it wouldn't spoil the fear.

"Ariadne!" he cries, shocked at my appearance. I look just like her, raven hair and ruby lips. He does a double take and nearly falls over.

"Not quite," I whisper, my voice unearthly, almost demonic. The fear surges through his body like electricity.

I rush toward him and place his throat against my lips. My teeth are like blades as they rip into his pulsating skin. There's a hot splash against my tongue as the blood spills into me. I'm a lioness with the urge to tear the flesh from his bones, and if I don't get control, I'll drain him in an instant.

I want this to be slow. I want to relish it. And I want him to suffer for what he did to her.

He cries in agony, in pain. He doesn't understand what is happening. I plunge my teeth deeper into him, scratching against the fragile bones in his neck.

He's in hell, and I feel sated.

I leave his body on the bridge. Let the vermin find him before the cops do.

She's groggy and half-dead when I pull her from the river.

The cut on her thigh isn't deep enough to do any real damage. Her attacker was too hesitant, too inexperienced. Not an expert in death. Not like me.

She coughs up water, and it splutters from her lips. Her breathing is erratic, but her lungs sound clear. Her skin shakes violently from the cold, and the blood is retreating deep within her body, turning her blue.

I scratch my teeth across my lips and feel the cold burst of blood across my skin.

Pressing my mouth to hers, I let my liquid wet her lips. I hold her head to my mouth, and like a newborn, I urge her to drink. She suckles at my lip, and it fills me with an indescribable peace.

For an instant, I remember what it feels like to be alive. I'd cry if there were tears within me to shed, but that part of me turned to stone centuries ago.

There's a rosy hue to her cheeks now, and she looks revitalized. It's time to get her home and tuck her in. She'll sleep for hours and not remember a thing; I'll make sure of that.

The house is empty, as it always is. Her mother is dead, and her father is drunk somewhere, at a bar or in a ditch. Or in jail, if he's lucky.

I lay her down on her bed and strip the garments from her skin. It pains me to see her so fragile, so delicate and vulnerable. She's breath and life and blood trapped in a fragile shell. And it will all dissolve. One day, she'll be bones in a grave, sleeping for eternity, as I cannot. But I'll always remember her as she is now, young and ripe, with a scar on her heart that may never heal, that may destroy her in the end.

But I'll watch over her as long as she lives, and I'll remember her always when she is gone.

Forever.

I wipe the blood from her lips, and it's as though I was never there.

She's my descendant, with my emerald eyes and a pout in her lips that I once wore like jewelry. There are others like her, with traces of my blood in their veins. I watch over them like a spectral mother, protecting my young from the predators of the world. There's a little part of me, of my darkness, within them, a little piece of eternity mingled with their mortality.

We are the children of the dark.

This story appears in *Night Hunters*, edited by Danielle Rose.

5 THE ANATOMY OF INSOMNIA

here is an ancient family in Dubrovnik, one which predates the Garibaldis of Monaco and the Romanovs of Russia by centuries, whose members die a torturous death before the age of forty. In their blood is a fatal disease that causes them to wake up one morning and never return to sleep—not until they die. The human body can endure months of wakefulness before its organs cease to function and its brain withers. This interlude, the period between life and death, is described

as being in a perpetual state of sleepwalking.

—————————◆—‹•••›◆‹•••›—◆—————————

During the night, I dreamed that we returned to Segesta. The temples were washed with limestone, as they had been in ancient times, and anemones grew near the ruins of the sacrificial pit, their petals tangled and entwined. There was something terrifying in the color of those flowers, and I imagined the petals repeatedly sprayed with blood from the victims of Aphrodite.

Andonetta picked one of the unformed buds and placed it behind her ear, her onyx hair riding the wind like a loose scarf. She smiled at me, just as she did when she was alive, and her eyes were those of a child, wide and liquid, shimmering with a violet luminescence. That's how I want to remember her eyes, playful and unburdened, not the bloodshot, tortured orbs that are burned into my brain.

The temple faded, vanished before us, and the sky became leaden.

"It's come for me. It's finally come," she whispered, her voice a specter across her barely parted lips.

She turned to face me, her eyes met mine,

and the ethereal violet irises were too large, too wide. I realized, in my unconscious fog, that her pupils were like pinpricks.

Then she dissolved, and the dream was no more.

When I awoke, my skin was bathed with sweat. Groping in the dark, I switched on my bedside lamp and reached frantically for the mirror that was hidden under my pillow. The breath was trapped in my throat, and my heart slammed violently against my ribs, a caged animal in my chest.

I held the mirror to my face and pulled my eyelids back.

They were normal.

My pupils were not the pinpricks of death, one of the first signs of fatal familial insomnia—the rare genetic disease that has plagued my family since the Renaissance.

I breathed a heavy sigh of relief and stared into the shadowy night. The doors to my balcony were open, and the wind ravished the damask curtains, making them beat furiously. The angry waters of the Adriatic seemed to seep into my villa, the waves twisting into faceless, amorous bodies, tempestuous and wild. The distant lightning slammed into the horizon, illuminating the nearby island of San Croce, a shadowed silhouette against the inky, moonless sky.

I returned my mirror to its hiding spot and coughed dryly, causing the naked body in my bed to stir. It was a woman, asleep on her stomach, her thick brunette hair a tangled halo around her head.

"Vittorio," she murmured groggily, a wayward hand caressing the pillow by her side.

I wasn't sure of her name, so I didn't reply immediately. My mind was still hazy from the dream and the alcohol of the night before.

"Go back to sleep," I muttered, my voice sounding harsh and authoritative.

She nuzzled her chin against her shoulder and smiled with hooded eyes.

"You were such a gentleman last night." She let her words linger, and I waited for the insult that never arrived. She had the accent of a village girl, and her features were plain under the layers of mascara and rouge. The cigarettes and spirits on the nightstand hinted to the lost sequence of events, to a night I couldn't remember.

I abandoned the bed and walked to my balcony, sighing heavily into the salty sky.

I curled my fingers around the metal railing and stared at the sea, at San Croce. The island was originally home to a mental asylum, a brutal place in which many of my ancestors had died, wasting away from perpetual insomnia and misdiagnosed with insanity. It was a bitter reminder of my family's history, and it blemished the view from my villa, a scar against the pristine horizon. But now, in the hazy throb of lightning, it was nothing more than a distant phantom, a series of medieval towers and catacombs that had been converted into a tourist museum. I habitually visited the archives, the dank, moldy cellars that were off limits to the tourists, and searched the records for hints about our fatal disease. So far, I'd only met with disappointment—with fresh fuel for my nightmares and no inkling of a cure.

There was something alluring about the island that night. It seemed to beckon me across the waves, a siren whispering ancient secrets in my ear. My ancestors, my dead family, were entwined in the ivy of the towers and the bitter salt that washed onto the soil.

I shook the phantoms from my mind. The adrenaline of my dream was wearing off, and my fingers pulsed against the cool metal of the railing. Pain pooled in my hands, hot and searing, as if sharp spindles were embedded under my nails. Irritated, I examined my hands against the blackened night and struggled to make out my fingers. The air smelled salty, and despite the potency of the sea, I detected a hint of copper mixed with something repulsive, like wet mold. Something faintly putrid.

Or was it the scent of blood?

A thick flash of lightning burned across the sky and briefly illuminated my hands. I was momentarily startled, and my first instinct was to think that my mind was playing tricks on me.

My fingers were caked with dry, gritty blood.

A searing noise broke my confusion— there was a loud scream from inside.

I rushed into my bedroom, the damask curtains a wild tangle against the wind, beating the air furiously like bat wings.

"What is it? What's happened?" I barked at the brunette, half expecting to see her butchered.

She was sitting upright in my bed, a white duvet clasped against her breasts, hiding her nakedness.

"The sheets," she said helplessly, her eyes fixed on my side of the bed.

In the dim lamplight, I couldn't fathom what she was saying. I rushed to the bed and pulled the duvet to the ground, alarmed at her horrified disposition. The linen hit the marble floor, and a faint gasp escaped her lips, her small hands flying to cover her mouth.

There was dirt, thick stains of dirt, covering the sheets where I had lain. Where my hands had rested, the dirt was mixed with blood, and the faint outline of my fingers remained. Coagulated, densely clotted blood that looked black against the white linen.

Blood that could not be my own.

The panic prickled through my limbs, and the bile rose in my chest. Stars invaded my vision and I felt faint. This tableau was surely the first manifestation of the disease. It was one of the signs—a period of lost consciousness, of disconnection between my mind and my actions.

In that horrible moment, mortality was tactile, and I was aware of the countdown to my expiration.

The sleepwalking had begun.

———◆—‹•∙>◌‹∙•>—◆———

I was restless for the remainder of the night. Trying to sleep was terrifying, and as the hours dragged on, I grew agitated and then distressed. My mind was wired, so I distracted myself with research into fatal familial insomnia.

Andonetta, my sister, had died less than a month earlier. She was fifteen when the disease crippled her and sixteen when it ended her life. It generally took around two hundred days—a little longer than six months—from the first manifestation of symptoms until the victim succumbed. In that time, I had watched Andonetta slowly decay from the inside out.

I still couldn't bring myself to visit her at our family's sepulcher, to lay anemones at her tomb. They were her favorite flowers, and she had been enchanted by their beauty ever since our summertime visit to Segesta, just days before the disease had become apparent.

"It's the blood of Adonis," she had whispered to me, her eyes on fire as she inhaled the scent of the fragile flowers. "Or so the myth says. Where the boar severed his groin, these flowers sprang from his blood mixed with the earth. That's why they plant them at the temples of Aphrodite."

My poor little sister, who had been as delicate as her beloved flowers. I could still hear the phantom echoes of her heels against the marble floor of the parlor, the smell of her jasmine perfume and cherry-scented skin.

Later that morning, as soon as the sun broke over the horizon, the brunette made a flimsy excuse and rushed from my villa, her makeup a mess and her clothing disheveled. She sped off on her tiny *motorino*, and I was glad for my solitude.

I sipped on a bitter espresso and tried to work up the courage to visit my dead sister. The family tomb was located on our property, a short walk from the villa in which I resided. I could go now, if I had the strength. It was an hour before the next ferry for San Croce arrived, and the walk to the tomb was barely five minutes. Plenty of time to spend with her, with the other members of my family, bricked up behind marble and stone.

I threw the remains of my espresso in the sink, almost shattering the glass. Absently, my fingers massaged the stubble of my jaw and the cleft of my chin, a nervous habit from my youth. I hadn't shaved for days, and my hair was thick and black.

"The fatal disease is not the only thing that the good doctor Venero left me," I muttered to the empty villa, referring to my Venetian ancestor. He was presumed to be patient zero for fatal familial insomnia. The original mutation occurred in his brain at an early age and was then passed on to four of his six children. The disease made its way down the generations, ravaging my family, randomly appearing in those unlucky enough to inherit the affliction. There was a fifty-fifty chance of illness with every new Parisi born.

And despite my family's wealth, none of us could cheat death.

My father had died in his late thirties, and my sister had been one of the youngest at sixteen. There had been a brother at some point too, one who was stillborn, and the genetic testing on his tiny corpse revealed a host of anomalies, including the fatal insomnia gene. My mother, to this day, is still alive and well, but I haven't seen her since I was eight. Not since Andonetta was born. She had handed the child to my father, newly emerged from her womb, and refused to look at her.

"I cannot lose another," she had whispered, and then returned to her family in northern Slavonia. I don't resent her for the decision—it's a special kind of anguish that leads a mother to abandon two young children.

Dismissing the memories, I quickly

scanned the rustic pieces of parchment that were spread across my dining table.

I had discovered a series of sketches of my ancestor Venero while searching the San Croce archives. The museum's curatrix was somewhat of a friend and had allowed me to borrow the papers for further analysis. Friend, perhaps, is not the right term; she regarded me with pity, having encountered so many of my ancestors in the records of the asylum. I was awkward and apprehensive whenever I met with her. The taboos of my family—disease, mental illness, incest—were charted and documented for tourists to admire. The sketches had been part of a private collection that had been misplaced in the archives for centuries, and it had given me an intense thrill to discover them.

In the first sketch, Venero was a young man with rustic features and a prominent, aquiline nose. The outline of his jaw was well defined and culminated in a cleft chin, so similar to my own. There was something sensuous about his dark eyes and wide mouth—the mirror image of my appearance when anger or lust possessed me.

There was a small inscription under his portrait—*Venice, January 1689.*

I gently placed the brittle document to

one side and examined the next sketch. The sepia-colored paper was dated three months later.

Venero looked significantly aged. There were dark troughs under his arabesque eyes, and shadows had formed under his cheekbones. He was almost forty in the first sketch, and he looked as though he had aged twenty years in a few short months.

The final sketch was the most disturbing. It was dated July 1689, just days before his death. Venero was almost skeletal. The skin hung loosely over his cheeks, but was sucked in sharply between his teeth, revealing the grossly prominent bones of his jaw. His eyes bulged from their sockets, wide and alarmed, and the blood vessels were a network of roots across his eyeballs. This was the face of a man who had gone without sleep for more than six months, sleepwalking throughout the asylum like a phantom. One horrible detail had been omitted from the other sketches, but that was all too visible in this final one.

The hideously small, pinprick pupils.

The sweat pooled at the base of my neck, and my mouth grew dry and chalky.

It was like a time bomb in my blood, the perpetual waiting for insomnia and death. The fear of sleepwalking.

Had last night been my final night of sleep? Had I even slept at all? The blood, the dirt on my sheets, and the cuts on my hands—they were telltale signs of sleepwalking, of the fatal insomnia. But what had I done? Had I murdered someone? Eviscerated one of my farm animals? The endless questions burned in my mind, and I had no answers.

There was no one left to watch over me. I was the sole survivor of my bloodline, the final Parisi. I would need to entrust myself to a hospice, or an asylum, depending on how rapidly I deteriorated.

But before I could make such a decision, I resolved to visit my sister one final time—before my mind abandoned me.

The air was crisp and the sky was endless over Dubrovnik as I walked to my family's tomb. I clasped the anemones in my hand and tried not to crush them on the short journey.

The sepulcher resembled a Doric temple, with broad columns and white-washed walls. *Domus Parisi*—house of Parisi—was etched into the facade. I remember thinking how fitting the title was; we spent more time dead than alive.

There were two sections to the mausoleum: the subterranean burial chamber, which had been constructed in Roman times, and the first floor antechamber in which the newly dead were placed in coffins. It was forbidden to open the tomb for a year after a fresh body was placed inside—the corpse must first turn to bones and dust before it could join our ancestors in the pit of remains.

As I approached the sepulcher, a distinct smell invaded the air. It was pungent and intensely repulsive, like wet mold mixed with musk. By the time I reached the stairs to the structure, it was overwhelming. I removed the handkerchief from my pocket and held it to my mouth and nose, trying not to gag.

My eyes scanned the entrance, and I felt the small hairs rise on the back of my neck. Something was not right with the tomb.

The sound of a woman sobbing permeated the air, the stifled cries of a young girl.

The breath jammed in my throat. *How could this be?* my mind screamed.

The sobs were coming from *inside* the tomb.

I dropped the flowers and rushed to the thick marble door. It was slightly ajar.

"Andonetta! Andonetta!" I screamed, my body pushing the frame with all my strength. The door slowly gave way and revealed the antechamber inside.

The smell of rotting flesh rose to meet me, and I was ill prepared for its intensity. My throat quivered, and the saliva pooled in my mouth. I felt my stomach cramp violently.

But the shock of what I saw froze my limbs, overriding my reaction to the decay.

There was a woman standing inside the tomb before Andonetta's coffin, her back to me. She was dressed in a black gown with a silk-and-lace veil—I had buried my sister in those very robes.

My mind scrambled. There had been some kind of mistake. She had never really died—she must have been trapped in a deep coma from the insomnia. And I had buried her alive, my own flesh. I had entombed her in the sepulcher like a medieval criminal.

"Andonetta," I whispered, my voice hoarse and penitent.

She whirled to confront me.

The face was not that of a sixteen-year-old girl, not the Andonetta whom I wished to remember. Her wrinkled cheeks were bathed with tears, and deep aubergine troughs marred the space under her eyes.

It was the face of an old woman.

———————◆‹••⟩◆⟨••›◆———————

The ghostly apparition flew into my arms, the black lace and silk trailing behind her.

"Oh, Vittorio! Vittorio!" she sobbed into my chest, her small fists pounding my sternum.

I had been holding my breath the entire time. The air evacuated my lungs as relief, and disappointment, flooded through me.

This was not my Andonetta. It was Dagmara, her childhood nurse.

"Vittorio, who would do such a thing? It goes against God," she wept bitterly, her emerald eyes glassy and confused. "Your poor sister," she continued, gesticulating wildly at the coffin.

I held Dagmara at arm's length and searched her face for an explanation.

"What are you talking about?" I spat, my voice cantankerous.

"She's been defiled!" she hissed. Her eyes flashed wildly in their sockets, and her long, wet eyelashes were matted to her skin. She collapsed helplessly into my arms, and I held her fragile body against mine. I felt her shoulder blades, rigid and cramped, the bones jutting from her back.

My eyes slowly grew accustomed to the darkness within the tomb, and I eventually understood what Dagmara was saying—why she was so distraught.

Andonetta's coffin was slightly ajar, the heavy mahogany lid misplaced at an odd angle. I saw four slim, pallid fingers resting against the lip of the wood, the nails black and surrounded by greenish meat. There were large welts on the back of her hand, as though sharp nails had dug into her skin and the flesh had fallen away. Black blood snaked down her exposed fingers, sinuous lines across her rotted flesh.

The same blood that I had found on my sheets the previous night.

❖

I blinked, and I was sitting upright in my bed, the nighttime air slicing my face like an icy whip.

What had happened? A moment ago, it had been morning, and I was in Andonetta's tomb with Dagmara. Now it was night, and I was back in my villa, alone in the dark. My eyes were horribly dry, and the skin of my eyelids felt like razors as I tried to blink. I

MASQUERADE & OTHER STORIES

hadn't slept at all; my eyes had been open the entire time. Another fit of sleepwalking.

I switched on the lamp and a dim sepia glow flooded my vision. The antique clock at my bedside revealed that it was three in the morning. Almost an entire day had vanished.

I placed my head in my hands and sighed heavily. What had I done this time?

A body stirred under the sheets next to me, and I was dismayed to find another faceless woman asleep in my bed. There was a half-emptied bottle of vodka on the bedside table and an ashtray filled with cigarette butts.

I tried to piece my fragmentary memories together. I must have visited the bar in Old Town Dubrovnik and seduced the brunette in my bed. The air was laden with the scent of perspiration and stale smoke. It was the only rational explanation for the presence of the woman. She was asleep on her stomach, so I couldn't see her face, just her onyx hair, fanned across the duvet, contrasting beautifully with the white linen. I doubted I would recognize her anyway—even my regular memories were becoming hazy and obscure.

Was this how the remainder of my existence would play out? Helplessness and fear clutched at my insides. Was this to be my

- 81 -

life—long periods of sleepwalking cut with brief flashes of consciousness?

Andonetta had known the sleepwalking would never cease when she awoke that morning in June, just months before she died. She sensed that her last night of sleep had vanished, evaporated like wasted wine, and that she was not meant for this world for much longer. There were periods where she would flutter in and out of consciousness, when her eyes would be wide open, but she would be unresponsive, her body enacting her dreams and maneuvering as though she were awake.

In the final month before she died, the sleepwalking had grown progressively worse. On a particularly horrible occasion, I had spoken to her for more than an hour through a translucent dressing screen in her boudoir while she attended to her hair and applied makeup. When she emerged, she was the image of a corpse, with ethereal white robes and garish, blood red lipstick across her mouth. She began to vomit uncontrollably, and large, undigested pieces of offal were thrown from her lips. We discovered later that she had stolen a large quantity of raw meat from the cellar and eaten it all, dreaming that she was at the court of our ancestor Massimo

XVI, founder of the Parisi line. When consciousness returned, her eyes were branded with deep charcoal circles, accentuating the tiny, permanent pinpricks of her pupils.

I never let her leave my sight after that, and she would chain herself to my bed each night until she died.

I examined my arms and fingers for clues from the night before. There was still dirt and blood caked under my nails, but something else drew my attention—the addition of a long, jagged cut across my forearm, reaching from my wrist to elbow.

Bewilderment gnawed at my mind, and suddenly, I couldn't think with the faceless woman in my bed.

"Get up," I hissed, nudging her shoulder with my hand. She didn't respond, continuing to sleep through my words.

I was a brutal fiend, kicking her from my bed like an unwelcome animal. For all I knew, she was a nice village girl who had helped me home and provided a few hours of sexual distraction.

"Hey," I repeated, shaking her a little harder, but still she slept on.

I sucked in an agitated breath and realized that the smell from the tomb had followed me to my bed. I placed my nails to my nostrils and inhaled deeply—they were putrid, the smell of my sister's decomposing flesh. The guilt and disgust were overwhelming, and I needed solitude. I wanted to break down without a witness.

The woman stirred faintly beneath the duvet, but made no effort to rise. My temper flared and I jumped from the bed and briskly walked to her bedside. I seized her roughly by the shoulders and shook her violently.

"Wake up!" I growled. "What's wrong with you?"

But the problem was not with her—it was with me.

She seemed to crumble in my arms. Her skin was too loose and pulpy. I feared my hands would go right through her as I squeezed, and her bones made a horrible crunching sound as they collapsed under the force of my fingers.

I recoiled from the duvet in horror. She appeared to squirm under the linen, her body writhing slowly, unnaturally. But she did not make a sound, and her face was still buried in the pillow with the jet-black hair strewn about her like ink.

Slowly, mechanically, my hand reached for the duvet, and I threw it back in a single, violent gesture.

There was no longer a woman in my bed. Just a sodden pile of decomposing flesh, strewn with worms—their tiny, bloated bodies squirming from a puncture in the corpse's back.

The force of my actions had dislodged her head. It rolled from the pillow and fell to the floor, the hideous, vacuous face staring up at me with rotted skin and exposed bones.

To my horror, the eyeballs were partially intact—the eyelids and lashes had been eaten away by vermin, but the hepatic eyeballs were not entirely devoured.

Two arctic irises burned into me, the soft lavender gaze turned to stone by death.

And the irises were two accusing witnesses, for they had seen everything that I had done in my sleepwalking trances.

They had witnessed my unconscious crime, the defilement of my sister's corpse.

The pinpricks of death had seen it all.

This story appears in *Sleep Walking*, edited by Chris Bartholomew.

6 VIOLET

had believed her eyes to be azure, but as I stared at her that morning, sunning herself in the courtyard, I realized they were violet. Luminous, violet eyes that contrasted vividly with her onyx hair.

"She's a real beauty, isn't she?" Roman said, placing his toolbox on the ground and joining me by the foyer's window. I felt slightly embarrassed having been caught staring at her.

"Yes, she is," I replied awkwardly.

"She's lived here for years. If I'm not mistaken, it's the apartment directly beneath yours." He shook his head absently, his hand rubbing the stubble on his chin. "Her family is all gone. They died in the fire last winter. It's a shame no one speaks her language. She's always calling out to me, but I can't understand a damn thing."

I nodded my head absently, and we stared on in silence.

Roman sighed heavily and picked up his toolbox. "You let me know if there are any problems with your gas connection or the water." He patted my shoulder and turned to leave. "And enjoy your new place. It's an icebox in winter, but the radiator will keep you nice and cozy. Unless you have a female friend to do the job." His eyes lit up mischievously, and I smiled mechanically in reply.

"I'm newly divorced, actually. Living on my own for the first time."

"Well, if you want my advice, get yourself a companion like her." He pointed to the courtyard.

"She'd do the trick."

Late that evening, I sat alone in my living room with a bottle of bourbon for company. The tiny studio apartment was scattered with unopened boxes, the summary of my brief existence packed into cardboard shells. My wife had taken most of our belongings in the divorce, along with our seven-year-old daughter.

And there I was, a cliché at forty-five, alone and drinking myself into oblivion.

There was a sudden tapping sound in the hall, and a shadow passed along the gap under my door. Someone was standing outside.

I opened the door uncertainly, not waiting to hear a knock. To my surprise, it was the violet-eyed beauty. Her features were drawn with anxiety, and she rushed into my apartment before I could say a word.

I wasn't quite sure how to respond. She seemed disheveled and alarmed.

"Are you okay?" I said dumbly.

I didn't understand her reply, but there was a look of pain in her violet eyes that I recognized, a reflection of my own loneliness.

"Let me get you something to drink." I fumbled in the dim light for a glass. It wouldn't be right to offer her bourbon. I opened the door to the fridge and realized it was almost completely empty, apart from a small milk carton. I poured her a glass, and she sat at the table across from me.

We sat in silence for a long while. There was no point in trying to make conversation, which was oddly liberating. No need for petty social constructions or small talk. Or perhaps that was the alcohol invading my mind.

It took her almost an hour to finish the glass of milk, and she seemed slightly more relaxed by the time she was done. But there was still a shade of fear in her violet eyes, which made me pity her.

"I need to lie down," I whispered, standing unsteadily. "The bourbon has gone straight to my head." I spoke more for my benefit than hers. I pointed to the decrepit couch near the window. "You can sleep there if you need to." I made a sleeping gesture with my hands. She seemed to understand.

I staggered to the bed and collapsed, drifting into sleep.

———◆—<•·◦◊◦··•>—◆———

At some point during the night, I became aware that she was sleeping in my arms. She was curled by my side, her hair like silk against my skin. I sighed softly and embraced her, causing her to stir and stretch her limbs lazily.

A pleasurable sound escaped her lips, and then her rhythmic breathing resumed. Her body was warm and comforting, and she didn't pull away from me.

———◆‹•·›◗◖‹•·›◆———

I was groggy the next morning. She had awakened before I did and was sitting on the windowsill, bathed in sunlight.

"Morning," I said gutturally.

Startled, she turned to face me, as though I had broken her thoughts.

Her violet eyes searched my features. The look of panic had returned, worse than the night before.

She leaned out the window and looked down to the street.

We were six stories up. It made me feel uneasy, as though she would fall, and my head was already spinning.

"You want a cigarette?" I asked.

She ignored me.

"What am I saying? Of course you don't," I muttered under my breath.

The next moment seemed infinite. Before my eyes, she suddenly let the front of her body hang out of my window, and then she pushed away from the frame with her legs.

I cried out in horror, half falling from the bed as I stumbled after her. She would surely be dead, a pulpy mess on the sidewalk below.

To my surprise, she had landed on the balcony of the apartment below mine. Her home, no doubt.

And then I understood why she had been so anxious, what had caused the fear in those brilliant violet eyes.

Her babies were on the balcony below, all six of them, crying with hunger. They had been out there all night in the cold.

She lay on her side and offered her breasts to them. All six suckled at her side, and she let out a contented purr.

I made some kind of stupid noise, an odd gasp escaping my lips. All six of her kittens stared up at me in surprise.

And they all had her violet eyes.

This story appears in *Colors*, edited by Jake Johnson.

This story was one of the winning entries in the Women On Writing winter 2013 Flash Fiction Contest.

7 MASQUERADE

aven't you heard, Gaetano? The Castello di Aubria is haunted." Emilio fastened the buttons on his tuxedo and tried to conceal the smirk on his face.

"Haunted?" Gaetano replied. "That's ridiculous. By whom?"

"Valentina di Aubria, the contessa's ancestor. They say she looks just like her."

"Perhaps it's just the contessa playing tricks." Gaetano ran a comb through his curls and examined his appearance in the Murano mirror. The thin fabric of his suit would pass for Veronese silk if the lighting at the masquerade ball was dim. He fastened the antique eye mask behind his ears, and its silver hues accentuated his pale-gray eyes.

"Tricks are your signature, Gaetano. Tonight it's the pauper dressed as a prince." Emilio's comment was harsher than he had intended, and he tried to soften his words by smiling warmly.

Gaetano clenched his fist in anger, a brutal stare imprinted on his features.

"I'm no match for you, cousin," Gaetano said with venom.

"Care to make a game of it?" Emilio asked. "My father's best bourbon for whoever can retrieve a souvenir from the contessa's private chambers."

"That's too easy—any child can steal a trinket. Let's make it interesting. Your father's best bourbon for whoever can steal a souvenir from the contessa herself."

"From the contessa? Do you mean a piece of her jewelry?"

"No, Emilio, nothing so simple." Gaetano smiled wickedly, and his pale eyes sparkled with amusement. "Something intimate— nothing less."

"Nothing less," Emilio agreed.

"Welcome, *signori*. A glass of champagne?" A maid dressed in an elegant baroque serving gown greeted Gaetano and Emilio as they entered the castle.

"Lovely, thank you," Gaetano said, accepting the beverage.

"Fabulously overdone, isn't it?" Emilio commented, surveying the opulent masquerade ball. Hundreds of guests dressed in lavish Venetian masks and gowns crowded the marble-lined ballroom of the Castello di Aubria.

"Have you seen the prize?" Emilio asked, becoming distracted by a blonde courtesan with leather-clad eyes and bright-purple feathers in her hair.

"No. In fact, I'm not altogether certain what she looks like..." Gaetano's words fell short. At that instant, he noticed a woman across the ballroom, dressed in a tight-fitting crimson gown, with long auburn curls snaking down her back. She chatted nonchalantly with a group of men, their features hidden by the traditional masks of the commedia dell'arte.

A soft laugh rose from her throat; the man dressed as Il Dottore had amused her.

Gaetano was surprised at the pang of jealousy he felt at her reaction. He instantly detested the well-dressed stranger, with his expensive shoes and gold watch.

The woman held an ivory mask surrounded by black feathers on a golden handle. She ran the feathers across Il Dottore's neck, down to his heart. It was an oddly predatory gesture, as though the feathers would slice open his arteries, and her features lit up with an intense flicker of pleasure. Her eyes slowly moved in Gaetano's direction, and she noticed him staring at her. She curled her lips in amusement, revealing a row of brilliant white teeth that were small and sharp. Her emerald eyes sparkled at him, and it made the breath catch in his lungs.

She whispered something in Il Dottore's ear, leaning her slender body against his. Gaetano felt the sting of jealousy rise in his limbs again, and he wondered why she paid the man so much attention, with his thinning hair and beady eyes flashing through his mask. Then, to Gaetano's pleasure, she abruptly turned her back on Il Dottore and began walking through the crowd.

"Well, cousin, it looks as though she's found you." A mischievous smirk played on Emilio's lips. "She's coming this way."

Her eyes remained locked with Gaetano's as she walked toward him. The guests moved from her path and averted their eyes as she passed through the crowded room.

"Gentlemen," she said, her voice like butterscotch across her lips, "I don't believe we've met." Her finger playfully traced over a wine-colored birthmark on her collarbone, just above the voluptuous curve of her breast. Gaetano stared at it, enchanted by the contrast of the crescent-shaped mark against her alabaster décolletage.

"I'm La Contessa di Aubria. Welcome to my masquerade."

———————•‹•·›◆‹·•›•———————

"Gaetano, how have I never encountered you before this evening?" She held his hand in hers as she pulled him through the castle's library. Emilio was indisposed, being entertained in a private chamber by three of the contessa's maidservants.

"I'm new to Umbria. My family is from the South. Perhaps you've heard of La Famiglia Pezzini?" Lying came naturally to him, and he hoped the small fiction would impress the contessa. The truth—that he was the illegitimate son of a cherry farmer—was likely to get him removed from the masquerade ball.

Her alabaster hand flew to her breast, and her lips parted in a sensuous smile.

"I know them intimately," she whispered in his ear, her face so close he could smell the perfume on her neck. "Come." She pulled his hand playfully. "I want to show you something."

He followed her eagerly, his footsteps clumsy and brutish as he tried to avoid treading on her long crimson gown. She led him to the rear of the library, through a door that was partially concealed by an elaborately carved wooden screen.

Behind the door was a small chamber, and the room was dimly lit with candles. Gaetano's eyes adjusted slowly to the flickering light, and his gaze lingered on the curve of her hip and tiny waist.

"This is the castle's most prized possession." She pointed her slender arm toward a wall, and Gaetano's eyes followed her bare limb, becoming distracted by her delicate fingers. He longed to kiss her hand, to place her fingertip upon his lips and taste her skin in his mouth.

"I present the original Contessa di Aubria!" Her voice took on a sinister tone, and a small, almost maniacal laugh escaped her lips. This distracted Gaetano from his fantasy, and he glanced hastily at the wall.

A tingle ran down his spine when he realized there was a life-sized portrait of the contessa's ancestor suspended before him.

"The resemblance is uncanny!" he exclaimed. "She looks just like you."

"Stunning, isn't she?" the contessa responded.

"Why is she hidden in this private chamber? She should be on display for all of Umbria to see. Beauty like hers—like yours— should never be concealed."

"I agree with you, my dear Gaetano. But many of my family would burn this portrait if I didn't keep it concealed. And there is also the matter of the superstition. Tell me, Gaetano," she said, leaning closer to whisper in his ear, "do you believe in ghosts?" Her voice had taken on a melancholy quality, as though she were confessing a horrible deed to him.

"Ghosts!" Gaetano exclaimed incredulously. "I've heard the tales of the Castello being haunted, but surely you don't believe in—"

"Oh, but I do!" she interjected, her eyes growing wild with animation. She edged closer to Gaetano, her small body pressing against his. "The original contessa was a wild and wicked woman, even for her age. Her sexual talents were well known to the aristocracy, and wealthy men from all over Umbria would travel great distances to be entertained by her. But her passions didn't stop there. She would kill the men, castrate her lovers, slitting their throats with a knife just like this one."

He hadn't seen the golden dagger in her hand, and she ran it across the inside of his thigh, gently tapping at his sex.

"A very wicked woman," he said, the blood pounding in his groin.

"Yes," she whispered, the word like a hiss through her parted lips. "Very wicked."

"And she looks just like you. She even has the crescent birthmark on her skin." He stared longingly at the delicate line of her neck, and then he let his fantasy take over. He was Gaetano of another age, of centuries past, the son of an aristocrat and not a peasant. He was making love to the original contessa, a lady of the Renaissance, and she was eager to share her sexual gifts. She was lust and danger incarnate.

His hands clutched at the contessa's crimson dress, identical to the garment in the portrait, and he pulled at the gossamer skirt until he felt the smooth skin of her thigh.

"You wicked, wicked woman," he whispered in her ear. In his mind, the two women were blending into a single being, ageless across the centuries. The doppelgänger and the original—merging to satisfy his ego, his sexual desire.

"Yes," she whispered eagerly. Her lips were upon his, hard and sensual, her teeth biting his mouth with enough gusto to cause pain. She pushed him onto the floor and climbed upon him.

"The original is much more delicious than the replica."

But he was never to know the difference.

There was a hot, fluid splash against his thigh, followed by a moment of confusion.

Then the panic set in.

"Calm yourself, my dear Gaetano." She stroked his hair lovingly and then produced the golden dagger, running it across her décolletage.

It left a streak of blood on her flesh, and he stared at her dumbly, thinking how perfectly the fluid matched the color of her dress.

There was a wild and hideous look in her emerald eyes that hadn't been there a moment before. It washed over her face until her features were contorted with malice.

Then she was lost in a state of frenzy, plunging the blade repeatedly into his body, his legs, his face. Dropping the dagger, she smiled contentedly at the portrait, her lips curling in the exact fashion of the original contessa. She could have been looking directly at a mirror were it not for the smears of blood upon her breasts.

———❖———

Emilio surveyed the grand ballroom in search of Gaetano. His hands absently adjusted his blond curls back into place, and he smirked, remembering how relentless the three chambermaids had been earlier in the evening.

"Well, my dear cousin," he whispered to himself, "I hope you are having just as much fun with the contessa."

A sudden drumroll roused him from his thoughts.

"Distinguished guests of the Castello di Aubria," a staccato voice resonated throughout the ballroom, "may I present to you Eva Angelina di Aubria, the sixteenth Contessa di Aubria!"

The crowd erupted into applause as the contessa appeared. She was dressed in a slimly fitting cobalt gown embellished with jewels—an utter contrast to her opulent crimson dress of earlier that evening.

The contessa greeted her guests warmly, and her eyes lit up at the sight of Emilio across the room. He waited impatiently as she was detained by a tall, skeletal woman with a golden mask and then an elderly man who seemed in no hurry to part with her company. He noticed that the guests no longer stared at the ground as she walked past them; they interacted freely with her as she slowly made her way toward Emilio.

He was brimming with anticipation when she finally offered her hand to him, and he eagerly accepted it, allowing his lips to linger on her fingertips for a little too long.

She's expended my cousin and now wants to compare my skills, he thought, his skin tingling with eagerness.

"Contessa." He smiled, allowing his dimples to show. "I adore your attire. The blue is much more favorable than your earlier gown. It accentuates your eyes."

"My dear patron." She giggled sweetly and allowed her hand to rest in his. "I have no idea what you are talking about. What other garment? This gown only just arrived from Milano in the last hour. It's why I'm so tardy in making my appearance."

The comment caught Emilio off guard, and he wished he had Gaetano's penchant for inventing tales.

"I'm so sorry," he said clumsily. "My mistake. I thought I had seen you in crimson earlier this evening."

"Oh, my dear." She laughed elegantly. "I never wear crimson. It is forbidden by my family. It was the color of the original contessa, the first matriarch of this family. And we all know what a scandalous being she turned out to be!" An innocent smile lit up the contessa's features, and Emilio realized that her eyes were a light shade of brown, not emerald as they had been earlier. And the birthmark, the small crimson crescent, had vanished from her collarbone.

"Why, the aristocracy would think I run around the castle murdering my lovers! We do, after all, look so similar. Ghosts, they say. It's so ridiculous! Unless you believe in that sort of thing." She giggled and squeezed his hand warmly in hers.

"Indeed," he whispered, the confusion in his voice slowly dissolving into realization, then fear.

"The Castello di Aubria is haunted."

This story appears in *The Evil Twin*, edited by Chris Bartholomew.

8 THE SPARKLE IN HER EYES

He sat in the café following her with his eyes, her fluid, effortless gestures like brushstrokes on a canvas. He remembered how her lips had tasted last night, when she had dashed the vanilla-flavored gloss across her mouth. She had worked late that night, the last barista in the café, and he had been the last customer, working on his novel while inhaling her perfume. He hadn't written a coherent sentence the entire evening, distracted by the curve of her calf encased by her sheer black stockings.

Seductive stockings, he had thought, with a long embroidered pattern that stretched from the heel of her stiletto to somewhere beneath her tight black skirt.

He had wondered where that pattern ended and how her skin would feel if he tore the stockings from her flesh and ran his fingertips over her legs.

But that was last night. When she still had that sparkle in her eyes.

Tonight she worked the graveyard shift again. They were not alone just yet; there was another customer seated at the bar, a man close in age to the novelist, perhaps a year or two his senior. But the man looked a haggard sixty, worn and beaten down by age, with thick, leathery skin and thin white hair. Antony was still young for fifty-eight. He could pass for a man in his early forties, or perhaps younger if not for the salt-and-pepper hair across his temples.

I must be doing all right, he thought, finishing his third espresso of the evening.

I'm still able to bed women in their twenties!

He let the cup clatter onto the saucer; a ringing, high-pitched noise resonated against the empty air. Louisa's eyes flashed up instinctively. After a year of waiting on him, she knew when he wanted more.

Her hands deftly maneuvered the espresso machine, the hissing and gurgling of the hot water cutting the silence as it blended with the ground arabica. A thick, black elixir dripped into the warmed espresso cup, and Louisa sprinkled the gold-and-saffron-colored cassia over it, just as Antony had taken it every day for the past year.

She walked toward him slowly, her eyes cast down to the floor before her. Her hand extended in front of her with the espresso cup; the other rested on her thigh. She could have been a pre-Raphaelite beauty, with her sensuous mouth and oversized amethyst eyes. Her thick, dark lashes scratched their way down her cheek, matching her thick chestnut hair, and he wished she would look up at him, even for an instant.

But he knew she was still angry from last night. And she had every right to be.

She placed his fresh espresso on the table and retrieved his empty cup. She turned to walk away, but he grabbed her gently by her wrist, her skin like peaches-and-cream against her black silk blouse. He could see the top of a lace camisole clinging to her bust, and he wondered if she had worn that especially for him.

"Louisa," he began, his voice sounding slightly harsher and more authoritative than usual, "we should talk about last night."

"There's no need to," she said softly, her wide mouth moving with indifference and settling into a hard line. "I understand completely. You're married, and you won't leave your wife. Last night was just that—last night. Nothing more."

She shook her hand free of his grip and returned to the bar, handing the other customer his bill and powering off the espresso machine. It hissed with irritation, and the hot steam exhaled from its metal fingers as the grinder wound down.

He wished that she hadn't brought up Rachel. Poor, patient Rachel, who tolerated his late-night escapades and never questioned him. Rachel, with her doe-like eyes and wide, homely hips, who took care of his children and kept his house immaculate.

He sipped his espresso and returned to his laptop. The harsh, white page with the innocuous words stared back at him. The popular courtroom thrillers that he now wrote were a long way from the tortured literature of his youth in Wales. But his fans preferred the formulaic novels of murder and rape to the elegant prose that he had struggled for years to publish.

He took another sip of his espresso and thought about last night. He had driven Louisa to his cabin in the woods, and she had guzzled amaretto liqueur—stolen from the café—the entire way there. He had rested his hand on her thigh, her skin warm beneath her panty hose. He could feel the strong, rhythmic pulse on the inside of her leg as his fingers played with her concealed skin.

He had grown impatient, ripping the nylon with his hands. She had laughed, a half-crazed, bitter cackle that had briefly alarmed him until she pressed her mouth against his, biting his lower lip.

The flavor of his espresso brought him out of the memory. It tasted different, odd, slightly bitter. He had almost finished the entire cup; only a thick black residue clung to the bottom. He brought the cup to his nose and sniffed.

Strange, he thought. *Like bitter almonds.* Perhaps the cassia had gone rancid.

That's what had attracted him to the café in the first place, the cassia that was added to his regular espresso. It wasn't the traditional chocolate-colored cassia available in the local supermarket and that tasted like old bark. This was an amber, saffron-flavored blend that only grew in Rajasthan and cost more than gold per ounce. That's what had lured him through the door, but he had stayed because of the pretty waitress.

He hadn't noticed Louisa as she returned to his side. She collected the cup and wiped the tabletop, her jasmine scent lingering about her. She seemed to take her time, putting more effort into the task than usual.

She's waiting for me to say something, he thought. *She wants me to say that last night wasn't a mistake, that it wasn't just a once-off.*

"I think the cassia has gone rancid," he said, a cough interrupting his words before he could continue.

He felt as though he would cough again, so he reached into his pocket and retrieved his handkerchief, pressing it to his lips to stifle the sound.

He noticed a bright-red splash of color against the fabric as he returned the handkerchief to his pocket and wondered if it was blood. But he didn't have time to check. She was staring at him now. And she looked like she wanted to speak.

"You know," she began, inhaling a ragged breath through her voluptuous lips as she spoke, "I read one of your short stories this morning. It's one of your earlier works.

Impossible to find. I had to write to a collector in Germany, and it took him almost six months to send it to me. I had been saving it for a special occasion, but after last night, I didn't see the point in waiting anymore." She paused, her voice harsher than he remembered it. Unconsciously, she drew her lips into an icy line with every breath.

"My favorite part," she continued, crooking her head to the side so that her chestnut curls fell in waves across her bust, "is when the heroine gets her revenge on her lover by mixing cyanide in his bourbon. What was that line that you used?"

His spine prickled with fear, and he felt his heart pound against his chest.

"A tawny whirlpool," he whispered, but she overtook his words.

"A tawny whirlpool in his glass." She smiled, her lips pulled back over her brilliant white teeth in an almost bestial snarl.

Tawny, he thought, *just like Rajasthani cassia. And bitter, just like cyanide.*

He coughed, the blood gurgling in his throat.

And there it was again.

The sparkle in her eyes.

This story appears in *Last Night*, edited by Dorothy Davies.

9 LAZARETTO

"Come…closer."

Grandmother is ill, and her voice is shaky. She reaches out her hand, skeletal and frail, and I feel a little scared to touch it. Her nails and lips have turned blue. She hasn't got long now.

"Listen…carefully."

She pulls me closer and whispers in my ear. "Under the stairs, in the tiny room…that's where I put her. She can't stay there. It's why we are all sick. Move…her."

She makes a choking sound like she's trying to spit out another word but can't. Her voice fades away, and the breath escapes her lungs. I'm terrified.

"Who's in the room, Grandmother? Who?" I scream and shake her body, but she's already limp. She was fine yesterday, caring for others in the ward. Now she's gone.

I'm half-crazed as I run down the corridor toward the stairs. I ignore the cries for help and the screams of pain that come from the dozens of rooms that line the hall. They call it death's hollow, the quarantine wing of the lazaretto where the infected are sent to die.

I fly down the stairs and nearly trip as I reach the lower floor. The tiny chamber under the staircase is locked, and I pound the wooden door furiously, so hard that my fists bleed. The door is old and decayed. As I hit it, part of the frame crumbles and the door gives way.

The room is almost completely dark. There's light coming in from the hall, but I can't see very well. My eyes adjust slowly, and I stretch out my hands as I stumble in the darkness.

"Hello? Is anybody here?" I ask of the blackness, but no one replies. "My grandmother sent me to get you. Do you need medical help?" She must be the first patient who became ill if she was locked down here by herself. How horrible, trapped in this tiny room, in the darkness. I wonder how long she's been down here.

My hand brushes against something, and I instinctively jump back. I realize it's just a bit of fabric, like the lace trim of a dress, and I feel a little relieved. I reach out my hand again, and this time someone clasps it.

"Mama?" she whispers. She sounds very young.

Her grip is weak. She must be sitting in a chair, alone and ill in this horrible little chamber.

"My name is Annalisa. I'm going to take you to the ward." I place my other hand on hers in a comforting gesture and give her a gentle rub so that she knows I'm a friend.

"I'm going to lift you up and get you out of here." I speak slowly, and I hope she understands. I put my hands around her torso. She's so thin; I can feel all her bones.

Gently, I try to lift her out of the chair and take her in my arms. She's almost weightless, like a handful of feathers.

There is a loud crunching sound, and the smell of rot hits the air. I try not to gag. She's been left to die in her own waste.

"It's all right. I've got you. We're going upstairs."

I rush toward the hallway with her in my arms. As I near the door, light floods my vision and my eyes readjust to the brightness.

That's when I look down.

It's not a girl in my arms. It's a skeleton.

I stare at her dumbly, thinking how pretty her white-blonde hair and lace dress are. The dress hangs limply in my arms, and my eyes search the spot where her legs should be.

I've ripped her body in half.

My foot slips and I fall to the ground. The door shuts, and the room is plunged into darkness.

Someone's screaming, and it takes me a moment to realize that it's me.

———◆◇◆———

"How long has this place been abandoned?" Josephine asked, breathing the question through chattering lips. This was what she lived for—ancient ruins gave her a blood rush like nothing else could.

"At least two hundred years," Arturo responded, his voice shaky from the cold. "I have it on good authority that the castle belonged to some kind of obscure Italian noble family who all died mysteriously in the thirteenth century. It was converted into a lazaretto soon after."

He failed to mention that the "good authority" was a black market antiquities dealer he had met in a beachside bar on the mainland.

There had been the faintest flicker of fear in the man's eyes when he mentioned the lazaretto. Arturo hadn't cared at the time; he knew Josephine would be wild with excitement once he told her about it.

They had been hiking for hours through the rocky mountainside of the Isola di Sophia, about six miles west of the Dalmatian coastline. The earth was coarse and difficult to navigate; the island wasn't on any of the local maps. The Adriatic air was icy, and the wind sounded like distant hounds baying at the moon.

"There's no risk of infection, right?" She threw him a mischievous grin, her emerald eyes glittering in the waning sunlight.

"No, of course not," he replied, his voice betraying his uncertainty. "Whatever disease was quarantined in the castle would have been wiped out after two centuries of solitude. Besides, broad-spectrum antibiotics would take care of anything else."

Or so he hoped.

The crumbling walls and steeples of the lazaretto seemed perfectly molded into the surrounding mountain. The road leading to the castle was almost nonexistent, overgrown with thorny plants and man-sized grass. As he surveyed the landscape, Arturo felt a slight tingle of apprehension in his abdomen. The idea of spending a night in the lazaretto, a towering mess of decaying architecture, was making him nervous. But he suppressed the sensation and focused on Josephine.

She seems to be her old self again. She's finally put it behind her, he thought.

A navy dusk was descending around them, and the curtain of night seemed to touch the castle first, before it descended on the rest of the island.

"We need to clear the citadel walls before sundown, otherwise we'll be camping on frost by morning," Josephine cautioned. She readjusted her backpack, and her sleeping bag almost tumbled from its anchor at the base of her neck. Arturo steadied it with his free hand, brushing aside her auburn ponytail as he did so. The brief contact with her bare skin enticed him, sending small slivers of electricity through his arm.

She hadn't let him touch her since the miscarriage almost three months earlier. A part of her had died with the child, and she'd become distant, withdrawn. But here, on the crumbling threshold of the lazaretto, she was alive again.

"Do you hear that?" he asked, forcing her to turn and face him.

"Hear what? I don't hear anything."

"Exactly," he replied. "Shouldn't there be more noise? What about insects or birds? Or even some bats?"

She smiled faintly and continued toward the ruins. "The whole island's gone dead silent with the dark."

"I'm exhausted. We've been exploring for hours. Let's set up camp in this room." Arturo yawned loudly and threw his sleeping bag on the ground. A large plume of dust spread into the air, drenching the flashlight in tiny flakes of debris. "Where exactly are we, anyway?"

"I think we're in the old contagion wing," Josephine answered. "They would have quarantined the terminally ill in this ward."

"I've got a surprise for you. Lie down and close your eyes."

Josephine compliantly spread her sleeping bag next to his and sat in anticipation, her small hands covering her eyes. Arturo reached into his backpack and produced three scented candles, a bottle of cheap red wine, and a box of Italian chocolates. He lit the candles and the scent of jasmine filled the air, making Josephine smile.

"You can open them," he said, leaning over to kiss her neck.

Josephine giggled and clapped her hands in delight. "I love it," she gushed, and returned his kiss.

But their intimate moment was cut short.

There was a sudden scream from the hall, followed by the sound of muffled crying. Startled, they both leaped to their feet.

"Is someone there?" Josephine called, her features pinched with concern.

Silence. Then the crying started again.

Cautiously, they both approached the door. Josephine was the first to peer outside as Arturo pointed the flashlight down the dark corridor.

"Hello!" she called, her voice echoing through the emptiness and then fading into silence. The sound of a young girl's sobs broke the quiet. It was faint, but unmistakable.

The hairs prickled on the back of Arturo's neck. He waved his flashlight in the darkness.

"Who's there?" he shouted.

"Be quiet! You'll scare her!" Josephine chastised. At that instant, the light passed across the form of a small child.

"There!" Josephine cried, her heart pounding in her chest as she snatched the flashlight from Arturo. She ran down the hallway, the light unsteady in her hands. "Little girl! Little girl!" she called, but there was no reply.

Josephine reached the end of the hall and turned to her left. To her surprise, there stood the child, at the top of a staircase.

Josephine gasped loudly. "You scared me!" she exclaimed, dropping to her knees and examining the girl. The child wore a white lace dress, and her hair was an odd shade of pale blonde, the kind of color that belonged to a much older woman.

"Where did you come from?" Josephine asked, extending her hand to the girl.

"There's someone trapped under the stairs. We have to help her," the girl replied, ignoring the question. She turned and walked mechanically down the stairs.

"Wait!" Josephine cried after the child as she followed her. Arturo was calling out from the hallway, unable to see through the darkness, but she was oblivious to his cries.

"What are you doing in this place? Where is your mother?" Josephine questioned, feeling the stir of maternal instinct. The child continued to walk slowly down the staircase. When she reached the bottom, she turned and faced Josephine so that her brilliant eyes were lit up by the flashlight.

"I live here. My mother abandoned me," she said, her voice quavering with emotion. "In there." The girl extended an alabaster arm toward a small door under the stairs. "She's inside."

Josephine looked quizzically at the girl. "There's someone in there?" she asked with apprehension.

"Yes. You have to help her. She's trapped."

"How horrible." Josephine's hands flew to her mouth, and she rushed to the door, forcing it open. The wood was old and badly rotted. The door opened easily.

Josephine swung the flashlight through the small chamber, examining the room. It was crowded with furniture, much of which was covered with dark sheets and a thick layer of dust.

But there was no one there.

"I don't see her," Josephine whispered, and the young girl crept slowly to her side, taking her by the hand. The unexpected contact sent a brief spasm of fear down Josephine's spine.

"She's under there." The child pointed to a long box-shaped object covered with a damask curtain. She began to pull Josephine toward it.

Reluctantly, Josephine removed the drape covering the box, and a small, stifled cry caught in her throat.

It was a coffin. A child's coffin.

"Promise you'll never leave me?" the child said in a gentle, almost meek voice. Josephine nodded instinctively. "Then open it," the girl commanded.

"Josephine!" Arturo exclaimed, standing at the entrance to the small chamber. His breathing was labored, and sweat drizzled down his neck. "What happened—" he began, but his words were cut short.

The door slammed shut before he could enter the room. He pounded his fists against the wood and screamed Josephine's name, but she could barely hear his muffled cries.

"Open it!" the girl repeated, and Josephine stared at her dumbly, compelled to obey.

There was a crude cross etched into the wood of the coffin, the kind of thing a child might scratch with a rock. Josephine traced her finger over it before she lifted the lid and let it clatter to the ground.

With trepidation, she looked inside, the skin crawling on her arms and back. There would be a body, the small, decomposing body of a child. And the image would be burned into Josephine's mind; she would never be able to forget it. It would be the lifeless body of a small girl, of the child she should have borne—the daughter who had died in her womb.

But there was nothing there.

The coffin was empty.

Josephine let out a deep sigh. She hadn't realized she'd been holding her breath.

There was a faint glimmer in the coffin. The light had caught something red and shiny. Josephine plunged her hand into the casket and retrieved a necklace with a small glass vial attached to it. She held it up to the light and examined it closely.

The young girl shivered, and her head jerked violently.

The vial was filled with blood.

Josephine glanced from the pendant to the young girl, and a scream caught in her throat. The child's face was decaying rapidly. The alabaster skin turned a putrid shade of green, and the beautiful blue eyes were gone, replaced with vacant sockets.

The vial shattered in Josephine's hand, and the glass seemed to move of its own accord, tracing a deep laceration down her wrist. She stared in shock as her own blood gushed from the wound, mixing with the infected blood of the young girl.

"Now we can be together forever, Mother."

This story appears in *Bloody Ghost Stories*, edited by Brianna Stoddard.

10 DON'T LET HIM SEE YOU CRY

hat's where the bitch is buried, boy." He spits the word "boy" like it's something rotten. He never calls me by my name. He never calls me "son."

He points an accusing finger at the unmarked tombstone.

His grip tightens on my wrist, and I hear a crunching sound before I feel the pain. Acid shoots up my arm and through my spine. My knees buckle. I bite down on my lip—hard. The only way I can stop myself from crying. If I cry, if I make a sound, he'll beat me until I can no longer walk.

"Don't you ever forget what she did to me." He shakes me and the pain is pure blackness. *"Your fucking slut of a mother!"* He barks the words at my face and throws me at the grave. I slam into the tombstone, my face scratching along the icy concrete.

He spits on me, on my mother's grave. The gravel crunches under his steel caps as he walks away.

I'm alone in the cemetery, with a blackened elm tree reaching its skeletal fingers down toward me.

I wonder why there's no name on her grave.

* * *

Marco awoke with a jolt. Electricity coursed through his limbs, and he scratched at his face, his fingers raking the stubble on his cheeks. Sweat drenched his undershirt. The darkness disoriented him, and his fingers probed the vacant air for the tombstone.

Where am I?

A jagged breath hitched in his throat, caught on a coppery fluid. He gagged, struggling to breathe.

"Marco!" A woman's voice cut the dark. Light flooded his vision. "Are you all right? You were screaming in your sleep." She wrapped her short robe tightly around her camisole. He couldn't help but notice the curve of her hip against the silk. She sat on the bed by his side and stroked his cheek with her soft fingers.

"It was just a bad dream, my sweet boy."

Something about the way she spoke, the way the words rolled from her tongue, reminded him of the woman in the unmarked grave.

"That's where the bitch is buried, boy."

His thoughts snapped from the lingering dream. Reality flooded back.

"Mom," he groaned, feeling awkward at her touch. He preferred to call her Aria, but she had been "Mom" ever since he was six, ever since she had adopted him. Claimed a stray as her own. Not that he remembered those days.

He coughed, and the taste of copper coated his tongue.

"You're bleeding," she said, her forearm dusting across his naked thigh as she reached for a tissue. It made him uncomfortable, and he pulled the bed sheets across his shorts. She dabbed at the blood on his lower lip and smiled at him.

"I bit my lip in my sleep," he mumbled. The dream cut his vision, the cemetery with the elm tree blurred into his bedroom. He rubbed his eyes, his mind caught between the two states.

"Do you want me to make you a hot cocoa?" Aria said, teasing the stubble on his chin with the tissue. She looked like a child with her oversized eyes and rosebud mouth.

"Don't you ever forget what she did to me."

He shook the violent thoughts from his mind.

"No, Mom," he said, turning away from her and licking the remaining blood from his mouth. She placed the bloodied tissue on his desk, causing her robe to spill open and reveal her cream-colored leg. His eyes followed the deep line of muscle along her thigh. He wondered if her legs were as soft as her fingertips.

"Do you want coffee and a *cigaretta?*" Aria giggled. She could usually mask her Slavic accent, but never when she said *"cigaretta."*

"I'm not legal yet," he said.

"It's never stopped us before." She hugged him against her body, and he wished she didn't feel so warm, so comforting. Her skin smelled of strawberries, and he could taste coconut as his lips brushed against her hair.

Her hand stroked a piece of bone that protruded from his shoulder. It never set right, and when winter came, it felt like broken glass under his skin.

"Was it that dream again?" she asked.

He pulled away from her.

"Yes," he replied. He couldn't stand it when she looked at him that way, her gaze imploring him, begging him to forget, to leave their miseries in the past.

"He won't ever hurt you—"

"I need some sleep, Aria." He turned away from her, pulling the sheets over his body. The thin fabric draped against him, clinging to the film of sweat that covered his skin.

She exhaled a long breath, running an alabaster hand through her hair.

"We're not in the old country anymore, Marco."

The blood seeped from his lip again, but he ignored the sensation and let it drizzle down his chin.

She stood, walked from his room, and killed the light.

It takes me an hour to walk home from the cemetery in the black rain. By the time I get home, my feet are bleeding. My shoes are too small and ripped at the toes. I crawl into the kitchen through a hole in the door. I think it's for a dog, but we've never had pets before. Maybe there was a bird once, when Mama was alive.

He's left his butcher's jacket and belt of knives in the kitchen, just as he does every night. I pull out the biggest blade of the bunch. It's the one he always waves at me. He says he'll cut my throat with it. Maybe one day he'll really do it.

I put the blade to my neck and hold it against my skin. I don't press as hard as he does, not enough to make it bleed. It feels cold, but not as cold as I do. I'm dripping wet with rain.

I hear him breathe heavily in his sleep. He's sprawled on the floor somewhere between the kitchen and the bathroom. He doesn't even make it into bed anymore. The air smells of bourbon. He's smashed the bottle again.

I stand beside him and stare at the sleeping beast on the floor. A strip of light from the hallway cuts across the lower part of his face. I finger the blade still in my hand. His body remains in the shadows. I can't see his eyes; it's too dark. The light falls across his lips and neck.

His neck.

I shake him with my foot. He mumbles something in his sleep.

I put the blade to his throat and press down, just as he does to me when he's mad.

"Elena." His voice is rough and clouded with sleep. "You bitch!" He raises both his hands as if to

strangle the air.
  I press a little harder…

━━━━●━<•••⟩◆⟨••⟩●━━━━

"Marco!" Aria screamed as a glass slipped through her fingers.

He stood in their kitchen, his eyes wide and vacant, his fingers curled around a blade. He pointed the knife before him, his hand dripping with blood, a crimson mess on the floor in front of him.

"Marco!" she repeated, shaking him. He didn't respond. "Marco, wake up!" She slapped him across the face, and the blade clattered to the floor. He blinked; his vision blurred as his eyes darted from Aria to his lacerated hand. Blood pooled at his feet.

"You should have left me in Ossetia," he said, his words flat and almost inaudible. "I'm a danger to you, to everyone around me."

Aria pressed a tea towel to his wound. "You were just a child." Her mouth quivered. "You were so dear to me. I would never have left you behind. I owed your mother that much." She dropped the tea towel and covered her eyes with her hands. His blood mingled with her tears and ran down her cheeks in cherry-colored streaks.

It weakened him to see her like that. He pulled her against his body and felt her shudder like a small, wounded creature. She felt so fragile in his arms, so delicate. He wanted to run his hand down her spine, to feel her protruding vertebrae against his fingers. But instead he clenched his fist, his nails cutting into his calloused palms.

"You were so young," he whispered into her hair, the scent of strawberries drowning his senses. "Why did you pretend to be my mother?" His lips were almost on her neck. "Anything else. Not my mother."

Don't do it. It's wrong. It's wrong. It's wrong.

"It would have raised too many questions," she muttered between sobs. "We needed to get away from Ossetia, as far away from that life as we could. No one would suspect a young mother with her child."

It's wrong.

"And there are others here, in the community, who watch us. The consulate, Ivanoff and his wife. If they realize who we are…" She didn't finish her thought.

He kissed her softly, his lips buried in the hollow of her neck.

She sighed, her fingers curling into his chest like a playful kitten. He lifted her against his chest. Her legs wrapped around his hips, and he could feel the hot pulse of her sex against his skin.

They abandoned the kitchen, his feet trailing black streaks of blood across the tiled floor.

———◄••⊃◆⊂••►———

The sound of screaming metal woke Marco. The other car had come out of nowhere—a green blur in his peripheral vision. He hit the brakes hard, swearing, his heart slamming against his ribs. The car skidded to a halt on the side of the road.

A fat hand slapped Marco's window.

"What's your fucking problem, asshole?"

Marco stared at the middle-aged man. A filthy sweat stain had formed down the front of his shirt. There was a knife in Marco's glove box. He could reach it in a second.

Doesn't he know how dangerous I am? Doesn't he know what I've done?

The memory scratched at his mind. Almost out. Someone had locked it away, but the cage was eroding.

"Hey! I'm talking to you! Open the window, asshole!"

Marco rubbed his temples. A constant migraine hammered behind his eyes. He shifted the gear into drive and sped off.

Are you cold in there, alone in your grave?

The decaying hands encircled him, pressing his face against the rotted breast. He couldn't breathe. The smell of putrefaction was everywhere. Maggots. The maggots had eaten her eyelids, exposing her eyeballs. The tiny veins had burst from the trauma. Red pinpricks around a blue sun.

"Elena." The voice scathed Marco's mind. His father. The butcher.

"You bitch!"

Marco growled and shook the steering wheel. The road snaked before him and the dividing line disappeared under his wheels. Shadows danced across his dashboard. The elm tree with the black hands. No. Just clouds against the sun.

He reached for the vial of pills on his passenger seat, fumbling with the steering wheel in one hand. The air was cold between his teeth as he sucked on the tablet, and he enjoyed the brief shock it gave his system. A small, pathetic cry escaped his throat, tickling the acid trail from the tablet. He dug his nails into his eyes.

If only he could sleep.

He arrived at Aria's dance studio within minutes, his mind numb from the narcotic. "Ave Maria" floated throughout the hall. Aria's favorite. She glided across the polished wood floor like liquid. He was momentarily breathless; she sucked the venom right out of him.

Every eye in the room was on her. Her peach leotard blended into her skin, the flesh-colored skirt like butterfly wings around her hips. It made the bruise on her neck stand out, like a black smudge on a porcelain doll.

My dirty fingers playing with forbidden things.

Aria's students followed her fluid moments with precision, mimicking the elongation of her leg and the delicate arc of her arm. She was oblivious to Marco's entrance. He slumped against the rear door, his reflection staring back at him from the mirrored wall. He looked older than his years. His eyes sank into aubergine troughs and his large, sensuous mouth was too severe for his face.

The music drew to a placid finale, and the young girls clapped their hands. Some scurried to the locker room; a few lingered around Aria, questioning her on techniques and rhythms. She spotted Marco in the corner and gestured for him to join her.

The girls turned to inspect the male figure in their presence. An auburn-haired ballerina blushed at the sight of Marco and whispered to her companion. They giggled behind cupped hands and flushed cheeks.

Aria smiled and embraced Marco, drawing him close to her side.

"Miss Konstantinova?"

Marco felt Aria's body stiffen at the sound of her name. A middle-aged woman with garish lipstick stood behind them. Her mouth pressed in a disapproving line as she eyed Marco's hand on Aria's waist.

"Hello, Mrs. Ivanoff," Aria replied, pulling away from Marco. He could sense her surprise at the presence of the woman, but she recovered her composure in an instant. "Audrey was just wonderful today. She's quite the star." Aria gesticulated absently at the auburn-haired child, avoiding the mother's eyes.

The woman ignored the compliment. "Is this your boyfriend?" she questioned, offering a plump hand to Marco. Her eyes glanced over his black jeans and faded shirt. A small sweat mustache had formed above her mouth.

"Oh, heavens, no!" Aria laughed a little too forcefully. "This is my son, Marco. Marco, this is the consulate's wife, Mrs. Ivanoff."

"Enchanté," he said, accepting the woman's hand and drawing it to his lips for a light kiss.

Give the old bitch something to gossip about.

Her daughter gasped and then giggled with her friends in the background. He glanced at them and smiled.

"Your son?" Mrs. Ivanoff almost spat the words, shaking her hand free of Marco. "But he looks, well, I mean, I just assumed he was your age."

"I was a child myself when I had him," Aria replied, her mouth drawn in a perfect smile, but her eyes glanced at Marco. She cupped a hand over the bruise on her neck.

"Yes, well, I'm sure you were. Come along, Audrey!" Mrs. Ivanoff snapped her fingers at her daughter, and the child scurried to her side.

The remaining students exited, leaving Aria and Marco alone in the dance hall. She stared at him, her teeth biting into her lower lip. He hated when she did that. It made the blood rush to his groin.

"What the *fuck* was *that*?" she hissed. She slapped repeatedly at his shoulder. "Kissing her on the hand? What were you *thinking*?"

He seized her by her wrists—he could fit them both into the palm of a single hand. She squirmed against him, but he was too strong.

"Are you jealous, Mother?" He pulled her a little closer.

"Let me go, Marco."

The anger in her voice excited him, and he pulled her a little tighter, squeezing her tiny wrists harder.

"Mother," he repeated, his mouth brushing against her ear.

Her wrist cracked.

"You're hurting me!"

"Don't you ever forget what she did to me—your slut of a mother!"

He let go of Aria, his face ashen. She rubbed her wrists, tears spilling down her cheeks.

"This is serious," she said. "If anyone ever found out, they would take you away from me. They would deport us. We would be murdered in Ossetia." She hugged her sides, and Marco could see the imprint of his fingers on her skin. "Do you want them to burn me? To slit my throat and hang me for the animals to eat? We would never survive. They think that I'm the one who did it. They swore vengeance on me. Your father—"

"I'd protect you."

"There is nowhere to hide from—"

"Stop talking about him!" Marco spat.

"The drunken piece of shit that beat me and mom every day. Who would beat me more if I ever cried from the pain. I remember, *Aria*."

"You remember?" She recoiled as though he had struck her. The hall was silent except for the sound of Marco's panting breath.

"Yes. No. I don't know. My head is a mess." Marco's pulse thumped deep within his abdomen, and he buried his face in his hands.

All he wanted, in that instant, was to be a child again. To curl his body against hers. Feel the touch of her nose as she smelled the infant skin of his scalp. But he had grown up too fast—and she not enough.

We're trapped in this lie. There's no way out.

Mama is giggling in the other room.

We've just come back from the ballet where Mama danced a duet with Sasha. It's the first time she's performed since she had me, and she's still so excited. She says she wants to perform all the time from now on.

She's dancing with Sasha again, but in the drawing room this time. I feel uncomfortable watching them through my keyhole. I shy away from the door, but I can still hear their laughter.

She's always happy when Sasha comes around. They eat French food and drink wine from Stavropol. They hold hands and kiss. They don't fight like she does with Papa.

There's a clap of thunder as the front door slams shut.

"Elena."

It's papa's voice, and he's angry. He's always mad. Why is he home so early? It isn't nighttime yet.

There's screaming, and I hear glass smash. I hope it's not the crystal ballerina. Mama was the model for that figurine—a translucent angel in mid-pirouette— and when the sunlight catches it, small rainbows appear at her fingertips.

"—you bitch!"

I crawl to my door and peek through the keyhole. I don't see Sasha anymore. Just Mama and Papa. It always makes me sick when they fight. The kind of feeling that makes me want to throw up.

I see him standing over her. She's on her knees, her hands out by her sides.

"You slut!" His hands are digging into her face. His slips his fingers around her neck.

I saw him kill a chicken once. Popped its head right off with his bare hands. He's trying to do the same to Mama.

I struggle to open the door and rush toward him. I'm screaming, but I don't know what I'm saying. I pound my fists on his legs, on his back. Anywhere I can reach.

But he doesn't notice me.

He always says I'm weak. Weak like a little girl. And he hates women—all women—but especially my mother.

Mama's eyes are so big, like they will pop right out of her head. The veins have burst, and there is a tear of blood running down her cheek.

She looks at me, and she is trying to say something, but the word never leaves her lips.

Papa jerks his shoulders, and there's a horrible cracking sound.

Crack. Crack. Crack. Mama's bones.

He lets her go, and she slumps to the floor.

Her eyes are wide and glassy, and I know she's no longer there.

—◆—‹•••›◆‹•••›—◆—

Marco's body was on fire. Something heavy covered his chest. He tried to sit up and realized that it was a limp arm. Naked legs were curled within his own. The room smelled of perspiration and a sweet, musky odor.

"Marco," Aria mumbled, "go back to sleep."

She scratched his chest with her nails, and he felt comforted by her touch. He pulled her closer to him, feeling the damp of her skin against his own.

He breathed in her scent and fell asleep to the sound of her rhythmic breathing.

———◆◆◇◆◇◆◆———

...I press a little harder.

He struggles and thrashes around, but it's too late. The knife slices through the right side of his throat like warm butter.

There's a gurgling sound as the blood foams from his mouth. He's vomiting thick, red fluid from the wound. The more he moves, the more blood escapes. It's all over me. Hot and sticky, and it smells like his butcher's shop.

I want to see the rest of his face, but the lights are still out—there's just that small strip illuminating his throat and lips.

Even in the darkness, I still feel his anger. It's like venom. His hands are clawing at me. I want to see his eyes, to see if he has that same look that Mama had when she died. I lean forward a little more.

Big mistake.

He grabs hold of my shirt and pulls me down. His other hand knocks me in the temple, and I see stars. Everything turns violet, and I'm not sure which way is up or down. I can't black out, or he'll break my neck too.

I stab the air with the knife, feel it sink into the deep fat of his belly. I do it over and over again. There's a howl—one of his animals being slaughtered. No. It's just Papa. Or it's me. I can't be sure.

Then everything is quiet, everything is still.

The lights flicker on, and I see the mess. Blood, hair, pieces of skin, and something white like offal.

Someone scoops me up. The knife clutters to the ground.

I look into the largest blue eyes I've ever seen. I put my small hand to her lips, and it leaves a crimson stain, like the juice of an overripe passion fruit. She smells like strawberries.

"Sasha!"

The gurgling sound from his dream awakened Marco. It had latched onto his mind and accompanied him back to reality.

The first thing he felt was the cold. He should have been tangled in Aria's bare limbs, but he wasn't. He stood in her bedroom by her side.

"Aria," he whispered into the darkness, "I remember. I remember everything."

She didn't respond, still sleeping.

"I remember you dancing with my mother. She only ever danced that once after I was born. And you were there. You were both demi-soloists, and you looked as though your bodies merged into one when you danced together."

He pulled the sheet from her legs, but she didn't stir.

"I remember who you were, before you were Aria." He shook her gently. She was cold—colder than he was. Her breath was heavier than usual, and it sounded wet.

The gurgling sound again.

It's not real. An aural hallucination. Not real.

A car passed by their house, shining its headlights through the bedroom window. The Venetian shades cut the light into slivers.

"I remember you—"

He saw it then. The knife in his hand, his fingers locked against it. He saw Aria, reaching her hand out to him. She opened her mouth to speak.

Blood poured from her throat.

I remember you when your name was Sasha.

This story appears in *Dangerous Dreams*, edited by Dorothy Davies.

11 ALL SORROWS

e seemed to drink me in with his jewel-black eyes. He let out a heavy breath, as though I had defeated him, worn down his resolve. Those liquid black pools moved slowly over my naked body, lingered on my bust, the small of my waist, the curve of my hip. I had ambushed him, lain in his bed waiting like a snake that hides unseen from its victim, then strikes at the prey with venomous lips. He was almost twenty years my senior, a man of thirty-three, but I was by no means a child at thirteen. Poverty

and hardship had broken me, given me insight beyond my years, or so I thought in those days.

The communists had taken power fourteen years earlier, the year before I was born. They had overthrown the king and promised a new era, equality and brotherhood for the masses. We did get equality in a way—we were all equally poor and starved. Royalty was replaced with politicians. They outlawed religion and individuality, and made themselves the new aristocracy. We lived in a broken country with a shattered political system, and anyone who didn't side with the communists was severely disadvantaged. My father had refused to sign their ideological papers. We were farmers not philosophers, and the pitiful land that we had owned was taken away. We were left with a scrap of coast that was so drenched in brine that almost nothing would grow. Our poverty and starvation was inevitable.

Signing those papers was never an option for my father; it would mean spitting on the graves of our loved ones. We, as many other families, had relatives and friends who had died trying to preserve those few basic freedoms that we had all taken for granted. My family, and a few others in our village, continued to practice our ancestral customs in secret. Every aspect of our rituals had been infected with fear. When we bathed the Madonna statue in the salt waters of the Adriatic, I imagined the sea was her tears, as though she wept for us, those lucky enough to survive the religious purging and unlucky enough to be left behind during the exodus. How naive I had been, to think that the religious icons that we infused so much of our hopes into could be of any help against the regime.

Many of my brothers and sisters had died in childhood; only seven of thirteen had survived. I should have felt some pity for those poor lost children, but my heart was so bathed with misery that sometimes I thought that they were the lucky ones. Of my siblings who survived, the eldest four boys had fled our small jewel in the Adriatic and tried to escape up north to Italy. My father's aunty had helped them; she was a nun and had been forced to flee to Rome with the inception of the new regime. Nuns and priests who stayed behind risked being murdered in the religious purging that followed. She had written to me once, having discovered that my brothers had been captured and were rotting away in labor camps or prison.

My father had a meager job far away in the city. His rations were very little, barely enough to feed a grown man, let alone a family. Those who hadn't signed the communist papers were the new class of slaves. He left my mother, my two sisters, and I to take care of our small farm and home on the coast while he was gone for months at a time.

Father wasn't there when the communists came every month to take a share of the fruits of our land. Painfully, they would count out how many potatoes we had, how many olives and grapes had grown that month. They would take the allocated share for the State, and when there wasn't enough, they would take the furniture in our home to compensate. When they found the small amount of grain that I had hidden in our cellar, they beat my mother until she passed out from the pain. When there was nothing of value in the home anymore, my mother having burned the remaining furniture for firewood rather than have the "men with suitcases" take it, they punished us. They raped my two older sisters. Mother would hide me in the cellar of the house so that I wouldn't see what happened, but I could hear the crying and screaming. When I helped bathe my sisters—Constantina and Jolanda—after the men had left, I understood exactly what had taken place.

"You're lucky that you're only a child—you hold no interest for men," Jolanda had whispered to me as she sat shivering in the metal tub that was used to wash our bodies and clothes. I had helped her dry off and dress in the rags that were her attire. The clothing fit her poorly; we had stitched the fabric so many times that it was worn and thin. I helped her to the plank of wood on the floor that was her bed.

"Get out of here, Katica, as soon as you can. Find a man and run away. No one will marry me now because I am…unclean." She whispered the last word with venom in her voice. I did not realize at the time what she was planning, I thought her broken down and weak. But she would prove me wrong.

The frost came and our small daily ration of flour and potatoes ran out by the end of winter. Father wouldn't be back from the city for three more days, and he would bring barley and olives when he came. Mother had become ill, and I feared that she wouldn't last three days without some kind of nourishment to sustain her. Constantina and I decided to steal bread from the Grdovic farm on the other side of the village. Their children were healthier than we were; their father had sided with the new regime and was being compensated for it. The two Grdovic daughters had pretty white dresses for church on Sundays. They had plump faces and rose-colored cheeks, enough food to feed their hunger. As Constantina and I crept into their kitchen through the open back door, we could hear them talking about an upcoming dance in the city.

"I'm going to wear my hair in two braids, and I'm going to use this purple ribbon on the ends." Ivana Grdovic was busily showing her sister Dragitca the beautiful thread of lilac-colored silk that she would tie in her hair. This angered my sister Constantina, but I urged her to hurry up and steal the bread that was still warm on the kitchen table.

"Whore!" Constantina whispered and spat on the floor. She took the bread and a few of the honey cakes that were next to it. We silently slipped out the back door through which we had entered and then ran like crazed witches back to our corner of the village.

Constantina tore apart the loaf of bread and tried to force my mother to eat it, but she refused to touch anything that had been stolen. She scolded us, saying that we would attract evil spirits with our crime. She wanted us to throw away the bread rather than eat it, but instead, I wrapped it in cloth and buried it in the yard where she wouldn't find it. I thought hunger would get the better of her after a day and she might change her mind.

The following day, Mother grew extremely ill. Her fever was high, and she babbled incoherently, anguished in her delirium. I tried to soothe her with cool water and some warm milk that our goat had yielded that day. When she fell into a fitful sleep, I rushed to the garden and dug at the earth with my hands to retrieve the bread I had hidden. I would prepare it for her with the rest of the milk, and I prayed that it would be enough to give her some strength. I hadn't buried the cloth-covered bread very deeply, and I found it easily.

I sensed something was wrong as I dusted the dirt from the wrapping with my fingertips. As I reached inside the cloth to pull out the bread, I heard a sharp hiss. Something cool and wet laced my fingers. I inadvertently shrieked and threw the bundle as far away from me as I could. My cries had roused our farm dog's attention, and he eagerly ran toward the wrapped bread. He stopped sharply before he reached it, a low growl escaping his throat as he crouched close to the ground poised to attack.

A black snake was slowly revealing herself from the wrapping. She slithered protectively across the food and arched her back in defiance of the dog. Her body was fat with lumps, as though she had swallowed a mouse or rat. It made my limbs prick with electricity just to look at her—that beaded black skin and those hypnotic dark-yellow eyes. She was beautiful in her own deadly way. The hair on the back of the dog's spine was raised with instinct. I sensed he would try to pounce on the snake and risked being bitten. I sprang to my feet and ripped a thin branch from a nearby pear tree that had been killed in the recent frost. I used the stick to toss the snake as far as I could from the bread, half shutting my eyes from terror as I did so. She made a horrible noise as she hit the ground, and it chilled my blood to hear it.

I hugged the cloth-covered bread to my breast as I ran back into the house. In the ice-cold kitchen, I removed the wrapping and inspected what was left of the food. My heart sank with disappointment. Much of the crust had been devoured. Worms and dirt filled the holes left by rats. Why had I buried it? I cursed myself, and hot tears wet my cheeks. I would have been less tortured if I had thrown it away.

My self-pity was broken by a loud banging noise at the front of the house. I rushed to see what it was.

Father had returned early! I shook with happiness at seeing him and the box of food in his hands. There was another man with him. A tall, thinly built foreigner with a mess of jet-black curls on his head and piercing black eyes. He spoke to my father with a heavy Italian accent. I rushed toward them, anticipation and excitement making my voice sound more girlish than my years.

"Father!" I exclaimed, wanting to wrap my arms around him in embrace and kiss his cheeks. I would have done so had he not been such an indifferent man. Words were spilling from my lips about Mother's illness and the shortage of food, but I was not conscious of what exactly I was saying. He rebuked me harshly.

"Katica, be quiet!" I felt he would have slapped my face had the stranger not been with him. He gestured to the foreigner. "This is Andrea." My father's voice was deep and authoritative. With his cold, gray eyes, he looked over to Andrea, who was slightly taller.

"He will be staying in the village for the next month to oversee the construction of the new mill. The communists have brought him all the way from Venice, so please show him some hospitality and prepare us a meal." He pushed the box of food into my hands and gestured for Andrea to follow him out into the farm.

Andrea hesitated before he went outside. His gaze lingered on me, but he didn't say a word. He approached me; his eyes seemed glazed as they explored the bare nape of my neck and the exposed top of my bosom. He leaned in to whisper to me.

"I am a priest and your grandmother's cousin. But no one is to know that, or the communists would surely kill me."

I stood in shock, the box of food trembling in my hands. The look he had given me was definitely not from the eyes of a holy man.

Over the next two weeks, I visited Andrea every day at the site of the new mill. He instructed dozens of the village men on building the new structure, which was to be the most modern and sophisticated building in our town. He was staying with the Grdovic family; they had converted a shed on their land into a dwelling for him. I had been charged with preparing his daily meal, as our house was closest to the work site. Every evening, I would make my way to Andrea's room and collect the food to be prepared for the next day. He was given a generous allowance of flour, vegetables, and even dried meat. I hadn't tasted meat in over a year.

"Take half for yourself," he had instructed me, his pitying eyes lingering on the top button of my dress, which had become unfastened. That ration of food was enough to feed my mother and two sisters as well. His kindness gave me courage. He would be leaving our village in the upcoming weeks, and I intended to go with him.

"You're very young for a priest. I don't think I've ever seen one as young as you—or as good-looking." I made my voice as soft as I could; I knew it would sound sensual and tempting to him. Nature had blessed my two sisters and me with natural beauty. But I knew poverty and starvation had dulled my features, made my face and limbs seem hollow. My emerald eyes had shadows where before there had been none, and my thick black hair had lost its luster. But I would use all my wits and cunning to make him desire me, at least for long enough to get away from my country.

My words seemed to electrify him. He became conscious of his lingering stare and averted his eyes. Perhaps I had underestimated his devotion to chastity. I panicked; I had been too assertive and risked repulsing him. I quickly changed my strategy.

"I'll prepare the meat just as you like it. And I'll mix some olives into the bread, especially for you. I've heard that is the Italian custom, and I'm sure you must be homesick by now." I lowered my gaze piously.

He seemed somewhat relieved. He gestured for me to sit on the bench next to him.

"Thank you, Katarina." He had taken to Latinizing my name. "You have been very attentive." He paused, staring deeply at me. I had sat a little too close, and his hand brushed against the skin of my bare leg. He pulled it away as though it had been bitten. I didn't understand his reactions toward me. One minute he seemed tantalized, the next ashamed, confused. I had to act carefully, tread a very fine balance between being alluring and chaste. I knew he wouldn't take me of his own free will. His eyes and mind might fantasize about it, but he seemed to lack the courage to do it. I could feel the frustration burning in his body as I sat next to him. I baited it. I squeezed his hands gently; they were folded in his lap with his fingers entwined as though he were in prayer. My hand passed close to his groin in doing so. He moaned softly despite himself.

I thanked him for the food and left.

Later that evening, as I lay in a fitful sleep on the hard wooden floor, I was roused by the sound of stifled groaning. I was alone with my mother and sisters in the house. My first thought was that it was a thief trying to steal the food Andrea had given me for the following day. But as I awakened from my sleep-drenched haze, I realized that it was the sound of a female. I staggered through the darkness looking for a candle to light. The groans grew louder and then turned into whimpers of pain.

"Mama?" I whispered into the blackness, but there was no response. My fingers found the small white candle I had hidden in a gap in the floor close to where I slept. I made my way to the kitchen to light it. I stumbled through the parlor toward the sounds. I found my sister Jolanda curled in a ball, almost hidden in a corner of the house.

"Jolanda, what's wrong?" I asked, but she

didn't reply. She was shaking with pain. Her back was turned to me, and I grasped her shoulder gently to turn her over. Her body clenched at my touch. She was bathed in sweat and was clutching her abdomen tightly. My feet had stepped in something wet, and when I brought the candle closer to the floor to inspect what it was, I realized it was blood.

I rushed to where my mother lay.

"Mama! Jolanda's dying! There's blood everywhere!" My hysterical voice woke up Constantina as well. I was overwhelmed with fear. I sobbed to myself as we fumbled our way back to her in the dimly lit house. My mother took one look at the blood covering Jolanda's legs, and her face seemed to slump with sadness. She ordered Constantina to get more candles and to light the fire; they would need to boil some water.

"Katica, go and fetch the Italian. He is the closest thing we have to a doctor."

I didn't bother to dress myself properly. I ran out into the dark-drenched night. I ran until acid pumped in my veins and I was panting for air. I ran through the blackness, not caring what stones cut my bare feet or when branches scratched at my limbs. I reached the Grdovic farm, and I could see the main house illuminated by the fire of their hearth. The shed was shrouded in darkness; Andrea would be asleep. I banged my fists heavily on his door and called his name. He didn't respond. I was contemplating kicking in the door when it suddenly opened before me. Andrea stood there, gazing at me in shock as he pulled a shirt over his naked chest.

I must have looked crazed. My hair was disheveled, hanging in long black streaks down my back. My white nightgown was worn thin with age, and it hugged my sweat-drenched body. I could feel my breasts heaving as I gasped for air, and I felt my small, hard nipples press against the fabric of my gown.

He seemed to breathe my name. "Katarina." His face was painted with shock, but his dark eyes were liquid with desire.

"I'm not here for you! It's my sister, Jolanda. She's dying. There's a lot of blood. Will you please help us?" I was unsure what he could do to help her. But he was the most educated person in the village. There was no doctor, no hospital nearby. It would take days for us to reach the city, and we didn't have money to make the journey.

"Of course. Of course I will." His face grew serious, and he rushed back into the house to finish dressing himself and collect a bag that had been hidden under his bed. From behind the door, he pulled out a thick warm jacket and covered my shoulders with it. The lining was made of soft wool, and it felt luxurious against my skin. Grabbing me by the hand, he pulled me toward his motorbike, and I followed his lead by climbing on. I had never been on a bike before, and I clung tightly to his waist as we made the short journey home.

When we walked through the door, Jolanda was in the same position that I had left her. The house was properly lit now, and I could see the trail of blood that streaked across the floor. Andrea and my mother placed her on her back, and he began to look over her body, feeling her lower abdomen as a doctor would. Her legs were covered in blood.

"She tried to get rid of her child," he stated gently, and my mother silently nodded, with tears welling in her azure eyes. That's when I saw the iron fireplace poker by Jolanda's side, the tip red with blood.

"I can't do much to help her. She has an infection and needs a doctor. I'll give her some medicine and try to stop her bleeding." He went to his bag and retrieved a dark vial of fluid that he forced the semiconscious Jolanda to drink. Then Mother and Constantina continued to clean her up, and they moved her limp body back to the pallet of wood on the floor where she slept.

Andrea looked pitifully around our home—the small kitchen and a curtained-off parlor—as he washed his hands in a bucket of water. The oldest part of the house had been built in Roman times, and the loose bricks let in the cold winter air. The four of us slept on the floor of the parlor with rags instead of blankets, and there was nothing left of the furniture, not a table or chair to sit on. The pity in his eyes filled me with shame, but I stifled my pride and thanked him for helping my sister. He took a beautifully embroidered handkerchief out of his pocket and wiped away tears that I hadn't realized were on my cheek. He squeezed a vial of medicine into my mother's hands before he left.

<hr />

Jolanda was awake the next morning. She looked better than the previous night, but her abdomen was swollen with infection and her skin looked as gray as a cadaver. She refused to talk. Mother informed us that Andrea would make the distant trip to the city and fetch a doctor. I was relieved to hear that as I collected the bloodied and soiled rags from the previous night and took them into the yard to wash.

I was not yet finished my chores when I heard the rumble of a motorcycle at our front gate. I rushed forward, eager to meet Andrea and the doctor. I stopped short as the motorcycle came into view. It wasn't Andrea. The communist had arrived to take his ransom for the month. He was alone this time, which struck me as strange, as they always came in pairs.

My chest felt tight with fear. I recognized the tall, blond man as the officer who had raped Jolanda. I feared for her; in her weakened position, seeing him might put her into a state of shock. I rushed forward to intercept him before he reached the house.

"I have some food for you this month. The crops haven't recovered yet, but if you wait here, I can bring you the food we have."

He pushed me aside and paid no attention to my pleas. He entered the house without knocking and pulled the door closed behind him.

I rushed to the back of the house and entered through the kitchen. I ran frantically to the front parlor where Jolanda was resting.

I heard a scream before I reached the room, and my heart seized in my chest. I burst into the room, crying Jolanda's name as I did so.

My mind couldn't digest the image that my eyes were witnessing. The officer was on his knees, facing my direction; he wore an expression of confusion on his face. Jolanda was standing behind him, her eyes wild and crazed. She seemed bestial and possessed. The iron poker was in her hand. I saw a small sliver of crimson blood snake down the officer's forehead. Jolanda raised the poker again and let out an anguished scream, but this time Mother intercepted her hand before it could deal a final deadly blow.

The officer stumbled to his feet and almost crumpled to the floor again. Mother held on to Jolanda protectively and pulled her away from him. He uttered curse words and made a move to strike at Jolanda. If he hadn't been so weakened by the blow to the head, I'm sure he would have killed her with his bare hands. He stumbled out of the front door and onto his bike. He rode off shakily down the dirt path.

"What have you done, my child?" Mother whispered, her voice choked with emotion. "You've killed us all."

Sometime later, I was to learn that the officer never made it back to the city. Doubtless, he had intended to return with his comrades and unleash all sorts of hell upon my family. His head injury overcame him, and he crashed his motorcycle before he could hurt us more. But I didn't know this at the time.

Jolanda's courage had sparked a sense of urgency in me. We had to get out of this country, or at least out of the village, before we were murdered. I convinced my mother that we should abandon our house and take refuge at her sister's house, which was in a village farther up the coast. It was horrible trying to convince my mother to leave her home; despite our poverty, she had such resolution and pride. But Constantina and I pleaded, and eventually, she conceded.

"We can't run from them forever, Katica. They'll find us eventually." Mother whispered the words, drawing her lips into a harsh, thin line.

Not if I can help it, I thought to myself.

Jolanda was in a poor condition to make the journey, but I hugged her and urged her to stay strong. She seemed broken, in shock. I advised my mother and sisters that they should journey ahead without me, that I would wait for Andrea at his lodging and bring the doctor to my aunt's house with me. My mother reluctantly agreed, and we parted.

The Grdovic barn was empty when I arrived there. It wasn't hard to break in, and I took my time in deciding how I would execute my plan. Andrea was much older than I. He was a priest, but I didn't feel that mattered. I had to convince him to take my family and me with him back to Venice, or else we were sure to be murdered at the hands of the communists in retaliation for Jolanda's violence. I didn't believe that he loved me. When his eyes looked at me, it was not with tenderness—it was with lust. So I would use that against him. I would bait him with my body. I'd seen his resolution wear down over the past few weeks, and it was time for me to strike. The feverish look on his face last night when he first laid eyes on my body had told me as much.

I disrobed and climbed into his bed. The mattress was soft, comforting; it made my body slacken with pleasure just to lie upon it. I'd forgotten what it felt like to sleep in a real bed and not on the cold, hard floor of our home.

I had hours to wait. I suspected that Andrea wouldn't be able to procure a doctor, as they were notoriously hard to come by, even in the city. Trying to convince one to come to our village would be almost impossible. As the time ticked by, I mentally prepared myself for what would happen. I was still a virgin, and I suppressed my fear as best I could.

A rattle at the front door roused me from my thoughts. It was Andrea; he had arrived. He was alone, as I had suspected he would be. He entered the shed and shut the door behind him, not noticing me at first.

I slowly rose from the bed like a sea nymph rising from the water. I was naked, my heart pounding under my breast. His eyes fell upon me, and he was briefly startled. He didn't say a word. I strode toward him as confidently as I could, but I suspect my fear-laced eyes betrayed me. I didn't allow him to speak. I pulled him down to me by the collar of his shirt as my hand worked its way to his stiffened groin. He took me right there, on the floor.

Before he reached his moment of ecstasy, I stopped him. I laid out my price. He would have to take my mother, sisters, and me out of the country. We could part ways once we were in Italy, but he had to smuggle us out when he left.

"Anything! Anything!" he panted the words in sexual anticipation. And then he fulfilled his desires.

When it was over, I gave him instructions on where to meet me in three days' time. Then he watched as I dressed myself and left. I had a long walk ahead of me, and I needed to reach the village before nightfall.

———◆—<•••)◆(•••>—◆———

Three days came and went without any news from Andrea. On the fourth day, I became panicked. I didn't tell the others where I was going. I set out early in the morning and went back to the Grdovic farm.

The shed was empty when I arrived. All of Andrea's belongings, his satchel, his coats, they were all gone.

I bit back the bitter tears that threatened to spill. I was enraged. He had tricked me. I had gambled and lost.

Despondently, I slumped in front of the shed door. I didn't know what to do next.

"Katica?"

I looked up to see Ivana Grdovic calling my name. She had the face of a cherub, with plump cheeks and a halo of white-blonde hair. A haughty smiled played on her lips. "Are you looking for Andrea?" she questioned, her fingers coiling around the lilac ribbon in her hair.

"Yes," I stammered, trying to piece together a lie. "I was supposed to collect the food for his supper, but he's not here. Do you know where he has gone?"

"Oh, didn't you hear?" Her violet eyes sparked with interest. "It turns out he was really a priest. My father found him out and turned him over to the communists. He's sure to be deported—if they don't kill him first."

My heart sank with despair.

One day, I would leave my country. I would make a long and adventurous voyage across the world to faraway Australia. But it would not be today.

"Oh, Katica." Ivana tilted her head to the side, her rose petal lips pursing with false sympathy. "You're so broken. You feel everyone's sorrows, except your own."

This story appears in *Broken*, edited by Dorothy Davies, and *The Sydney Anthology: Read Me*, published by the University of Sydney.

12 PRETTY SCARS

our love was a branding iron, a tattoo of hot cuts with a serrated knife falling in sharp succession against my thigh. You left the prettiest scars, like the scallop-lined clouds I used to draw as a child. And you told me crying was forbidden." A small tear snaked down Natasha's cheek. After a decade, she could finally cry. It was not the cathartic weeping that she had longed for during all that time. Instead, it was dull and flat, an innocuous splash of emotion against the mosaic of her misery.

"I thought you a despot in those days, with lava where your heart should be." She reached out her hand to touch him, but stopped short of his face. Her forefinger traced the silhouette of his aquiline nose, his brutal, sensuous mouth, the cleft of his chin—identical to her own.

"Hating you was like breathing, a simple ritual. You'd drink the homemade wine and litter the yard with empty bottles. 'Tomorrow is another day,' you would complain, and then cut my pretty lip in two." Her hot, irregular breath was smoke against the icy air, materializing before her eyes in a thick cloud.

"I never thanked you for the beatings. Never thanked you for the acid in my chest or the needles in my blood. The way I'm terrified to have a child of my own because it takes me back to my own dark days, when you were my shadow and I thought the sun would never rise."

He stared back at her with vacuous, blanched eyes. The small veins in his eyeballs had burst like tiny red stars around a blue sun.

"You left something under my skin—a jagged piece of glass or the terra-cotta Christ I smashed when you died." Even though they were alone, she still couldn't bring herself to say *when I killed you.*

She tried to lock the freezer door, but it wouldn't quite close. His fingers were caught near the seal, curled in midair as though he would scratch her from his glacial grave. The ice burned her skin as she forced his hand against his chest. The sickening crunch of frozen bones and fingernails caused her lips to purse into a thin line of disgust.

"I'm like an eggshell, cracking up slowly and from within. I'm waiting for the baby bird, but instead, it's always the sanguine yolk." She pushed on his hand a little harder, and two of his fingers snapped off in her palm, crunching like ripe flower stems. The blood was crystalline and vermillion, glistening in the dull lamplight of her basement. She tossed the fingers into the freezer, and they landed with a dull thud against his cadaverous skin. For a moment, she couldn't distinguish his digits from the frozen intestines spilling out of the thick gash that ran from his collar to his groin. She slammed the door shut on his icy grave.

"*Sit tibi terra levis*—may the earth rest lightly on your bones," she whispered into the air. Underneath the weight of her emotions, she realized her mistake and laughed gently to herself.

"But you'll never be buried in the ground, beloved."

This story appears in *Serial Killers Iterum*, edited by James Ward Kirk, and *Fresh Ground V3*, edited by Jess A. Weiss.

13 THE BACCHAE

ournal of Dr. Lorenzo Lombardi, M.D., Ph.D., Psy.D.

During the night of the first of July, Violetta Mendez went into the basement of her house, loaded a revolver, placed it in her mouth, and shot herself.

Her neighbors didn't discover her body for six weeks. One of them remarked that she might have rotted for longer, but the electricity to her home had been suspended and the smell of decomposition grew too severe to ignore.

The police discovered hundreds of bottles of wine scattered throughout her home. In her basement, along with her putrefied body, were three freezers, each filled with human remains. Dismembered body parts. The coroner couldn't determine the weapon used in the murders, only that the limbs had been torn from the torsos.

All her victims were male.

And I cannot help but feel responsible for her actions.

—————————————•⟨••⟩◆⟨••⟩•—————————————

She came to see me the week before she died, arriving at my office at the same time she did every other Friday. The last person I'd see for the day. She insisted on coming a half hour after the previous patient's departure. Naturally, I objected at first, but she made it worth my time. She came from money, a privileged background, of that I have no doubt.

Although I'd known her for almost three years, I'd never actually seen her face. I often thought of her as the Lady in Mourning. Always wrapped in black, not an inch of flesh visible. Her previous psychiatrist had noted that the black attire was a manifestation of her perpetual grief. I agreed with this assessment, though I added my own: a post-traumatic recluse. Almost agoraphobic.

She wore a short-brimmed hat draped with a black lace veil always tilted to the left. It bled into her black dress so that none of her face—not even an eyelash—was visible. Her hands were hostages in black lace gloves. I wondered what her skin would feel like if I were to strip her of those gloves, let her flesh breathe.

That evening, the sun had clung to the sky far longer than usual. It must have been the solstice, for it's never that bright in these parts. Madeline, my secretary, had forgotten to close the curtains before she left for the day, and the sun bathed my patient in a gentle amber glow as she sat across from me.

Her small lace hands were intertwined, and a delicate elbow rested on the leather couch. She smelled of jasmine and something bitter, like sandalwood. Her covered face was angled away from me, toward the bottle of port near my window. The wine was an antique—for decoration, not for drinking— but it made me wonder if she had experienced some kind of substance abuse issue in her past. I noted the possibility of a resurfaced addiction in her file.

"Tell me, Violetta, how are you feeling today?" I began the session as I had always done, hoping to make some progress with her mental state. She'd been weaned off the antipsychotics and free of institutions for many years now.

"I'm fine, Dr. Lombardi. Just fine." Her voice was soft, feminine, with a faint Catalonian accent. It cut through the layers of veiling lace and lingered on my ears. She never spoke of her formative years, but I suspected that she was the product of a British education. The way she conducted herself, the gentle intonation of her voice, it reminded me of the ladies at Oxford or Cambridge from my youth.

"Of course you are, Violetta." I tried not to sound condescending, but my voice has a tendency to be clinical. Or so my ex-wife tells me. "I want to try a more aggressive approach today. We've been skirting around the issue for enough time now."

Her shoulders stiffened under the black silk dress. Attending weekly counseling sessions had been one of the conditions of her release. I'd been gentle with her up until then, but her treatment had stagnated and it was time for progress. We had been stuck in a holding pattern for years, a limbo of comfort and half-truths. Time to end the impasse, even if it meant being forceful. There's just something about a gentle female—the thin wrists and softly spoken words—that brings out the brute in me.

The veil shook, and a lace hand searched for a necklace on her bust. Her fingers twisted as though she were fondling a pearl, but there was nothing there.

"I'm not sure about this, Dr. Lombardi. I've been doing so well. Please don't alter our sessions." Her breath was elevated, giving her voice an urgent quality.

She shifted in her seat, and the light caught her veil in a way that I had never seen before. For an instant, her profile was illuminated: the outline of a Botticellian angel, with a delicate nose and sensuous mouth. But then she fidgeted, and her profile was steeped in darkness. She turned toward the port once again.

"I understand that you are anxious, Violetta. That is to be expected. But we are never going to cure you of the delusions if we don't try a more aggressive approach."

"Delusions?" She sounded wounded, as though I had betrayed her on an intimate level. "But I've been cured for some time now."

"Please, Violetta," I began, leaning forward in my chair, my eyes burning into the veil where I imagined her eyes to be. "There's a reason that I'm the best in my field and that you pay me so handsomely for my time. I've indulged you up until this point, and you are an exceptional, exceptional…"

Liar would have been the most accurate label (although utterly unprofessional).

"…patient. But I can see right through the façade. You've learned the art of imitation to perfection. Maintaining such a deception for so long will hurt you, and your mental faculties, in the long run. If we aren't able to make some progress—some real progress—I'm afraid that I'll have to recommend your return to the institution."

"You can't! You can't! You wouldn't dare!" She leapt from the couch, her voice shrill as I had never heard it before. "They are *not* delusions! Everything that happened was *real!* Everything that they did was *real!*"

There it was: the truth. The wound was open, now to let it bleed.

"The Bacchae?" I whispered, hoping my tone would placate her. She inhaled a sharp breath at the sound of the word. Again, she clutched at the invisible necklace, her fingers biting into the silk dress.

I'd never used the term before that day. This particular delusion had plagued her for more than a decade, and I'd gleaned the details from the transcripts of her time at St. Margot's asylum.

She turned her back to me and walked away from her seat, stopping at the bare window to stretch her lace-covered hand against the glass. I could only imagine what she saw through the prison of her veil. The window looked out onto the vibrant city, hedonistic and uninhibited in the evening twilight. Did she envision it dancing before her eyes, while she—trapped in her lace-covered coffin—was stagnant, wasting away, entombed by her tormentors?

"They aren't real, these Bacchae that you're fixated on. They're mythical—women who suckle serpents at their breasts and tear grown men limb from limb with their bare hands. Surely you understand it's only fiction?"

It sounded ludicrous when I said it, and I hoped that hearing it verbalized would have a similar impact on her.

She was silent for a long while, and when she spoke again, her words were soft, the outburst of the prior moment forgotten.

"I've seen them. With my own two eyes."

Her hand remained on the glass, and I could see her body slacken, as if she were unburdening herself of an invisible weight. She let her fingers slide down the windowpane and come to rest at the bottle of port.

"Those beautiful, seductive women who make wine and honey flow from their fingers. They do exist. I felt the wine—their god—inside me. And it made me do horrible, horrible things."

Her voice trembled and I could feel her words imbued with remorse. I knew the 'horrible things' she spoke of, and I made the critical mistake of resurrecting the violent episode.

"Violetta, you've assumed some guilt over what happened to Byron, despite being exonerated by the police. The weapon was never located, but they supposed—"

"There was no weapon," she spat. "It was the Bacchae who did it to Byron."

I paused, softening my voice before I spoke again. "It is quite common to construct a fantasy to shield one's mind from such events." I studied her, but saw no reaction to my words. "The police initially assumed the presence of others, but they never found any physical evidence to substantiate the idea." I leaned forward in my chair. "I have another theory," I said, relieved that she wasn't facing me, that she remained at the window.

"I don't think there was anyone else there that night. But I think Byron did something to you. Perhaps there was an unwanted sexual encounter, or some kind of abuse. In a moment of self-preservation, your psyche splintered and you assaulted him to spare yourself any injury. The propensity for self-preservation is astounding, and—"

"Do you think, Dr. Lombardi," she said, cutting me off again, her veil shaking and her voice now filled with acid, "that I would do *this*—"

She turned to face me and, in a single, fluid movement, ripped the veil from her face, sending the bottle of wine shattering against my marble floor. The shards spun from the force of her gesture. Port spread across my floor like coagulated blood.

"—to *myself?*"

A small shriek escaped my lips before I could contain it. The sound disgusted me—an unprofessional, reprehensible reaction to a patient.

Of course, I had wondered many times before that day what her face would look like. In truth, I had idealized her physical appearance in my mind. Her butterscotch voice had pervaded my subconscious and formed the image of a nymph under that veil.

But she was not a nymph, not an angel.

Half her face had been ripped away from the bone. Her scalp was uneven on the left half of her head, the side that the hat always tilted toward. The injury extended from her forehead to jaw. The skin was lumpy, thick and porous, as if it had been roughly reattached over the bone.

But most horrible of all was her eye—or rather, her eye socket.

Her left eyelid had been ripped away, leaving the remains of a skeletal cavity. It still terrifies me. When I wake at night, bathed in sweat with my heart pounding in my chest, it's her disfigured eye that I see, searching my face, imploring me, begging me for empathy. For understanding.

"Now, Dr. Lombardi, do you believe?"

———————●◦◦◦◦◦●———————

"If you could exist in any age, when would it be?"

Byron hung a languid hand over Violetta's shoulder and pressed the wine bottle to her lips. It was a cheap red, and her emerald eyes squinted at the taste.

She guzzled a mouthful despite the acidity and wiped the drizzle from her chin.

The wine looks like blood on his mouth. I wonder if things will get rough again, like last night.

A wide smile played on her lips.

"Byron, Byron, Byron."

She took another sip of the wine and then forced the bottle into his hands.

"Classical Athens, before the Peloponnesian War. I want to live like a *hataira* and be passed around from husband to husband! Now tell me what we are doing here. You've been so secretive all night." She tilted her head to the side, her short auburn hair falling about her eyes. She knew Byron couldn't resist the curve of her elongated neck.

"I would never pass you around. You have such beautiful skin, like snow." He traced her collarbone with his finger. She winced as he pressed into an aubergine bruise near her shoulder.

"I'm sorry about last night," he said. He leaned toward her and placed his lips upon her neck. She ignored the comment and continued to sip the wine. His mouth traced the line of her jugular and he worked his way toward her left ear, nuzzling his nose into her hair.

"Let's not talk about it. I want to get inside," she said, tugging at his collar. "It's freezing out here, and I want to get out of these wet clothes."

"Wet?" He examined her.

Violetta poured a small amount of wine on her bust and giggled. The smell of cheap alcohol and plums permeated the air.

"Well, I'm wet now," she teased, pulling him toward the museum.

The campus was deserted, haunted by the distant sounds of college parties and indistinct music.

They stumbled through the Gothic archways and across the manicured lawn of the central court. The night air had turned the dew to ice, and the grass crunched beneath their feet like tiny bones being crushed.

"She's just stunning. You have to see her. It's worth the risk. She changes our entire understanding of the myth." He sounded like a giddy child.

"I'm very excited to meet your artifact. Will you do your Ph.D. on it?"

"Definitely," he replied, slurring the word. "You ask such idiotic questions, Violetta."

There he is again, the beast beneath the schoolboy.

She chewed on her inner lip, hurt by the venom in his voice. Tears burned behind her eyes, but she bit them back.

Don't let him see you cry.

Instead, she tucked her hand under his sweater, feeling the hot skin of his torso. Her fingers played with the rough hair on his abdomen, and she scratched her nails against his flesh. He moaned and hugged her tighter against his side. He bit her on the shoulder, his teeth pressing into her bruise. She shrieked.

"What was that for?"

"Stop trying to distract me. Give me the bottle."

You're such a bastard when you're drunk.

The entrance to the museum was lit by soft amber lights, accentuating the Gothic curves of the door. The sandstone arches were tangled and crossed like muscle fibers on an anatomy diagram, stretching the length of the museum. Violetta flung her head back and tried to trace their elaborate pattern with her eyes. The floor rocked beneath her.

"Maybe this isn't such a good idea, Byron."

"Why are you afraid? I'm the one taking all the risk, bringing you here. You should be thankful. I could've taken anyone, but I chose you." Byron struggled to swipe his staff card across the gray plastic box on the museum's door. He was successful on his fifth attempt. The glass entrance hissed open as the doors parted.

Violetta dug her nails into his skin, hard enough to make him wince.

"Wait!"

"Stop talking, Violetta. Your voice is so fucking annoying. I need to remember the code."

He punched a six-digit combination into the keypad to disarm the alarm, but the light continued to flash red. Swearing under his breath, he took another long, deep drink from the bottle. "Seven, zero, seven, three," he muttered, his attention focused on connecting his fingers to the keypad, "two, four." The light flashed green, and the alarm chirped as it was disarmed.

Byron took her by the wrist, his grip a little too hard, and led her toward the center of the museum. The Egyptian exhibition was the key attraction, the main hall littered with sarcophagi and papyrus scrolls. They passed the Etruscan display and moved through the Roman quarter.

"Byron, let's go back to your apartment," she said.

"What I have planned for you is better than fucking." A grin crept across his lips.

He led her to a small, blackened room at the very end of the museum, cordoned off by a thick red rope. Violetta strained to see into the area, but it was too dark. A faint prickle of adrenaline rushed down her spine.

"That's where she is!" Byron halted before the entrance.

The fidgety, drunken demeanor drained from his features. He grew silent, as though he had entered a religious space. Byron inhaled and extended his hand toward the rope.

"Wait!" Violetta grabbed his elbow. "We should go back. We'll be expelled if we get caught."

He shook free of her grasp. "I need to see her again!" he hissed, his eyes like two dark slits. "She's burned into my brain, worse than an addiction." His nails grated his cheeks, pulling down on his eyelids, revealing hepatic eyeballs. The veins had popped around his irises. Tiny red stars around a black sun. "I haven't slept in almost a week. Something keeps dragging me back to her—to the artifact." He panted in her face, his breath heavy with wine.

The skin on Violetta's neck shivered.

It's the alcohol making him cruel.

She tried to step away from him, but he seized her, his nails cutting her skin.

"Come with me."

"Byron, please, you're hurting me," she whimpered. "Not again. Not like last night."

He let go of her. "I'm sorry," he said. He tried to embrace her but she recoiled from him. He took her hand instead. "I don't know what came over me. I'm just not myself right now. Look, do you remember the crystal swan I gave you last summer?"

"Yes," she said, struggling to meet his gaze. His eyes were terrifying when he was drunk.

"It was so expensive. My entire week's allowance. I gave you that swan because you are mine. And I'm showing you this," he paused, forcing her to engage his stare. "Because. You. Are. Mine." She smiled despite herself. He kissed her, and she let him.

"Come on," he urged as he unhinged the rope. They stepped forward into the darkness, Byron dragging Violetta by her trembling hand.

Their presence triggered a sensor, and an aureate glow flooded the display. Violetta's eyes took a moment to adjust to the lighting, and she struggled to make out the large, curvaceous object that loomed before them. Her pulse throbbed deep within her abdomen.

"The Amphora of Dionysus," he whispered. Byron circled the display, his eyes wild and agitated, darting in his sockets like tadpoles. "She's amazing, isn't she? Pulled from the bottom of the straits of Messina in an ancient shipwreck. Someone went to great lengths to ensure that this vessel would never be broken, sealing it in a bronze coffin." Climbing onto the stone step on which the amphora was displayed, he placed his hand against its neck. "She's like ice," he said, the breath catching in his throat, "and not a scratch on her."

Violetta clutched at the pearl necklace around her décolletage, her fingers toying with the small white marbles.

Byron's hands slid up the neck of the vessel, caressing the black pottery like a lover. His fingers slipped into the opening at the mouth.

"Hand me some of that wine," he said.

"What? Why?"

"The seal is still intact. Two and a half thousand years at the bottom of the ocean, and she's been saving herself for me."

She handed him the bottle, her fingers unsteady. Byron poured the remainder of the wine into the amphora and worked his fingers inside the opening.

"The seal is dissolving," he said. "I've almost got it loose! I can smell him inside!"

"Him?" Violetta cried. Images of a dismembered body flooded her mind.

"It's Dionysus. He's inside. He's in the wine." Byron's nostrils flared as he sucked in the scent. "Grapes, and plums, and black cherries from Illyria."

Damn it, Byron! Don't do it!

Byron's hand worked its way out of the vessel. He clutched a pulpy black mess in his fist: the remains of the amphora's seal.

"Pandora's Box was never really a box. That's a mistranslation," he said, speaking to the vessel. "It's actually a jar, an amphora, just like this one. It's a symbol of the womb." He plunged the empty wine bottle through the amphora's neck.

Violetta took two steps back, but could not turn away. A gurgling sound filled the air.

"All the horrors in the world, trapped inside a bottle," Byron said.

Violetta clutched at her pearls until the necklace almost broke.

The cheap wine bottle was filled with what looked like tar. Some of the ancient wine slithered down the side toward Byron's fingers, a viscous black snake nipping at his hands.

"Dionysus," he whispered, placing the bottle to his lips.

"Byron, no!"

But Byron ignored her, throwing his head back to drink the wine. When he finished, he let out a slow, satisfied breath, then turned to face her. He clutched the handle of the amphora as he tipped the bottle in her direction. His cobalt eyes looked black in the soft lighting. When he smiled, his teeth were dripping with tar.

"I can feel him inside me!"

Then everything went dark.

A hissing sound seeped out of the shadows. It surrounded them, rising from all directions.

They were no longer alone in the museum. A woman laughed in Violetta's ear. Voices erupted all about her. Pottery shattered across the museum floor. Byron howled, choking on his saliva. The sound jabbed at her ears.

"Byron!" she shrieked, her hands outstretched into the darkness.

She groped at the vacant air. His screams were smothered by laughter. Wet, slippery hands clutched at Violetta's skin. She heard a tearing sound and felt cold fingers on her naked abdomen.

Nails scratched at her lips. When she opened her mouth to scream, the fingers pushed inside. She tried to bite down, but her throat flooded with a bitter fluid as thick as honey. She swallowed reflexively. Nausea ripped through her insides.

The ancient wine caught in her throat and she gasped for air.

Laughter burned in her ears. Hands forced her to the ground. She couldn't breathe. The small room was crowded with women, their silken gowns scraping her limbs. Jewelry scratched at her skin. The whispers grew louder, frenzied; voices drowning her in confusion. She could discern a single word.

"*Sparagmos.*"

She had never heard the language spoken aloud by native speakers. It had been dead for more than two millennia. But she understood the meaning of this word.

They were going to tear her to pieces, limb from limb.

She writhed against the hands. Fingers clutched at her necklace, tearing it upward, and a shattered pearl caught on her open eye. She shrieked as her eyelid was torn from her face. Nails scratched at her pants, tearing her jeans to pieces. They were lifting her, pulling on her limbs.

Byron wailed, a smothered, desperate cry, like a wolf in a steel-toothed trap. The sound echoed in the small chamber.

Crack, crack, crack.

His crying ceased.

Something sharp pierced her earlobe. Hot pain bit at her face. She heard the tearing sound before she felt it, a large piece of skin being ripped from her face. Her mouth opened to scream, and cold air rushed into parts of her head that she had never felt before.

She shook the hands away from her arm. Her fingers flew to her cheek. A hot, sticky fluid drenched her hand. Her teeth were exposed all the way along her jaw, all the way to where her ear should have been.

The fingers pulled at her hips, tearing her panties. A sharp stab burned in her other ear. Someone was screaming, repeating a word. A loud, authoritative cry resonated above the hysterical laughter.

"*Gyny.*" Woman.

They had exposed her sex, leaving her naked.

The laughter stopped. The hands fell away. Violetta hit the ground with a moist thud.

A single hand rested on her remaining cheek. A soft hand, with rings on each finger. Something juicy and warm was placed upon her tongue, like firm jelly. When her quivering jaw locked against it, an intense copper taste rippled over her palate.

"*Omophagia*," the unseen woman whispered to Violetta.

No! The word snapped in Violetta's mind, but she no longer had a mouth to scream.

They were eating Byron, eating the raw flesh from his bones. She had tasted him. Tasted his coppery entrails.

They were the Bacchae, the women of myth.

And now she was one of them.

This story appears in *In Vino Veritas*, edited by Dorothy Davies.

14 SANDSTONES LIKE SEPIA

lthough I've only known you for sixteen weeks, I will love you until I am dust.

I whispered the words in his lavender ear and entwined his fingers with my own. They were marble, hard as stone, glacially cold. The ebony was seeping into his wrist, barely visible past the cuff of his military uniform. It could have been a stain of ink, but I knew it was nothing so benign. His blood was discoloring, turning black. His skin had taken on a pallid tone. There were hepatic speckles across his hands, wayward drops of paint from an artist's brushstroke. He seemed so small in death, shrunken, surreal—as though the unnamed artist had carved him from stone and laid him out on the crimson silk. Just a statue. An imitation of life. Not the real thing.

My eyes strayed to his face. The lustrous crop of auburn hair, so like my own, had dulled, turned tawny in the flickering candlelight of the church. I resisted the impulse to touch his cheek. The stiffness of his hand had shocked me, sending a brief ripple of alarm through my chest. The bones of his face seemed more prominent in death than they had in life. And in a day, there would be nothing left of his flesh. He would be burned, like medical waste. Then the ashes would be sealed in our family sepulcher, dusting the bones of our ancestors, piled upon each other. The thin line of his lips, those eyelids sewed shut, they would all dissolve. I would never see those onyx orbs again. Gone. Just sunken cheeks, streaked with ivory and lavender.

And it was my fault that he was going in the ground.

In the confines of the church, my mother and her sisters raised their mourning wails. The sound reverberated off the walls and drowned everything in sorrow. It was our tradition, our ritual. Deeply inhaling the scented air, I attempted to join in the half-chant, half-screaming song—but the sound choked in my throat and a heavy, raspy breath escaped my lips instead. It was an obligation to the dead, this hideous cacophony. It kept away the pollution attracted to bloodshed, or so the old widows had told me in my youth.

But I no longer believed such superstitions.

Wetness tickled my face. Tears chased each other down my ashen cheeks. In the golden reflection of the tabernacle, my eyes were two violet drops in a sea of liquid crystal. The small chest glittered with jewels that pulsed in the inconstant candlelight.

I looked over his dark-navy jacket, the crisp white collar blossoming out upon his neck. I placed his favorite knife in the coffin upon his chest. Then I felt around in my pocket for the smooth, cool metal object that was tickling my thigh through the thin fabric of my dress. His cigarette lighter. How he had loved that thing. Flicked the small metal latch backward and forward to watch the blue-gold light reappear. Traced his fingers over the elaborate engraving in the metal. The baroque letter *R*. His name had been Romano. Just another lazy Sunday afternoon in our small cottage on the side of the volcano, flicking the lighter and following me with his eyes.

"We've all lost a child. It will get better with time."

A gnarled hand clutched my elbow—one of my aunties, veiled in black. Only the white flesh of her neck and cheeks broke through the flatness of the color. Gelatinous orbs looked at me with pity, laced with blame. Her lips were bloodless, her mouth moving in a soft monotone of comfort. She whispered that last word through her solicitous stare and glazed emerald eyes.

Time. I had nothing but time. I was only twenty-eight.

"You can try again."

Try what again?

Back at home, in the small cottage, I laid two plates on the kitchen table. He wasn't there.

I placed the bitter almond biscuits on his red silk handkerchief. Filled his glass with the honey-spiced wine. Lit a small red candle in his honor. Inhaled the cinnamon smoke of the flame and sprinkled a sulfur crystal upon it. I watched as the honeycomb-yellow powder melted into a drop of viscous red foam.

Il giorno della morte—the day of the dead. The only day I set the table for two. I no longer believed in the custom, but it felt wrong not to perform it.

I sat and flicked a cigarette lighter as he had done. It bathed the room in amber.

A crescent moon watched me from behind lace curtains and frost-bitten glass. The patterns in the lace created luminous figures who danced upon the cottage floor and across my toes. I could see the Doric temple from the window in my chamber. The remains of the Greek theater and cemetery lay just to its side. They lit up the ruins at night. Sandstones, the color of sepia. The Christians had tried to build a church over the pagan site, but abandoned it when lava erupted and almost drowned the temple in flames. A sinewy, red-gold snake, flowing down the side of the volcano, the tear streaks from the ancient god trapped below the mountain. That volcano was littered with superstitions.

Snakes carry the souls of loved ones. The widows' words ricocheted in my mind. I could see the small silhouettes of the women as they left the honeyed cakes and bitter almonds for the serpents. *Take the sweet biscuits. Let me know he still lingers.*

But you will never be a snake. You will

never be buried in the ground.

Just a few drops of blood. Maybe it's not so bad. Plenty of women bleed when they are pregnant.

But the acid in my gut and the red snake down my thigh tell me differently. My body has betrayed me. And your father, Raphael, had those long, rounded lashes—like spider legs shooting from his eyes. He is already in the ground, but you cannot go with him.

You are too little.

My mother drops her plate with honeyed cakes and bitter almonds. The spiced wine splashes the stone floor of the cottage. Mixes with the small red drops of you.

She starts to wail, and her sisters join in. There is no church, no coffin.

There never was, and there never shall be.

Just the sandstone, sepia temple, with the ancient statue of the goddess in the middle. The one the Christians threw into the sea but that washed back to the black soil of the volcano. I would have named you Romano. And I can fit you in the palm of my hand.

Although I've only known you for sixteen weeks, I will love you until I am dust.

"We've all had miscarriages. It will get better with time. You can try again." My aunty, the black-wrapped widow.

But you will never be.

This story appears in *Songs for the Raven*, edited by James Ward Kirk, and *ARNA*: A Literary Journal, published by the University of Sydney.

This story was one of the winning entries in the Women On Writing winter 2012 Flash Fiction Contest.

15 THE BURNING RITUAL

rancesca, she's come for me. I told her everything. I'm sorry.

Marco

The letter was crumpled and stained with crimson. He had been clutching it in his hand when he died, years ago, and she had pried his stiff fingers open to reveal the mess of paper and ink. It was little more than a sepia leaf now, with Marco's elaborate writing painted across it, the letters large and dark, not his usual uniform script. He had pressed the pen forcefully against the paper, almost tearing it in some places, hinting at the panic and fear he had felt in those final moments—in the minutes before he killed himself.

The image of his mutilated face was branded into her mind. It took a special kind of self-loathing to do that much damage to your own body. His cheeks were streaked with dried blood from the wounds in his eyes, and a pair of horrible black caverns stared at her where his eyeballs had been. A thick gash across his throat had sprayed the room with blood, painting his torso red. She had thought it all a horrible joke at first, until the smell of decay had made it real.

The train rocked unexpectedly, and the Veronese landscape became a blur of colors in her peripheral vision, jolting her mind from the memories. The young girl by her side let out a small, stifled cry, and Francesca instinctively took her hand in a comforting gesture.

"It's nothing, just old train tracks. Where's your mother?"

The little girl was silent for a long moment, her azure eyes searching the ground. Eventually, she replied in a sweet, seraphim voice.

"She's gone to fetch dinner. You were sleeping when we arrived."

Francesca nodded her head absently. "What's your name?" she questioned, noticing the nervous look that lingered on the girl's features.

"Angelina," the girl replied, her small lips like tiny pink jewels against her porcelain skin.

"That was my mother's name," Francesca whispered pensively, unable to contain the words before they left her lips. She was always so careful not to reveal details of her identity, not even to a child. But hearing her dead mother's name had briefly shocked her, disarming her guard.

Every November second, on the Day of All Souls, Francesca would perform a burning ritual, incinerating her old identity and adopting a new guise.

It was the subtle details that made the difference: newly shaped eyebrows, a different shade of rouge, and highlighted hair could transform her from "Joan Hestia" to "Francoise Pachen."

She collected passports and nationalities as though they were a hobby, the only mementos she kept from her former lives. Her brother was the only one she had kept in contact with, the only one who knew her as

Francesca. But he was gone now, dust and bones in a faraway grave, and she was perpetually on the run.

"What's your name?" the young girl parroted, her thin legs swinging beneath her seat, causing her small frame to sway in time with the motion of the train.

"Ruby—Ruby Renaldo," Francesca replied without hesitation, and the young girl smiled sweetly at her, mouthing "Ruby Renaldo" before opening her thin novel and returning to her page.

"Excuse me, signorina." An elderly ticket inspector opened the door to their compartment and smiled apologetically. "Passport, please."

He ignored the young girl and studied Francesca with his eyes, his gaze lingering on the curve of her neck as she swept her auburn hair to one side.

She handed him her documents, and he fumbled with her passport and ticket.

"Thank you, Miss Renaldo," he said, purposefully brushing her hand with his as he handed back the ticket. His tongue traced a slow, wet line across his bottom lip, and it sent a shiver of disgust down her spine.

"It's Missus, actually," she said coldly, and folded the documents into her purse.

He was noticeably offended and shut the door loudly as he exited the compartment, muttering an insult under his breath.

Can't he see I'm with a child? she thought angrily, glancing at Angelina.

Even if she's not my own, she's young enough to be my daughter.

It was then that Francesca noticed the cover of the book Angelina was reading. The artwork was disturbing—a young woman, wrapped in a long cerise garment, with ominous black wings protruding from her back. They were the type of wings that belonged to a fallen angel, with edges like razors and curled talons at the apex. Serpents encircled her waist, and her eyes were ablaze with a deep-red flame.

"She's an Erinys," the young girl said, not moving her eyes from the book. "An ancient Greek demon, one who takes vengeance upon those who spill kindred blood." There was something disturbing about Angelina's voice. It was no longer the honey-sweet cadence of a young child, but the deep, resonant tone of a much older woman.

"They hunt and torment the offenders until the vendetta of the dead is fulfilled." A disturbing smile played upon the young child's lips.

"Where did you get that book?" Francesca whispered with horror, the air catching in her lungs.

"I didn't get it anywhere," the girl replied, slowly raising her eyes and locking her gaze with Francesca's. "It was written for me…"

A faint hissing sound permeated the air, so soft that Francesca almost didn't notice it at first.

"…about me." Angelina curled her mouth into a snarl, and her eyes were no longer azure, but a deep crimson. Her lips twitched, and they revealed a row of sharp, tiny white teeth.

"I've been looking for you, Francesca."

———◆<••◦◆◦••>◆———

"This will never work, Marco." Francesca played with a strand of her long onyx hair, a nervous habit she had picked up in her childhood.

"It has to. It's the same poison she used on Dad, and he was twice her size." Marco maneuvered the syringe like a deadly surgeon, slowly stabbing the metal tip into the sugar cube.

The mention of her dead father wounded her slightly, scratching at the grief she had locked away in that deep, black chasm where her heart had once been. She couldn't believe it had come to this, that her blasé, ordinary world had disintegrated, that her life was so unrecognizable from three years earlier. The Francesca of thirteen had been a loving, devoted daughter, living a cloistered existence that revolved around her family. Now, at sixteen, she was plotting her mother's murder with her drug-addicted brother.

"You've put too much into the sugar cube; she'll notice something's off." Francesca poked the cube with the nail of her index finger, and it crumbled into a crystalline mess. "See? Just leave the syringe with me. I'll take care of it." Her voice was flat, dispassionate. She had loved her mother once, but that was a distant memory now.

"Quite the little poisoness, aren't you?" Marco handed the syringe to his sister, and she wrapped it in a tissue before slipping it into her pocket.

"Death is too good for her," Francesca whispered, her eyes hard and glazed with a faraway look. "She deserves much worse for what she did to Papa, for what she did to us."

Marco was silent, his cracked lips pressed into a thin line. He looked ill, with pallid skin and hepatic streaks under his eyes. And there was that disgusting thing on his wrist, the spot where he had plunged countless needles into his vein so often that a pulpy mass of flesh had risen. He picked at the spot nervously, the blood vessels and skin protruding like a fat boil against his bony arm.

"Stop it!" she chastised, taking his hands in hers, feeling his fingers tremble and his frayed nails scratch against her. It pained her to see him like this, at the very edge of his existence, a skeletal shadow of his former self.

She curled her body into his arms and rested her cheek against the hollow of his neck. He sighed softly, the cool air of his breath tickling her skin as he wrapped his arms around her.

"You're all I've got left. I love you, sis." He kissed her neck gently, and she didn't stir.

"I love you too, Marco." She pulled away from him slowly, and his eyes had that horrible, tormented look within them. "You should go, before they get here."

He nodded compliantly and tucked his hands into his pockets. "I'll be watching you the whole time, so don't be scared."

"I'm not," she replied flatly, her eyes dull and dispassionate.

"I don't feel anything anymore. That part of me died along with our father."

"Francesca!" Angelina called, her voice rising with a gentle intonation, a common characteristic among the Italian aristocracy. "We'll take our coffee in the parlor."

"Yes, Mother," she replied with forced sweetness.

Angelina and her new husband, Raùl, entered the parlor and sat on an antique silk chaise, one of the many items that had been purchased with the profits from her late husband's death.

Money tainted with blood of the dead, Francesca thought, her brows knitted with anger. *The proceeds from the business of murder.*

Francesca rushed into the parlor with a silver tray loaded with sweets and delicacies. It suited her to act the role of a slave in her own home—it kept her mother and Raùl appeased, and there was no need to turn her out if she served them faithfully.

"Where's the coffee?" Angelina's lip curled with annoyance.

"It's almost done. They sent the wrong one this week. It's an amaretto blend. I hope you both like it despite the bitter aftertaste." *And the poison center.*

She glanced from her mother to Raùl and felt the familiar tingle of disgust that rushed through her blood every time she looked into his black eyes.

You defiled my father's bed while he was still alive.

The thought bit at her mind, but her features remained frozen, an ice sculpture of cordiality and respect.

"I'll run and fetch it now," she added, her fingers brushing against the syringe in her pocket.

"Yes, do that," her mother ordered, her eyes narrowing slightly.

In the kitchen, Francesca poured the steaming espresso into two small cups and filled a pitcher with ice-cold water. She arranged the items on a silver tray, taking her time to ensure the layout was symmetrical, just as her mother always demanded.

Marco stirred from his spot in the pantry, and she felt his eyes watching her.

Carefully, she removed the syringe and placed six drops of the amber fluid into each cup.

"That's too much!" Marco hissed from the shadows, opening the pantry door frantically. "If they screen their blood, they'll find evidence of poison."

She placed her finger to her lips and indicated that he should be silent, shaking her head calmly.

"There won't be any bodies to find when I'm done."

Raùl had his hand on her mother's thigh as he whispered something tawdry in her ear. His eyes remained locked on Francesca as she bent over to collect the empty coffee cups. She felt his gaze gravitate to her bust, and she suppressed the urge to tear at his face with her nails.

Angelina giggled like an adolescent and ran her tongue across his earlobe. She coughed abruptly, turning her head as she wiped at her lips.

"Bring us some brandy," she commanded, her eyes not leaving Raùl.

He laughed in his boorish, masculine way and threw a plate against the tray in Francesca's hand, the ceramic hitting the silver so hard that it almost shattered.

"Yes, bring us some brandy!" he echoed, his voice like venom and his black eyes watching her with masked desire. Angelina coughed again, but this time she couldn't stop. Her chest began to heave violently, sucking the air into her lungs between violent spasms. Her delicate hands flew to her face, and when she finally composed herself, there was a splash of blood against her lips.

"Raùl," she whispered, but he seemed unresponsive. His eyes had become dull, and he shook his head in disorientation. He clutched at his abdomen and stood as though he would strike Francesca, but his legs gave way beneath him and he stumbled to the floor.

A look of horror flooded Angelina's face. "What have you done?" she spat, her lower lip shaking violently and her eyes welling with distress.

"Nothing that you haven't done yourself, Mother," she whispered in reply. Francesca had fantasized about this moment for years, ever since she discovered that her mother was responsible for her father's death. Now that it was here, it was all happening so suddenly, too quickly, more brutal and horrific than she could have imagined.

"You put greed and lust before your own family, murdering my father so that you could marry his cousin! You disgusting, foul creature! Driving your own son from your home so that you could bathe in wealth with your lover!" Her voice shook with anger, more passionate and resonate than it had been in years. The emotions that had died with her father were bubbling to the surface, coursing through her veins with fury and disgust.

"No! No!" her mother whispered, sinking to the floor. Raùl was bent over in convulsions, the vomit foaming at his lips as he choked on the fluid in his throat. "It was never like that." Her voice was growing softer, the distressed look in her eyes fading slowly.

"He never told you that you had a sister. We had a daughter, long before you and your brother. He killed her. That bastard murdered my little girl. That's why I killed him. I needed Raùl to help. Not for money. For vengeance."

A violent spasm shook Angelina's body, her back arching at a horrific angle before her muscles turned limp.

"For vengeance," Angelina whispered, clinging to the word as the breath escaped her lips for the final time.

Her eyes glazed over, and her body became stiff and lifeless.

Francesca dropped the tray, and it clattered against the marble floor. "Mother! Mother!" she hissed, shaking Angelina's limp body.

But it was too late.

She was already dead.

"You're the one my brother wrote of," Francesca uttered to the Erinys, her mind consumed with memories of her dead mother. Angelina, who was now nothing more than a charred skeleton buried in the basement.

"You don't have to run anymore," the demon coaxed, her voice like a silken whisper in Francesca's ear, soothing and inviting.

Francesca was tired, so tired of running, of habitually shedding her skin. The black wings encircled them both, plunging them into darkness and blotting out the external world so that it seemed a hazy, distant dream.

"I can make this pleasurable, if you yield to me. Or I can show you horrible things, make you gouge out your own eyes."

Snakes hissed in the darkness, and Francesca felt a moist sliver against her thigh.

"Just like my brother," she whispered, surprise flooding her voice. "I thought the guilt had gotten to him, that he couldn't stand the memory of my mother and her lover burning in that pit, that hole we dug for them in the basement. But it was you all along, wasn't it?"

The Erinys ran a long nail across Francesca's cheek, causing a rush of fear down her spine.

"Tell me of your mother's murder. Did she scream? Beg for her life?" The demon's hand squeezed Francesca's jaw so that she couldn't look away, and the haunting crimson eyes burned into her, forcing her to speak.

"I thought she screamed when I set her on fire. But she couldn't have. She was already dead." The red eyes momentarily flared in the blackness, illuminating the delicate feminine features that were contorted with rage.

"The scream of the Erinyes, of my sisters. We were born from the crime of a child against his kin, of the spilled blood of Ouranos." The demon's voice was horrific, an intense screech paralyzing Francesca, causing her to drop to her knees, her hands flying to cover her ears.

"She deserved it," Francesca spat, screaming into the darkness, the bile rising in her chest. "That whore murdered my father and ruined my family! Where were you when my father was murdered? Where was justice for my father?"

"There are no blood ties between husband and wife. Her crimes do not concern me." A talon scratched at Francesca's abdomen, tearing the entrails from her body. She screamed in agony, in fury, catching the white intestines as they slipped through her fingers.

"I would do it again. A thousand times over. I spat on her grave, and I would burn the earth she rests in if it meant I could kill that bitch one more time!" Francesca screamed into the ground, the pain tearing apart her body.

"Yes," the demon hissed, a hellish cackle spilling from her lips. "Resist me. Fuel my wrath. I'll enjoy picking the flesh from your bones."

This story appears in *Demonology*, edited by Dean Drinkle.

16 ETERNITY, AS IT IS IN MORTALITY

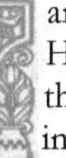armelina, Carmelina."

He whispered her name into the darkness and tried not to inhale the scent of death. She was badly rotted. Her alabaster skin had already turned ashen, and her rosebud mouth had desiccated. But he didn't see any of that. He only saw her as she was in life, young and fearless, and with a scar on her heart from too many hardships at an early age.

He carried her in his arms and laid her on their bed. He had done this many times before: on her sixteenth birthday when she had begged him to take her virginity, on New Year's Day when he had proposed, and last month when she had died.

The virus had spread rapidly through her body, but something had gone wrong. She hadn't reanimated like the others, the mindless corpses who had leveled their city to an urban war zone. She should have awakened by then, her dead cells hungering for warm flesh. But she was still a corpse, her features softened by death as though she were sleeping, painted with decay. To him, she was as lovely in death as she had been in life.

He stroked her auburn hair and traced his tongue over her mouth. Her sensuous, erotic mouth had always been his point of weakness.

"Carmelina," he said, running his hand across her breasts. They were hard, cold, and the skin cracked where her flesh had turned black with decay. He bit her nipple, gently at first, and then sucked on the tip, his hand clenching her breast until his fingers broke her skin.

"I'll keep you here with me forever. They can't have you. He can't have you."

She had always been a free spirit, and he had tolerated her affairs for years. But the last one had proved fatal. Joe—or had his name been Jack? He was the one who had bitten her, turning ravenous during their liaison. Not that it mattered; the entire city had gone to hell in a matter of weeks.

He ran his hand up the length of her thigh, tickling her with his finger and drawing juices from the chasm between her legs. He parted her labia gently and traced small circles around the cluster of nerves in her sex, an action she had adored in life. Her hand twitched suddenly, and there was a faint spasm in the corner of one eye. He didn't acknowledge these gentle movements. In his mind, she was still alive, biting his lip and digging her nails into his shoulder blades.

"I don't care what they say. The virus won't change you."

He whispered the words between kisses, his tongue tracing the hollow of her navel. "You'll remember me. You'll love me and come back to me as you always have." Her flesh became moist and pulpy from his saliva, sticking to his skin, and a viscous fluid oozed from the wound.

"It's the apocalypse outside. But in this dark room, it's just us."

He entered her, his body like fire, hers like ice. His strokes grew faster, more urgent, until he was on the verge of climaxing.

His hands dug into the skin of her back, and his fingertips connected with the bones in her rib cage. He squeezed her body against his, his hips writhing against her dead flesh.

He pulled out, teasing her, the tip of his cock stroking her clitoris with short, sharp strokes.

Then he was back inside her, her icy flesh wrapping around him.

There was a loud moan, and it took him a moment to realize it was coming from his throat.

His climax was intense, harder than he had experienced in a long time. The release was exquisite, better than it had been during her lifetime, and he rode the orgasm like a hot wave.

He collapsed next to her on the bed, his body drenched in sweat and his heart beating furiously against his ribs.

"Let the city burn. Kingdoms crumble and rulers flee, but still my heart belongs to thee." It was part of the poem he had written for her when he proposed, and she had fallen to her knees, tears spilling down her cheeks.

That's how he remembered her, not as the zombie who lay before him.

Her right leg began to shake, and there was a violent shudder throughout her limbs.

Her back arched sharply, at an impossible angle, and the bones in her spine made a horrible crunching sound. Her face became contorted, and her eyes rolled back in their sockets.

"No," he whispered. It wasn't as he had imagined. She was animating, the virus was awakening her body. She would be fractured—a mindless creature.

She would want his flesh.

A deep snarl rose in her throat, signaling her awakening. Rotted teeth protruded from her face, horrifying, jagged stubs in a sickening shade of brown. Her head shook from side to side and lunged forward, biting the air. The action reminded him of a shark attacking its prey.

"Carmelina," he whispered, but she did not respond.

The sound of his voice caused all her senses to focus. She was crazed, starved—ravenous as all newborn creatures are. Her body convulsed and hurtled forward, her teeth making contact with his neck. She latched onto his flesh, biting deep and hard, repeating the action over and over.

A large piece of his skin was torn away, and blood spilled from the wound, thick and hot, splashing over her face and washing over his body. Her hands dug into his back and she wrapped her thighs around his waist, grinding against him as she tore the larynx from his throat. He wanted to run, to escape the creature in his bed. But he had hesitated for that brief, fatal moment. It was still Carmelina to him, and he wanted to believe that the memory of sex, of love, and of a life together would override the instincts of her new species.

How wrong he was.

They were together again in death, as they had been in life.

Together in eternity, as they had been in mortality.

This story appears in *Love at First Bite*, edited by Danielle Rose.

17 THE HOUSE OF ATREUS

Children are a rare and precious thing in my family. Not many live beyond the age of twenty.

I would joke with my cousin Evgenia that it was some kind of family curse. Only one or two members from each generation would survive; the rest would perish before their time in horrible accidents or go missing and never be found.

It had been that way since the gods roamed the Earth, or so my father used to say.

All but a few were fated to die young.

—◆—<•••>◆<••>—◆—

"Evgenia, I'm scared." My voice was a whimper through trembling lips and quickened breath.

"Whisper, Naia, or they'll hear us. Every word echoes in here." She cupped her petite hand over my mouth and drew me to her side. Her hazel eyes were wide with fright, and as she pressed me to her chest, I felt the flutter of her heart against my body.

We had crawled into the air duct of my basement, a cavity in the wall large enough to fit two adolescent girls. Replacing the ornate iron screen, I felt like a prisoner in some kind of elaborate baroque torture cell, with flowery bars and icy walls.

"We should be able to see almost everything they do down here," she mouthed into my ear, her lips tickling me as she whispered.

"I wonder what it is. Do you think they do drugs?" I joked nervously, the anxiety still bubbling through my stomach. Irrational thoughts were distracting me, the kind of ridiculous fictions that only a teenage mind could invent.

I expected Evgenia to rebuke me, but she

grew oddly silent. Her skin turned pallid, and her thin fingers curled around the iron screen. She was like an ethereal being, some kind of fae creature trapped in a jar, with her wild hair and scarlet mouth.

"No, it's nothing like that." Her lips barely parted as she spoke. "It's something much worse."

"Dmitri, grab the other side."

I awoke with a start. My arms were numb, and my back was stiff. I turned to face Evgenia, my bones crunching as I moved. She was curled into a ball at my side, her features pinched and disturbed as though troubling dreams were floating through her mind.

We must have been asleep for hours. Icy air was blowing furiously through the vent— much harder than when we had crept into our hiding spot. Someone had turned on the ventilation, and a distinctive smell filled the air—acrid, like rot mixed with mold.

Evgenia whimpered in her sleep. Her lower lip trembled as her throat constricted in small spasms. A violent shudder passed through her body, and her eyes burst open with a start.

"Where am I?" she whispered, her hands rubbing her face.

"We're still in the vent. Look"—I pointed at the grate—"our fathers are carrying something into the basement, but I can't see what."

She rolled onto her stomach and propped herself up on her elbows, peering through the screen. I did the same.

"Dmitri, the other side! You're making a mess." My father sounded angry, scolding his brother. They carried something long and heavy, wrapped in layers of plastic sheeting. My father gripped one side of the object, my uncle the other.

"What is it?" I whispered, my heart pounding against the floor beneath me.

My uncle groaned as thick, black fluid seeped from the plastic onto his shoes.

"It looks like—" The air caught in Evgenia's throat, and she swallowed dryly. "A dead body!"

"All right, Alex! He's heavy! You should have drained the blood properly. That's why he's making a mess."

A prickle of dread washed over my spine. Evgenia grasped my hand, and her skin was clammy despite the cold air. I wanted to cry, to run away screaming.

Our fathers are murderers. The thought echoed through my mind.

They threw the corpse onto a large metal bench, their actions uncoordinated and clumsy. The body didn't land properly, and the top of the head slipped through the plastic. I caught sight of thick black hair, tightly curled and matted with blood.

Evgenia gasped sharply at the sight, and her small body stiffened against mine.

"I know who it is." Her voice choked with emotion, the words shaky and unsteady. "I'd recognize that curly hair anywhere. It's Nick."

Nick was her brother, my twenty-year-old cousin. He had just graduated from business school and was supposed to be working at an internship in Athens.

Lies our fathers had told us to cover up their crimes.

"I don't want to believe it." The tears spilled down her cheeks and washed onto my bare arm. They felt hot against the freezing air blowing through the vent. "My mother warned me before she died. She used to tell me the old legends of the House of Atreus— of our ancestors. Tantalus murdered his son, chopped him up into pieces and fed him to the gods." Her eyes were wild and her tear-stained lashes flitted like insect legs across her cheeks.

"The gods cursed him and his bloodline. That's where it all started, and it got worse with each generation. Incest, virgin sacrifices, matricide"—her voice trailed off to a small whimper—"Thyestes eating the flesh of his children."

Her breathing was erratic, and I feared she would hyperventilate. The air duct felt tight and claustrophobic, as though the metal walls were closing in on us.

Suddenly, my uncle let out a horrible sound. I peered out again. He and my father had unwrapped the body and were standing over it, my uncle with an ax in his hand, my father with a long knife. They stood with their backs to us, their bodies obscuring our view of Nick's corpse, and I was thankful I didn't fully witness what happened next.

"We have to do it, Dmitri. It's the only way to protect ourselves, to suspend the curse." My uncle mechanically nodded in agreement, and a stifled, guttural sob escaped his lips.

Then they began to hack Nick's body into pieces.

Evgenia and I closed our eyes. We huddled against each other, sobbing into our clothes, trying not to make a sound. Trying not to be discovered.

"One of us will be next," she whimpered, her hand squeezing my hair in nervous repetition. Her words stabbed at me, and I felt a heavy numbness spread throughout my body. I must have been in shock, for suddenly, nothing felt real. It was all a dream, some kind of hideous illusion.

There was the horrible sound of flesh being hacked, of metal hitting soft, pulpy skin. Of bones breaking and limbs ripping from sockets. My uncle and father polluted the air with their inhuman cries and grunts.

I shielded my eyes from the sight; each separate and distinct sound burned into my mind.

But there was one sound I could not interpret, like something sloppy and wet being thrown against hollow metal.

I summoned the courage to open my eyes for an instant. It was like blinking—I saw the image in a flash, and then my eyelids closed and the world was dark again.

My father threw a piece of flesh into a large metal cauldron, a heavy wrought iron pot with strange symbols branded into the facade. A flame burned under it, and my uncle filled the pot with water from a hose. Behind them, the plastic sheeting lay across the metal bench, now unwrapped, sodden with remains and curls of thick black hair. The basement was covered in blood and pieces of bone and offal.

Evgenia continued to whimper by my side, and I was thankful she hadn't witnessed what I had seen.

"It's nearly over," I said, trying to comfort her.

But the worst was yet to come.

They had been boiling Nick's body for over an hour—not that time had any meaning in our icy cell. The night seemed never ending, and we were trapped in infinity.

Evgenia remained curled at my side, a wounded creature waiting for death. But I no longer kept my eyes shut. I watched in silent horror as my father and uncle began their ritual.

They washed themselves of the blood and doused the basement with bleach, eliminating the evidence of their crime. My father changed into a crimson robe, my uncle into black. They looked ridiculous, as though they were dressed for a costume party, and it made the tableau all the more horrifying.

Reading from an old, decayed book, my father began to chant over the cauldron. His voice was as I had never heard it before, staccato and lyrical, the words spilling from his lips like a morbid song. He spoke an ancient Greek dialect, quite different from our modern tongue, and I found it difficult to understand all that he said.

"For the crime of Tantalus, we atone…sacrifice…upon the altar…"

The words had a palpable effect on Evgenia; her limbs clenched and she sank deeper against me.

"Don't be frightened," I soothed, but my shaky tone betrayed my intentions.

My uncle joined in the ritual, producing a small golden vial from a pocket in his robe. He tipped its contents into the cauldron and inhaled the scent deeply. The air became perfumed, a sweet, musky odor mixing with the sickening stench of boiled fat and blood.

There was a small gasp in my ear. Evgenia had opened her eyes, and we both watched, paralyzed with fear.

Abruptly, my father stopped his song.

Unlocking a cabinet, he retrieved a long golden spear from an arsenal of torture devices. He thrust the weapon into the air and stabbed deep into the cauldron, skewering a large piece of Nick's remains. It looked like a thigh bone covered in pale-gray meat.

He raised the flesh to his lips, grinding his teeth momentarily as steam rose from the caldron and obscured his face.

Then he bit aggressively into the remains and ate the flesh.

I was sick to my core. My stomach contracted, and I felt bile rise in my throat. An odd quiver fluttered at the back of my tongue, and I couldn't contain the vomit anymore. I turned my head away from Evgenia and threw up. In the confined space, the vomit splashed against the wall and smelled rancid.

When they had finished their gruesome feast, my father threw the blanched bone back into the pot.

"Just one more to go," he said solemnly, a sympathetic hand resting on my uncle's shoulder. "I know this is hard for you, Dmitri, but be strong. The ritual will protect our family and ensure that at least one of our progeny will survive. I mourn for their generation. At least fate spared me my brother, but whoever survives from among our children will grow up alone."

My uncle appeared defeated, his olive skin turned hepatic in the dull basement lighting.

They removed their robes and exited the basement.

"It's me. I'm next," Evgenia whimpered, a sickening look flooding over her features. "He named me after Iphigenia, the virgin sacrifice. I'm the same age she was when her father killed her."

"We've got to get out of here," I responded, knowing that either one of us could end up like Nick if we were discovered—boiled and butchered in an antique cauldron.

Frantically, we pushed at the screen that sealed the ventilation duct. It gave way, and I crawled onto the basement floor, my limbs unsteady and weak after hours of lying in a confined space. I reached for Evgenia and pulled her to her feet.

Tentatively, I scurried toward the basement door. I tried not to look at the cauldron as I passed it, but my head turned involuntarily. Something caught my eye, drew my vision to the murky contents of the pot.

I should have run screaming for the exit, but instead, I was transfixed by what had boiled to the surface of the cauldron.

There were four hooves floating in a thick layer of melted fat—black curls surrounding each one.

The remains weren't human—it was a sheep.

I could breathe again. For the first time that night, the world was no longer a dark and sickening place. Our fathers weren't murderers, butchering my cousin as penance for an archaic curse. They had slaughtered a sheep, taken part in some kind of bizarre ritual—strange, but ultimately benign.

"We were wrong!" I exclaimed, glancing about for Evgenia.

But she wasn't there.

A burning pain exploded behind my right shoulder. Acid sliced through my torso. Hot blood ran down my leg and dirtied my feet.

I stared in disbelief as Evgenia pushed the spear deeper into my body.

"Iphigenia should have murdered Elektra and spared herself." Evgenia's mouth trembled, and her eyes were frenzied, darting back and forth in their small sockets. That beautiful, fairylike creature whom I had loved as a sister was gone. She was an inhuman thing, spoiled by fear and grief, sickened by generations of misfortune and an endless legacy of brutality.

She pushed the spear again, and I felt bones crack deep within my body. The tip jutted out of my abdomen, the golden metal dripping with my blood.

"All but one are fated to die young."

This story appears in *Dreadful Legacies*, edited by George Wilhite.

18 THE LADY OF THE LAKE

e used to come here as children, before the murders began." Mischa tightened her jacket around her body, shivering violently. She was unsure whether it was the cold wind or the memories that were making her feel uneasy.

"My mother used to tell us about the Lady of the Lake—a spirit who haunts the waters where women die violently. We even had a painting of her in our living room. She was this beautiful woman with flowing garments and skin so pale it was almost blue. But her eyes were hollow and blacked out, like fish had eaten them. It scared the life out of me."

Orazio said nothing; he just listened and took her hand in his. She rarely spoke of her family, and he realized how difficult this was for her.

"I was always too scared to look in the water, but Rochelle was fearless." Mischa ran her palm across the frozen surface of the lake. Her warm skin left a clear streak against the frost.

She tried to see through the ice to the black waters beneath, but the surface was too thick. Her reflection stared back at her with large, haunted eyes and quivering lips. The image was disturbing, as though she were looking at a corpse trapped beneath the surface.

"I thought you didn't remember those days," Orazio said.

"I've blotted out most of that period, but I'm starting to remember fragments. My therapist says it's my brain's way of coping with Rochelle's disappearance."

"Is he trying to get you to remember what happened?" he questioned.

"Yes." She sighed heavily, suddenly exhausted by his questioning.

"Do you really think that's a good idea? It's been more than ten years. Maybe your brain has erased the memories for a reason." Orazio placed his palm under her jacket and touched the warm skin on her back. She shivered; his fingertips felt frozen. Then he leaned closer and cradled her chin in his hand, running his thumb across her lower lip. She hated when he did that; it made her feel like a child. She was like a puppet in his arms, with no will of her own.

Mischa was silent for a long while before she responded.

"I'm not sure. But I can't shake this horrible feeling," she whispered, gathering the snow before her in a heap so that it covered her reflection. "I think Rochelle is trapped beneath the water."

———————•‹•·›◆‹·•›•———————

"Rochelle, wait for me!" Mischa called into the darkness, but her older sister didn't hear her cries. She was too fast. Rochelle jogged the path through the woods every morning, and the inky night didn't slow her down.

"Rochelle!" Mischa called again, but there was no response.

The air was glacially cold, and frosted branches scratched at Mischa's face. She pushed them away with her trembling hands, and they snapped in her fingers like tiny bones.

She could hear the water hissing in the darkness, and she knew the lake was nearby. It wasn't winter yet, and it would be another week or two before the lake began to freeze. It was far too cold to swim, and she wondered why Rochelle would sneak out of the house on such a frosty night.

The dim moonlight cast a silvery glow across the lake, but the light was distorted by the violent movement of the water. The lake was usually calm, but now it seemed animated, crashing over rocks in turbulent waves and foaming onto its banks. It looked unnatural, as though the waters were enraged.

Mischa could see her sister on the other side of the lake. She wasn't alone. There was a man with her, his head covered by a hooded jacket that obscured his features. They both gesticulated wildly, and Rochelle threw her hands in the air as she typically did when she was upset. She turned away from the man, her hands covering her face. She was crying.

Mischa averted her gaze and stared at the ground. It was an intensely private moment, and she felt like an interloper, spying on her sister. She began to walk the length of the bank toward the bridge. She could wait there for Rochelle, and they could walk home together. Rochelle would undoubtedly be furious at her for sneaking away, but it wasn't safe to be alone at night anymore. There was a killer out there, murdering young girls like Rochelle and Mischa.

Hanging her feet through the rails on the bridge, Mischa watched as the water rushed beneath her. She wondered how long it would take Rochelle to break up with her boyfriend. He was comforting her now, with his arms around her.

As Mischa spied on the couple through the darkness, she realized something didn't seem right. The way he held Rochelle was dominating, almost predatory. Rochelle's body had gone limp; she was hanging in his arms, her head rolled back so that her long hair almost touched the ground.

Mischa's heart began to thud in her chest. Was Rochelle drunk? Had she passed out?

The man suddenly dropped her. He let her fall out of his arms and crash to the ground. Then he bent over and picked something up, something dark and heavy that Mischa couldn't discern.

He held the object in his arms and stared at Rochelle, who lay in a crumpled mess on the ground. Then he raised his arms above his head and brought the object down hard, connecting it with Rochelle's skull.

Mischa inadvertently shrieked, and her hands flew to her mouth. The man raised the object again, and Mischa realized it was a rock. He brought it down, over and over again, and she watched as he beat her sister's head until it was a pulp of bone and blood.

He picked up Rochelle and cradled her, her body hanging like a lifeless doll in his arms. With horror, Mischa realized that he was heading toward her; he was making his way to the bridge. Instinctively, she sprang to her feet and ran toward the bank, the adrenaline pumping in her veins like acid. She hid behind a nearby tree and forced herself to watch as he approached.

He stood in the center of the bridge, the highest point above the water. The railing was as high as his waist, and he effortlessly lifted Rochelle onto it, resting her body on the metal so that his hands were free to touch her. He stroked her face and stared at her, his expression obscured by his hooded jacket. Then he began to remove her clothes. Bile rose in Mischa's throat. The tableau seemed surreal, as though she were at the theater watching a horrifying play.

He ran his fingers over Rochelle's thighs, working his way to her hips. Her crystal blue eyes were wide open, and her skin was like alabaster in the moonlight. Rochelle's arm hung toward the lake, a streak of marble against the black night. He had stripped her of her outer layers, and she was almost naked, just her undergarments remaining. Dark fluid dripped from her skull into the water below, and her head was misshapen; part of her skull was missing. He wrapped the large rock in her jacket and tied it to her feet, binding her legs together with the rest of her clothing.

Gently, he placed his arm under her neck so that her head was upright, and he cupped her chin in his hand, staring at her lovingly. He was doing something odd with his thumb, perhaps fiddling with her lips. He leaned forward and kissed her.

Then he let her go, and she fell toward the lake, her body appearing weightless, as though she were already fluid, already part of the water.

She hit the surface with a sickening crash.

Then she was gone.

"Mischa! Mischa, wake up!" Orazio screamed in her ear, shaking her.

She awoke suddenly, her body bathed in sweat despite the cold air.

"What happened?" she asked groggily.

"You were crying in your sleep, calling out your sister's name." He pulled her to his side and wrapped his arms around her. He was naked, and his body felt warm and comforting, but she gently pulled away from him. She didn't want to be touched.

The dream was seared into her mind, and the memories were scratching through the surface of her subconscious. She could still feel the emotion of that night, the paralyzing fear of watching her sister fall into the lake. And Rochelle's crystal blue eyes, frozen in death, staring at her lifelessly.

Mischa stumbled from the bed, her limbs still heavy from sleep. Flicking on her night-light, she hastily dressed herself.

"Where are you going? It's the middle of the night," Orazio questioned, his voice filled with concern.

"I'm going to find my sister. I remember everything."

"This is a bad idea, Mischa."

They stood at the center of the bridge, overlooking the frozen lake.

She ignored Orazio's comment, absorbed in her memories.

"The water wasn't frozen when it happened. It wasn't winter yet. He stood here, exactly as I am. He placed her on this bar." She rested her hands on the railing, feeling the cold metal through her gloves. "He touched her face as though he loved her."

She imitated the killer's gestures, cradling the empty air as though it were her sister. It filled her chest with pain to remember the lifeless body, the horribly misshapen skull and marble skin.

"He did something before he kissed her, before he dropped her in the water. He held her chin…" Her voice trailed off as she mimicked the action, cupping the air, moving her thumb over invisible lips.

Then she realized what the killer had done.

It was the same action Orazio had used on her earlier that day, tracing her lower lip with his thumb. She stared at him dumbly, the voice caught in her throat.

"I always knew you would figure it out one day," he said. There was something sinister in his features, a brutal look in his eyes that hadn't been there a second earlier. She had never seen him look so cruel. "You're just like your sister, always messing with my business."

She turned to run, but he grabbed her by the wrist. He pulled her to his chest, wrapping his arms around her torso. She lost her footing briefly and struggled to regain it. He was holding her tightly, and she writhed against him. He brought an arm around her neck, trying to choke her, but she whipped her head backward before he could tighten his grip. The back of her skull connected with his nose, and he howled in pain.

She didn't feel the blow to the side of her head. It came out of nowhere. It was painless; she only felt a splash of hot fluid against her cheek. The stars seemed too close, as though they were directly before her eyes.

Then she was falling—falling slowly through the air—and the stars were rushing away from her, giant streaks of lightning in the black sky.

There was a shattering sound as she hit the ice, and her body plunged into freezing water.

The coldness was exquisite, the most intense sensation she had ever felt—so cold it burned her skin like fire, confusing her senses and disorienting her mind.

It wasn't black under the ice as she had feared. It was crystal blue, like Rochelle's eyes. She was floating in those large irises, those beautiful, dead eyes.

Rochelle was suspended in the water before her, her hair a dark halo around her face. She was marble, her skin so pale it looked blue and her mouth like a purple rosebud. Her arms floated at her sides, and she was like an angel with amputated wings, frozen in crystal.

But her eyes were missing. The sockets were black and cavernous, the nerves floating loosely where those beautiful crystal orbs should have been.

Mischa screamed. Her lungs filled with icy fluid. Rochelle was the haunting, beautiful image from her childhood.

She was the Lady of the Lake.

This story appears in *Beneath the Waves*, edited by Chris Bartholomew.

19 SECOND SIGHT

hat old gypsy lady is giving you the *mal'uocchiu*," Irma whispered into her espresso, her lips curling with amusement while her eyes remained serious. "Expect some sort of life-altering disaster in the next few days!"

"The evil eye again?" I questioned, scoffing under my breath.

"Quick, throw this at her!" She poured a few sprinkles of salt into her water bottle and handed me the mixture. I compliantly threw the liquid over my back. The white crystals made a mess on the collar of my charcoal jacket, and a waitress eyed us with annoyance burned into her features. We giggled like adolescents.

"Oh great, she's coming this way." Irma smirked to herself and stared into her coffee, her eyes hooded with mischief.

I felt the breath on my neck before I saw her. She was very old, with shocking white hair and pallid skin etched with wrinkles. Monstrous cataracts impaired her vision, making her eyes seem an odd shade of pale blue. She leaned over with difficulty and whispered in my ear, speaking in an ancient Sicilian dialect, the kind that was only spoken in isolated villages.

"There is death in the sea," she said cryptically, her voice guttural and more masculine than I had expected. She clutched my shoulder, digging her nails into my skin. "You have the gift. The second sight. The dead follow you." Her jaw quivered slightly, and her gelatinous eyes bore into me, staring beyond me.

I said nothing, but my blood turned cold in my veins, and the hairs prickled on the back of my neck. She didn't wait for me to respond.

She just turned her back on me and walked out of the café.

She's wrong, I thought, the sweat pooling at the base of my spine. *It's not the dead who follow me; it's I who follow them with my visions.*

"Crazy old peasant," Irma remarked awkwardly. We were silent for a long while, sipping our espressos uneasily. Irma dropped her empty cup a little too forcefully, and the loud chime of the ceramic caused us both to jump and then laugh anxiously.

"Well...I can't believe it's been more than five years. You look amazing, Amara." Irma smiled affectionately, her azure eyes alight with excitement.

I hadn't seen her since our college graduation, but she still looked like her twenty-year-old self, with tanned skin and an addiction to scented cigarettes. It was a humbling feeling, having coffee with an old friend in our favorite café, as though the whirlwind of the last five years abroad had vanished and I was back in my old skin.

"I'd been meaning to come home sooner. It's just that Kristos's work..." I couldn't finish the sentence. Our hands had accidentally brushed together as we both reached for the plate of *amaretti*. The floor fell out from under me, and my head began to spin. The café turned black, and a vision flooded my mind.

I saw Irma sitting beside a hospital bed, her cheeks streaked with tears and her lower lip quivering. Her mother was incapacitated, hooked up to a respirator, and the incessant beeping of the machine reverberated through my mind. Then the tableau changed, and I was looking across the Mediterranean Sea on a moonless night, the dark waters cut by flames. The sea was scattered with burning debris, and the stench of ignited fuel was overwhelming. The smell was so intense it trapped the air in my lungs and I struggled to breathe.

I snatched my hand away from Irma, as though I had touched a piece of the burning wreckage. The vision vanished, and I was back at the café again, surrounded by the chatter of a roomful of strangers. I felt the familiar creep of anxiety in the pit of my stomach, a feeling of guilt and helplessness. People would die in a fiery wreck at sea, some kind of sunken cruise ship or ferry disaster. And there was the vision of Irma's mother, sick and confined to a bed. How could I tell Irma of the horrors I had seen? Tragedy painted her future, and I felt powerless to stop it.

My heart pounded furiously against my ribs, and all my senses were heightened. The smell of gasoline lingered, causing me to struggle for breath. I tried desperately to regain control of my body before my consciousness shut down.

"Amara, are you all right?" Irma asked, her features flooded with concern. She sounded like an aural hallucination, as though she were speaking to me from underwater. I quickly steadied myself, and my pulse began to slow.

"Did you see something? Did you have another vision?" she asked in a hushed, secretive tone.

Irma was one of the few people, along with my husband, Kristos, who knew about my gift. My curse. Visions of death and tragedy had plagued me since I was a child. Sometimes I saw the future; other times it was the past. The visions hijacked my mind and ripped me out of reality, paralyzing me. I was nothing more than a passive observer, a mere onlooker.

I wasn't the only one with the curse. Other women in my family suffered from these apparitions. My mother had warned me before she died to never try to alter the course of fate. Never. Those were her dying words to me.

"No, I'm fine, Irma. Just jet-lagged," I replied apologetically. "We visited with Kristos's parents last night, and I'm still exhausted."

"Do you still have seizures after an…episode?"

"I haven't had a seizure in years. My doctor in London gave me some pills that work brilliantly." That wasn't entirely true. Alcohol, and then a brief affair with heroin, had extinguished the visions. The pills just put me to sleep when the anxiety was too much.

Irma smiled warmly and took my hand in hers, the concern genuine in her eyes. My skin tingled for an instant, and I held my breath, expecting her touch to provoke another vision. But nothing happened.

The moment was cut short by a sharp buzzing sound. My phone had vibrated, stirring me from my thoughts. It was a voice message from Kristos.

"Didn't you say your flight to Rome was at seven?" Irma asked, staring anxiously at the clock on the café wall.

"Yeah, I'm meeting Kristos at the airport in Palermo. His company chartered a small jet for him and the other executives."

There is death in the sea. The words of the gypsy woman lingered in my mind, and I felt relieved that we had decided to fly out of Palermo rather than catch a ferry to Bari, as we had originally planned. But guilt also flooded my mind. At some point in the future, there would be an accident at sea. People would die horribly, burned alive or drowned beneath the inky waves. I could stop it, prevent a tragedy, if only I could decipher the visions and find a clue about the timing or location.

"You'll never make it. The traffic is horrendous this time of night." Her words sobered me a little. I still had a life to live, full of mundane, ordinary things, like rushing to the airport. I would figure out something on the plane when I had time to think through the vision. I could find a way to warn the Coast Guard or somehow have the ship grounded.

I glanced at my watch and swore under my breath. I wasn't quite ready to say good-bye to Irma; she was one of the few people who made me feel reassured, as though no matter how much the world around me changed, I could always come back home.

I stood to leave, and we embraced for a long moment.

"How's your mother doing, by the way?" I asked, my voice slightly unsteady as the vision of the hospital bed flashed through my mind again.

"She's great! We just celebrated her sixtieth birthday. Her doctor says she'll live to see a hundred."

"Let's hope so," I whispered.

———◆◆◆◆◆———

The night was windy, and icy rain scratched at my skin.

I struggled to find a taxi willing to take me to the capital in the tempestuous conditions. Eventually, with much begging and bribing, I was on my way to Palermo, my wet clothes clinging to my body and soaking into the cheap seats of the taxi.

I tried to call Kristos, but there was little reception in the villages. Periodically, my phone would tinkle and another voice message notification would pop up on my screen, but each time I tried to retrieve the message, the connection failed.

"They won't be sending planes out in this weather," the driver muttered, a cigarette hanging from his lower lip. His comment made me feel a little more relaxed. Perhaps I wouldn't miss my flight, after all. The airport was pure chaos. A monitor at the entrance informed me that all flights had been grounded or delayed due to the storm. I took my time checking in and tried calling Kristos again, but this time his phone was out of range.

The receptionist who took my ticket was surly and in a foul mood. She glanced over my papers and snorted. "This flight boarded thirty minutes ago," she said, handing back my papers without making eye contact.

"What?" I spat, astonished. "But every single flight on the front board was either delayed or grounded!"

"They're commercial flights. Private planes follow a different protocol. I can book you onto the midday flight to Rome tomorrow, but it will cost extra." Her fingers slapped at the keyboard furiously, and she sighed heavily.

"No. No, thank you," I replied uncertainly. "I'll need to check with my husband first." I fumbled with my papers and my small suitcase as I left her desk. Anxiety fluttered in my stomach. Kristos had an important meeting to attend early the following morning and a conference call later that evening. He would be furious.

But my concerns were unfounded. In that instant, a mop of jet-black hair and a red tweed jacket caught my eye through the crowd of people. It was Kristos, and it was sheer luck that I had seen him when I did. He was one floor below me, wandering aimlessly in front of a *chocolateria* with a confused expression on his face. He was clutching a small bunch of roses in his hand. It made me feel even guiltier; not only had I made him miss his flight, but he had been thoughtful enough to buy me my favorite flowers.

"Kristos! Kristos!" I shouted, half my body hanging across the railing. But he didn't hear me.

As I rushed down the escalator to meet him, I had the sickening sense that something was wrong. It wasn't a vision—I was still firmly planted in reality—but my body reacted as though I were having an extrasensory experience. Every noise was suddenly too loud, and my hands flew to my ears. The sound of people chatting, of luggage being dragged across tiles, and a hundred other innocuous noises ripped through my head. I groaned in pain, and my vision blurred.

I steadied myself on the railing and stepped off the escalator. My senses adjusted quickly, and the odd sensation passed. I hurried to the *chocolateria*, but he had already left. Looking around anxiously, I searched the crowd for the red tweed jacket. I spotted him about to turn a corner to enter the departure lounge, the flowers clutched in one hand and his small corporate suitcase in the other.

"Kristos!" I called again, my voice a little too loud and shrill, causing the people in my immediate vicinity to turn and look at me uneasily. It was useless; he couldn't hear me.

I tried to dial his number again, but his phone was still out of service. He must have shut it off in preparation for the flight and forgotten to turn it back on.

I rushed down the corridor in the direction of the departure lounge, stumbling through the thick crowd of travelers. I turned the corner a little too eagerly and almost lost my footing. I expected to see Kristos sitting in the corporate lounge working on his laptop or reading the financial section of the newspaper.

To my surprise, the lounge was empty. I stared in disbelief at the unoccupied chairs and vacant buffet.

"I'm sorry, signorina. The lounge is closed." The usher smiled apologetically, his eyes quickly surveying my disheveled appearance. "Maintenance," he added cordially, taking me by the arm and leading me back around the corridor.

"But my husband," I protested, shaking his grasp from my elbow. "He just walked in here. The man in the tweed jacket with the roses. Where did he go?" I frantically glanced around the empty lounge for a sign of Kristos, but saw nothing. "Perhaps he's in the restroom?" I pointed to the rear of the area, where heavy damask curtains partitioned a section of the lounge.

"Impossible," he replied, a slight note of agitation entering his voice. "You must be mistaken. The lounge has been closed for the past half hour. And I remember il signore with the flowers. We spoke over an hour ago. He said he was waiting for his wife, and he would take his coffee by the window, to watch out for her in the crowd."

"But he was just here!" I objected, stubbornly ignoring the usher's words.

"Signora," the usher insisted, his voice abandoning all charm and growing authoritative. "I assure you there is no one here. You are mistaken. Please, it isn't safe for you to enter this area. They are about to start construction."

Dejected, I let him pull me back into the corridor. I stood there stupidly, travelers bumping into me as they scurried about the airport. The harsh fluorescent lights burned into my eyes, disorienting me. I couldn't be mistaken. I had seen Kristos in the very clothes he had worn that morning, the very jacket I had picked out for him. There had to be some kind of mistake.

There was a sudden, piercing scream from the crowd.

People were gathering near one of the departure gates. I couldn't make out what was happening, but several people were yelling at the counter supervisor. Some were even crying.

Numbly, I walked toward the commotion as faceless strangers rushed passed me, anxiously joining the growing mob.

"What's happened?" I asked an elderly lady who stood at the fringe of the crowd.

"They say a plane's gone missing, but they won't release any of the details yet."

"Gone missing?" I said. "But I thought that no planes had taken off tonight because of—"

How ignorant I had been. At least one plane had taken off.

That's when I saw him again. My Kristos. Clutching roses in his hand. But now the petals had fallen away, and only the barbed stems remained.

Half of his face was badly burned, so deeply that I could see the charred bone escaping the flesh. His eyes were a mangled mess, and the hair on his head a waxen black pulp, mixed with the melted skin of his scalp.

My phone tingled again. Another voice message. I blinked and he was gone.

I clung to hope. Perhaps I was just seeing things, my mind playing tricks on me. My fear from the vision in the café had gotten the better me. Perhaps I had imagined the entire thing.

With shaky hands, I pressed the call button to retrieve my messages. For the first time that night, the service worked.

"Amara, where are you? It's six thirty and we are about to board."

"Amara, pick up the phone! They won't hold the flight for you."

"I just spoke to Irma. She said you are en route to the airport. I'm going to board the flight and hope you make it in time."

"Damn reception. I'm boarding right now. I need to make that meeting tomorrow morning. If you get stuck, just catch a later flight and I'll see you at the hotel. Love you."

There was one final message.

"Ama…something wrong…plane…"

Static hissed in my ear.

And the phone went dead.

This story appears in *Gifted*, edited by Danielle Rose.

20 PIT OF DARKNESS

er eyes fluttered open. They were heavy, painfully dragging against her clouded vision. She fought against the disorientation, the hazy, dreamlike state that clouded her mind. Her lips were parched, and her mouth was chalky, her tongue a swollen pulp of flesh between her teeth. Intuitively, she knew something was wrong, and a pang of panic prickled the tiny hairs on the back of her neck. She tried to stand, but her body wouldn't comply. She lifted her left hand and then her right, hearing

a metallic clink each time and feeling the cool brush of steel against her wrists. Her legs wouldn't move, no matter how hard she writhed.

She didn't understand. What was that thing, the long, white snake in her arm? Where were her clothes? A ripped shirt barely covered her breasts, and her legs were completely naked, her sex hidden by frayed underwear. Her pulse beat violently, and the sound of blood rushing through her ears whipped her into a state of alarm.

She was lying in a bed. Some sort of white fluid was feeding her intravenously through her left arm. The air was cold and damp, causing her skin to shiver violently. She didn't recognize the room. It wasn't a hospital, and instinctively, she knew that it wasn't her bed—but she couldn't remember what her own bed looked like. She couldn't remember a thing—not her name, her face, or what year it was.

She continued to survey her surroundings, and nothing seemed familiar. Her first thought was that she was in some sort of medieval dungeon, with clay bricks for walls and a dirt floor. It was deep underground, where no light could permeate, a subterranean chamber dug into the earth. Dirt stairs were carved out of the wall opposite her, but the room was so dark that she couldn't see where they ended. They seemed to disappear into the darkness, ascending into the unknown blackness.

A flicker of light caught her attention. She noticed a small table hidden in a corner of the room, decorated as though it were some kind of religious altar. Thick crimson candles were scattered across a black satin covering. Some of the candles were new; some were little more than melted pools of bloodlike wax. There was a small gold chest in the center of the altar, and it caught the dim candlelight, shimmering with a faint, haunting glow. She wondered what horrible things were locked inside.

Directly behind the altar hung a large mirror, the frame elaborately decorated with gold and carved with exquisite detail. A woman fashioned from ivory was surrounded by flames, the fire wrapping about her naked body.

The image was intensely disturbing; whoever worshipped at that altar praised destruction and death. It sent a brief thrill of disgust through her body.

Her eyes searched the floor despondently, tears burning against her cheeks. It was then that she noticed the large hole dug into the ground in front of the altar. A shovel lay near it, tossed innocuously by the side of a pile of dirt. The darkness obscured her vision, causing the hole to blend into the shadows. Despite her confused state, she realized exactly what it was.

A grave.

Her throat constricted, and the air was trapped in her lungs. The walls seemed to rush toward her, suffocating her. She tried to focus her vision, to calm her palpitating heart and hysterical breath. The harder she stared at the mirror, the more disoriented she felt, until it became a horrifying thing, a black pool of emptiness reflecting her death. Her murder. Waves of intense dizziness hit her mind, making her feel as though she were falling, as though the ground had disappeared beneath her.

Where am I? Who did this to me?

The rancid air jolted her out of her delirium. There was the smell of mold mixed with something else, something indistinguishable. It was like the scent of musk, almost sweet. She breathed a little more deeply and involuntarily gagged. Not musk— it was decay. There was something rotting in the basement with her.

She held her breath and raised her hand to cover her lips. Her hand stopped short midway. She tried again, but she couldn't connect her fingers to her mouth. Her hands were chained to the bed.

"No!" The word escaped her lips. She pulled harder, again and again, tugging at the metal clasp and chain. Her blood pumped violently through her limbs, electricity coursing through her veins.

Then she saw the burns, the horrible scars on the inside of her arms, her fingers, her thighs. Some of the scars were fresh, still raw and the color of aubergine. Others were much older and had healed, distorted pools of flesh blending into her olive skin.

"How long have I been down here?" she whimpered, her voice a crackled sob through bloodless lips.

"Please be quiet. Please! He will hear you." The frightened voice of a small child cut short her thoughts. Her eyes darted wildly across the darkened room, looking for the child, but her vision was still hazy, her eyelids heavy with delirium.

Then she spotted him. He was in a corner, small and frightened, his dirty knees tucked against his chest, his arms wrapped around them. She couldn't see his entire face; his lips were buried against his thin arm, his eyes hidden by shadows. Tears had washed away slivers of dirt from his cheeks.

"Please, please don't make him angry," he pleaded, his fragile voice quivering between sobs. He bit the sleeve of his shirt, stifling the whimpers that fluttered from his lips.

"Make who angry? Where are we?" Her voice was hoarse, almost inaudible. She was unsure if she had spoken aloud or merely thought the words in her mind. She coughed, swallowed, and tried again.

The child shook violently and didn't respond.

"What's your name?" she whispered, trying to soften her voice and sound reassuring, but her parched throat made the words abrasive, almost brutal.

His large dark eyes looked at her with alarm, with fear.

He stood, wiped at the messy blond curls that had fallen into his eyes and carefully walked toward her. His small, naked feet softly thudded against the bare dirt floor beneath him. Standing shyly at the side of her bed, he touched her gently, avoiding the burns on her shoulder. She guessed his age at six, perhaps seven years old. His jewel-black eyes searched her features imploringly, and a faint flutter of recognition stirred in her mind, but she couldn't quite place him.

"Don't you remember me, Mama?"

———————❖⟨•••⟩◆⟨•••⟩❖———————

It was cyanide. That thing in her vein. Or some other kind of poison diluted with her intravenous fluid. Not enough to kill her, but enough to incapacitate her, to keep her in a perpetual dreamlike trance. The smell of rot had roused her from another brief bout of unconsciousness. She wiggled her toes, her fingers. Her legs were finally starting to respond. She repeated the small movements, but they seemed so burdensome, so unnatural.

The child sat on the edge of her bed, his hand still on her shoulder, so light it could have been a feather. The tears welled in his eyes, then spilled over and snaked down his small, hollow cheeks.

The wooden ceiling above them shuddered suddenly, and it sent a rain of dust and dirt down around them.

"Daddy's home," the child whispered, mouthing the words so quietly that she barely heard what he had said.

Fear bubbled in her stomach, making her feel ill. Her throat filled with bile and her body convulsed to vomit, but nothing was expelled. She tasted acid in her mouth, and it felt as though dried blood had crusted her lips. She tried to wipe at her face but failed; the chain was too short, and it made a loud banging sound as she repeatedly tried to free her hand.

The metallic sound of the chains scared the boy, who jumped off the bed in a fluid, catlike motion. He scurried back to the corner of the basement, his small body disappearing into the blackness.

The basement door opened slowly, and there was the heavy thud of feet against the stairs.

His legs were the first thing she saw. There was something horrible in the sight, the body half-hidden, shrouded in darkness with just the legs visible. Long, muscular legs, wrapped in black pants, the kind that belonged to an athlete. He descended slowly, the light revealing his form in small segments—the lean torso covered in a tight-fitting shirt and the tanned arms that held a small collection of knives wrapped in cloth. The silver blades jutted from his fingers like razors.

His face was unremarkable, so plain and average. If she had passed him on the street, she wouldn't have looked twice, except for his scar. A horrible, twisted piece of flesh snaked across his right jawbone, distorting his skin from chin to ear. It looked like it had been melted, acid poured directly onto his flesh. It hardened his features. His small mouth was locked in a harsh line, and his black eyes were like stones in their sockets.

He walked toward her, his boots kicking the earth into small plumes of dust, and she couldn't help but think that this was where it would all end, where he would murder her, bury her in that foul-smelling dirt.

She expected him to speak, to explain what he wanted with her, but he didn't utter a word. He threw the knives on a silver tray near her bed, the loud clank of metal making her muscles clench involuntarily.

He walked toward the altar, inhaling a long, deep breath as he did so. He seemed to take pleasure in the hideous smell. His shoulders slackened slightly, and his nails dug into his fists so that his knuckles were white and bulbous against his flesh. Opening the golden box, he uttered words that she couldn't distinguish, but they sounded foreign, perhaps Latin or Italian.

It terrified her to watch him before the altar, mesmerized by whatever it was he had hidden in that box. She could see his reflection in the mirror, a distorted flash of black eyes and scarred skin against a pool of darkness. He turned to face her, and his gaze lingered on the hole in the ground, the crudely dug grave.

He walked toward her, a faint smile upon his lips, and he watched as her battered body writhed against the dirty mattress. He took pleasure in seeing her squirm, in hearing the chains that bound her arms and legs clatter against the bars of the bed.

The man placed the small golden box on the metal tray and then selected a scalpel from his knife collection.

"No! No!" she shrieked, her muscles tensing with fear as the man cut into her thigh.

"Be still, or this will take me twice as long!" he barked, the spit foaming at the corners of his mouth.

A stab of pain shot through her right leg. Her body convulsed, and she involuntarily jerked forward, the motion cut short by her shackles. He dug the scalpel into her flesh and then inserted his fingers under her skin. He probed into her leg, his nail scratching at her bone. She howled in agony, and black stars danced before her vision.

"Tell me why you did it!" he spat the words at her, his face so near she could smell his putrid breath, see the yellow stains on his teeth.

"I want to know why! Why me? Why my family?" His screams blended with her cries as he twisted his finger, scraping her thigh muscle. There was a tearing sensation deep within her leg, and he finally pulled out a thin piece of pulpy flesh covered in blood. He held it up to his eye and examined it. A hideous smile crept across his lips, and his face lit up with pleasure.

"This is a ligament from your leg," he said nonchalantly as he placed the gelatinous flesh on the tray near his knives. "The human body has hundreds of such ligaments. I will tear every single one from your flesh unless you tell me why!" The small muscles in his jaw bulged as he screamed the words, his body shaking with a brief, intense spasm of fury.

She said nothing, unsure how to respond. Her mind was a jumbled mess; she didn't know her own name, let alone her captor or why he was screaming at her.

He's deranged, she thought, the realization filling her with terror. *He's had some kind of psychotic break and thinks I'm to blame for whatever horrible things have happened to him.*

Angered by her silence, he reached into his pocket and retrieved a small purple vial. He poured a clear liquid directly onto her open wound. A sickening smell filled the air, like burned meat, and it caused her to gag, the odor hitting her before she felt the pain. Her flesh was on fire, the skin of her thigh burning with intense pain. It was some kind of acid, melting her thigh into a messy pool of red flesh.

Her body went into shock from the pain. She began to shake and break out in a cold sweat. She fought the urge to black out.

He laid his hand upon her forehead and wiped the matted hair from her eyes. She felt violated, disgusted. She cried bitterly and tried to wiggle out of his grasp.

"I'm not done with you yet," he whispered, grabbing her by the chin and staring into her eyes.

"Please, please let me go." She struggled to form the words, her voice shaking, her vision blurred with tears, with terror.

"Let you go?" He laughed sarcastically, his eyes glaring with disgust. "Like you let those children go?"

He snatched the golden box from the tray and thrust it into her face, pulling back the lid. The stench of rot flooded her nostrils, and she squeezed her eyes shut, terrified of what lay inside.

"Look!" he spat, the anger making his voice tremble. "Look at what you've done! Open your eyes, or I'll carve them out of your sockets!"

Reluctantly, she forced her eyes to open, the smell of rot causing her stomach to spasm. It took her a moment to interpret the contents of the box, the horrible things that were hidden inside.

They were remains. The rotted, desiccated remains of tiny fingers. Children's fingers. Three of them. One still had a small signet ring, the type a young girl would wear.

"Why did you do it?" His tone changed. He was no longer angry; he sounded wounded, defeated. "Why did you murder those children?" A tear slipped down his mutilated cheek.

Hanging his head, he covered his eyes with his dirty fists, and his rigid body faintly shook.

"We've been at this for days, and you still won't talk."

The anger possessed him again. "Why did you break into my house, all those years ago, and take my son? Pour acid on my face to incapacitate me? Murder my wife? What sick ritual do you perform at this altar?" He flung his hand in the direction of the mirror, his features contorted with rage.

She couldn't respond. She had no idea what he was talking about.

He unlocked her chains, one by one, starting with her mutilated leg. She tried to kick him, to pound him with her fists, but her body was weak and she could barely raise her arms.

"You should have murdered me too. I never understood why you didn't. The three other families you targeted, you always murdered the father before you took the children. Why leave me alive? Why me?"

He lifted her from the bed and carried her in his arms, tearing the drip from her vein so that blood gushed from her flesh in a crimson fountain.

"You kept the children alive for years, raising them as your own, only to murder them when they turned seven. Why?" His eyes burned into her, but she remained silent.

He stood before the grave, the crudely dug pit, and she realized no one would ever find her remains down there. She fought against him, trying to twist her body out of his grip, but she was too weak and her movements were ineffectual.

"I'll never get an answer from you," he whispered, his voice hollow and defeated. "But the thing I can't live with—the thing that really burns my blood—is my son still thinks you're his mother." His eyes glanced toward the shadow-drenched corner of the basement where the young child was hidden.

Of course, she thought. *They have the same stone-black eyes.*

His arms relaxed, and he dropped her into the hole, into the rotted earth. She hit the ground with a moist thud, and the smell of decay intensified, becoming unbearable.

"You buried them here, in your basement, where their families would never find them. Why?" He roared the words at her one final time, and her body shook violently with fear. She opened her mouth to scream, to yell that he was sick and deranged, but the air choked in her throat and an unsteady whimper escaped her lips instead.

"Massimo!" the man ordered, and the blond-haired child scurried to his side. They looked down into the grave together as she groaned in pain, her limbs twisted beneath her at awkward angles.

"This woman is not your mother. She's a murderer. She hides her sins in this pit of darkness."

"Yes, Papa," the boy whispered obediently, his voice shaking with fear.

"Now help me bury the bitch so we can finally go home."

This story appears in *In the Darkness*, edited by Dorothy Davies.

21 THE CULT OF PERSEPHONE

hat's the spot where it happened." Daniele pointed his finger at a benign patch of grass littered with narcissus flowers, his dark eyes filling with intensity as he studied the landscape.

"Where the devil kidnapped Persephone?" Valentina's lip curled at the comment. Her words sounded sarcastic even to her own ears, but she hadn't meant to be cruel.

"No," he rebuked, slightly wounded at her

tone. "He's not the devil," he said harshly, and she instantly regretted upsetting him. "And it's not just Persephone who went missing."

This is it, she thought. *This is the reason he's dragged me halfway across the globe to this obscure town in Sicily.*

"My sister was also kidnapped."

———◆<•••>◆<•••>◆———

There was a melancholy stillness to the mountain range. A series of catacombs littered its side, honeycomb caves obscured by overgrown vines and monstrous plants.

Daniele had been quiet for the entire trek, despite Valentina's attempts to break the awkward silence. They had been friends for more than four years, since their first year at university, and she had never known him to act so emotionally, to be so volatile.

Penitently, she threaded her fingers through his, squeezing his hand so that their clammy palms were pressed together. She expected him to snatch his hand away, but he just stared at her with an odd, surprised expression on his face, his almond eyes like dark jewels examining her. She felt a tingle in her abdomen, the type she always got when he touched her skin.

"I'm sorry about before," he whispered, his words heavy and guttural. "It's just hard for me to be home. It stirs up so many memories that I would rather forget."

"I had no idea you had a sister. You've never mentioned her before." Valentina's words were probing; she desperately wanted to know the details of his sister's disappearance, but she felt ashamed to ask outright.

"She disappeared a long time ago. They never found her body, just enough blood to indicate that she couldn't have survived whatever happened to her. There's an empty grave somewhere," he murmured sotto voce, his expression pensive and distant. "We carried an empty coffin from the churchyard and buried it in the village cemetery, threw dirt on it. We buried air, her favorite brush, a well-worn doll—but not my sister. There's a tombstone with her name on it. But she's not really there."

"How horrible," Valentina replied, her amethyst eyes glazing over with a thin film of tears. "What do you think happened to her?"

"I'm not sure," he said meditatively. He pulled a small piece of crumpled ribbon from his pocket and unfolded it. It was tattered and worn, the crimson faded at the edges. "Someone sent this to me a week ago. The envelope was stamped from Rome, but there was no address on it, no note. My sister was wearing this ribbon on the day she disappeared, almost sixteen years ago."

He smoothed the ribbon over with his fingers and handed it to Valentina. She held it before her eyes, examining it closely. The worn edges looked burned.

"Do you see the markings on the back?" Daniele asked, and Valentina shook her head. He curled the side of the fabric, and she noticed a faint brown stain against the crimson. It was faded and almost impossible to see.

"It looks like—"

"A blade of wheat," he interjected, taking the ribbon back and gently placing it in his pocket.

"What on earth does it all mean?"

"The blade is a symbol of the cult of Persephone. They're an obscure sect that has hidden in the Sicilian mountains for centuries. They worship the *katabasis*—the act of descending into the underworld. They worship hell."

Valentina was silent for a long while, digesting his words.

"Like the Orpheus ritual," she eventually replied, her mind scratching at the almost-forgotten memories of an archaeological paper she had read many years earlier. "The initiates descend into a cave, symbolic of entering the underworld, and they're surrounded by utter darkness. The sensory deprivation is quite confronting. It makes the encounter intensely spiritual."

"The cult of Persephone is much more dangerous than that. Every sixteen years, a girl goes missing in these parts." He paused and squeezed her hand tightly. The tiny muscles in his jaw seemed to bulge, and all the color drained from his features, leaving him waxen, his jeweled eyes haunted and distressed.

"And tonight," he whispered, "I need that girl to be you."

―――――――――――•‹•·›◆‹·•›•――――――――――

The night was moonless, and Valentina stumbled in the dark, her foot catching on gnarled tree roots and overgrown grass. Brittle vines scratched at her bare arms, and the scent of narcissus flowers intoxicated her, disorienting her senses.

She had wandered in circles for almost an hour, exhausted by the uneven mountain terrain. Daniele had braided her hair with flowers, and she washed the makeup from her face until her skin was dewy and clear, all in an effort to make her look younger, like a teenager. Virginal and uncorrupted, he had called her, causing the crimson to flush across her cheeks. She had desperately wanted to kiss him then, but had lacked the courage. Instead, she sat in silence as he tied a ribbon in her hair, his calloused hands threading through her tresses as though he were playing a stringed instrument.

Nervously, she surveyed her surroundings as best she could in the darkness. Mount Etna was a gray outline against the onyx sky, a faint plume of smoke spilling into the air from its volcanic center. There were numerous caves before her, their entrances blotted out in the darkness, and she knew that Daniele watched her from one of those black hollows. She tried desperately to take some comfort in the thought, but the unnerving darkness was wearing her out. Each minute dragged her deeper into her own anxiety.

There was a snapping sound behind her—grass and twigs being broken. She whirled around in the darkness, her thick auburn hair a tangle in her eyes. She couldn't see anyone, but she could sense a presence.

"Who's there?" Her voice was meek and unsteady, and her heart pounded in her flesh, causing her skin to burn. Her eyes searched the darkness, but there was nothing.

She heard the sound of her neck cracking before she felt the pain. It was a horrible crunching noise that reverberated in her ears. A searing, hot acid flowed down her spine.

The night grew infinite, and she blacked out.

———————◆‹••›◗◆‹••›◆———————

When Valentina awoke, she was aware of an intense heat lapping at her naked legs. Her arms were painfully numb, and the back of her head and neck ached violently, throbbing in time with her anxious heart. Her vision was murky, and the world was a jumble of colors, browns and yellows mixing with an intense shade of vermillion. She blinked, and her vision slowly cleared.

Her feet were dangling above a deep precipice. With horror, she realized her body was suspended in the air, ropes biting at the flesh of her wrists. She looked down, trying to see how deep the gorge was, and the motion caused her body to swing like a pendulum. The sight of lava, brilliant and bubbling, flooded her vision, and she instinctively started kicking her legs in panic. She was *inside* the volcano.

The sound of women singing, their voices soft and melodic, filled the air. Valentina was surrounded; they encircled her, their bare feet treading the limits of the rocky cliff on which they stood, while she dangled before them, her body writhing in midair. The subtle glow of the molten rock made the women seem hideous, their eyes drowning in shadows, their features obscured by black-painted lips and disheveled hair.

Abruptly, the melody was disturbed by the entrance of a solitary figure. He was cloaked in black, his head covered by a hood and his hands hidden in black gloves. The women moved from his path as he walked among them, their white robes contrasting brilliantly with his dark garments. There was something shocking about his face; his features were distorted, the skin burned and thickly scarred. As he neared the edge of the precipice, Valentina realized that it was not a human face staring at her, but the vacant features of a mask.

His glacial eyes seemed to drink in her form, becoming vibrant at the sight of her twisting against the ropes. There was an awful pleasure in his black irises, and in the confused motion of her struggles, Valentina imagined the mask contorting into a vicious smile.

"Inferno," he boomed, his voice bass and resonant, making the hairs on the back of her neck stand erect. The women responded to him, dropping to their knees and bowing their heads. They were a sea of white robes and black hair, hundreds of them, all acting in unison at the commands of a single man.

"Persephone, queen of the dead, returned from Hades to resurrect fertility. She brought the secrets of hell with her to the surface." He threw his hand forward, and bright aureate crystals flew from his fingertips. They seemed to fall for an eternity before they reached the lava and disappeared in the flames.

Valentina's skin was burning, and she groaned in pain. It felt as though the fire were entering her, mixing with her blood, dissolving her skin from the inside out. Tears snaked down her cheeks, and they were like hot acid on her face. *Where is Daniele?* she thought, her mind growing foggy and disoriented.

"We offer this vessel, uncorrupted flesh, to Hades, to raise his bride from the inferno." The phantom figure pulled a long knife from his robe, the blade catching the fire in a brilliant shimmer.

Panic surged through Valentina's body as she realized what he meant to do. The rope that bound her hands and held her suspended in the air was attached to large rock on the ledge where he stood.

He raised his arms above his head and brought the blade down swiftly, in a sharp, whip-like motion.

The women became frenzied at the abrupt snap of the rope. In the obscured light, they were bestial and crazed, their movements wild and rapturous.

As the lava rushed toward her, Valentina threw her head back and howled. For an instant, she saw the phantom's eyes clearly, and he pulled the mask away to reveal his face, his features aquiline and exquisite, not at all like the hideous disfigurement she had imagined.

His mouth was sensuous, the lips crimson against his olive skin—lips that she had longed to kiss many times before. His almond eyes were black stars, glimmering in the dull volcanic glow of the cave, alive as she had never before seen them.

They were Daniele's eyes, intense and brutal, watching her as she fell into the lava, as

she dissolved into the fire.
    Watching her as she entered hell.

This story appears in *Hell*, edited by James Ward Kirk.

22 THE CAGE

he's clinically insane—lost it a few years ago. Her first victim was her closest friend, and then she progressed to killing random sexual mates." The doctor pointed at a young girl as he spoke to his students. She was like a caged animal, sitting on the floor of her cell with her hair falling into her eyes. Her arms were covered in horrible burn scars from stubbed-out cigarettes. She absently picked at one, digging her finger into her flesh and creating a pulpy wound.

"She liked to enucleate her victims—gouge out their eyes. You can see the motion she uses to pick her skin," he said, pausing to mimic her scratching gesture against the fabric of his suit. "It's very effective in removing the human eye."

There was a sudden spasm of panic in her features. Her body violently contorted and slammed against the wall, as though she were being pulled by unseen hands. She scratched at the air, fighting an invisible presence.

The doctor quickly swiped his access card against the keypad on her door and rushed inside. He struggled to restrain her and then plunged a syringe into her vein.

"This will help you relax, you filthy *whore*," he whispered in her ear, his voice low and guttural so his students wouldn't hear.

"I'm going to have some fun with you tonight. You're always so restless on Halloween."

She soaked in the burning water, dipping her head backward and fanning out her long black hair. It felt like silk when she washed it this way, merging with the water to become a dark halo. She closed her eyes and sank below the surface. Water like fire. It burned her eyelids, her lips, and the soft flesh of her neck. She found the pain soothing. It filled the emptiness.

Her thoughts were broken by the sound of her dog barking. It brought her back to the surface with a deep gasp of air.

How long was I under? she wondered.

A few seconds later, she heard the click of a key in the front door. Marie glanced at the clock. It was six forty-five; Vero would be letting herself in. She stepped out of the antique bathtub and reached for the nearest towel, wrapping it around her torso. The water dripped down her body and splashed messily on the floor.

"Maro!" Vero chirped excitedly as she walked through the house.

"In here," Marie called.

"You didn't have to get dressed for me." Vero purred like a satisfied cat and smiled cheekily. She rifled through her tote bag and produced a short black dress. "I've got the perfect Halloween costume for you. You can wear those black angel wings from last year. It's a classic bad fairy outfit."

"Or dark angel," Marie mused as she flicked through her closet in search of the wings.

Vero fiddled with the seam of her short skirt. "So, do you like it?" she asked, sashaying her hips from side to side. Marie burst into laughter when she realized Vero's costume was a modified version of their all-girls Catholic school uniform.

"Mrs. Spencer would have a fit if she saw you now!" she said, pointing to the school blouse that had been transformed into a boob tube top. Gone were the puffy sleeves and shapeless bodice; they were replaced with a tight-fitting, striped-green corset, which still had the original moss-green tie down the front.

"How do I look?" Vero asked as she pouted her lips and ran a glitter-painted fingernail through her hair.

"Perfect. Like an absolute whore. That guy you always flirt with on the ferry will be all over you tonight."

"That's the plan."

———————●—<••◦◊◦••>—●———————

The Halloween party was exquisitely staged. The subterranean university bar had been transformed into a hellish paradise, its entrance covered in black lace cobwebs and life-sized gargoyle statues. The bouncer, dressed as a ghoul, stamped their hands and laughed wickedly. Vero ran a fingernail down his chest as she passed him, much to his evident pleasure.

Marie's skin shivered as she entered the club, and she felt uneasy. She glanced over her shoulder and saw a man in a dark suit staring at her, his tongue tracing his lower teeth. His expression sickened her, and she turned to face him, but her vision was quickly obstructed by the growing crowd.

"I want to dance!" Vero screamed in Marie's ear, eagerly pulling her to the center of the club. They were surrounded by witches and horned devils. Angels and courtesans danced together as demons looked on from the second-story balconies. The air pulsed with music and colored lights, making the night seem surreal.

Marie and Vero squeezed their way through the crowd. Marie felt the tickle of her bare skin against the bodies of random strangers, their hands lingering on her waist and thighs as she brushed passed them.

There was a spiral staircase in the center of the main dance area, surrounded by an atrium of caged balconies. Alabaster limbs hung from between the bars, appearing lifeless in one flash of light, alive and dancing in the next.

"Let's head up top. I want everyone to see us!" Vero said, pulling Marie up the stairs toward the pinnacle of the atrium. Marie compliantly let herself be dragged up the wrought iron fixture, but she felt uneasy. She couldn't shake the feeling of dread in her stomach.

With a spasm of fear, she realized there was an odd snarling sound rising above the music. Marie pulled free of Vero's grasp, her skin shivering with adrenaline.

She stared into the pulsating darkness of the cage where the noise had originated. A witch sat upon a demon that ground his hips beneath her. They turned slowly and smiled at Marie in unison. There were maggots where their eyes should have been, and decayed lips sneered at her over long white teeth.

A shrill scream escaped Marie's lips.

"What's wrong?" Vero cried. Marie pointed to the cage, the air caught in her lungs. But when she turned back, the couple had vanished.

There was no one there.

Marie swore bitterly under her breath. *I'm losing my mind*, she thought.

"It's just the lights," Vero said, reaching her arm out and pulling Marie up the remainder of the stairs.

She's always pulling me up, Marie thought. *But I just keep sinking down.*

From the top of the atrium, they had a panoramic view of the club. The dance floor was a mosaic of flesh, painted with colored lights and fantastical costumes. Vero had already started dancing, and Marie found her body responding to the music despite her lingering sense of anxiety. Her hips slowly ground to the rhythm, and her hands clutched the bars of the cage. She let her head roll back, and her long hair tickled the small of her back.

It's Halloween, she thought. *In this costume, surrounded by a curtain of darkness, I can lose myself.*

She began to dissolve, and then she was gone, swimming in a sea of anonymity and rhythm.

The songs bled into each other, a seamless tattoo of international beats. The movements of the crowd were hypnotic—gruesome bodies swaying in a frenzied state of unison. She felt dizzy, outside her body. The blood pounded through her veins, and her breath became labored. She wanted sex more than anything else at that moment.

"You're giving out a strong erotic energy."

She heard his voice before she saw him, as though he were inside her mind. He sounded deep and guttural—the kind of voice she would associate with a cruel individual.

"It's like a pheromone. I can see it, smell it…" He grabbed her by the shoulders and spun her around, forcing her to watch as he ran his tongue across his teeth. "Taste it," he said.

She was alone with him in the cage. *What happened to Vero?*

A soft, subtle laugh escaped his lips. He towered above her, his jet-black eyes burning into her.

"Who are you?" she spat.

He slowly pressed his body against hers, forcing her to back up against the cage. He stood so close she could have gagged on his scent. The soft fabric of his suit tickled her bare thigh, and she felt an intense wave of disgust deep in her abdomen.

"You leave the scent of *whore* everywhere you go." He hissed the words through his thin lips. In the inconstant light, the bars of the cage cast long shadows over his features.

"Get off me! What do you want?" she screamed against the music.

"You know exactly what I want, *whore*. Show me what those bastards pay for." His fingers tightened around her neck and forced her higher against the bars, suffocating her.

He was panting in her face, his breath rancid and intoxicated. She struggled to breathe against his weight, her breasts crushed against his chest. He locked his eyes with hers, and in that instant, she understood what he meant to do.

"Don't fight me," he snarled, his voice almost bestial. He ran his fat tongue across her cheek, sending shivers of disgust down her spine.

She writhed against him as he dug his thumbs into her throat. She was trapped in those jet-black eyes, like dark prisms, and she was falling, sinking into unconsciousness. He released her, but it was too late. She was already broken, limp in his arms.

"Where's Vero?" she whispered helplessly.

"Vero died a long time ago," he replied, a brutal smile on his lips. "Don't you remember? You killed her."

He plunged a syringe into her vein. "This will help you relax, you filthy *whore*," he whispered in her ear.

"I'm going to have some fun with you tonight. You're always so restless on Halloween."

This story appears in *Halloween Shrieks*, edited by Dorothy Davies.

23 SOTTERRANEO

ristóbal, where are you?"
Sebastiano felt his way
around in the dark, his hands
stumbling upon an olive tree
in the process. His fingers
followed the thick trunk until
he detected a branch low enough to guide him
to the edge of the graveyard. He breathed in
short, palpitating breaths, and the scent of
olive flowers seemed nauseating in his anxious
state. He slapped at the sweat that drizzled
into his eyes, and his heart hammered like a
trapped animal in his chest.

"Lower your voice!" Cristóbal hissed through clenched teeth. "You'll give us away!" He crouched low, keeping his body close to the ground, listening to his feet crunch against the rocky soil. Once the earth became smooth, he would be close to the tomb. Silently, he dragged the ax behind him, careful not to cut into the ground with the blade. He focused his vision and tried to make out the sepulcher against the midnight sky.

Six more steps east, then twenty steps south, Cristóbal thought. They had examined the cemetery during the day, but in the black infinity of night, it all seemed different, as though the graves had become animated and moved around on their own. He could hear Sebastiano fumbling around behind him, tossing the earth with his boots and groping at the vacant air. Cristóbal swore silently under his breath and wished he had brought someone—anyone—else along to complete the task. But it wasn't his choice. The Domina had given him orders, and he had obediently followed. The penalty for disobedience was too severe to risk.

Finally, his gloved hands detected the tomb. He had studied its construction in detail and knew it by memory. They would have to remove the heavy stone door that barred the entrance—that would be the most difficult part—and then cut the wooden barrier away with the ax. The village women would not make their way to the graveyard for another hour or so; they were scattering sweets for the serpents near the Doric temple. But Cristóbal realized he would still need to hurry. The Domina would start the ritual once the moon was directly overhead, but the key ingredient was still entombed.

He tapped gently at the marble wall of the sepulcher to alert Sebastiano of his location. The sound of rustling leaves and panting breath broke the silence, and he reached out, seizing Sebastiano by the hands, pulling him close to the tomb. He removed his apprentice's leather gloves to reveal icy fingers that shook uncontrollably. Cristóbal squeezed them tightly until the agitated movement abated. He leaned toward Sebastiano, close enough to smell the saltiness of his skin, and placed his lips against his ear.

"We are in a sacred space now," he whispered, his voice rough and guttural. "Prepare yourself. We shall begin the ritual." He hesitated for a moment, picturing Sebastiano's sapphire eyes wide with terror. "It's always hardest the first time," he added, not wanting to seem overtly cruel.

Sebastiano sucked in a quavering breath and nodded silently in the darkness. He closed his eyes and tried to compose himself.

Cristóbal produced a small vial from his coat pocket. His fingers gently turned the elaborate bronze lid until it unfastened. The smell of copper pervaded the air, mixing with the rustic scent of olive blossoms and graveyard sage.

He turned the vial upside down, and blood leaked onto his fingertip. It felt warm despite the cold night air.

Standing on the balls of his feet, he pressed a single drop against the top of the stone that barred the entrance to the tomb and then placed two more at the barrier's base. They formed the points of a blood triangle.

He took a step backward, away from the burial chamber, and handed the vial to Sebastiano. Cautious not to spill its contents, Sebastiano fell to his knees and dug a small pocket in the ground. He slowly dripped three drops of the blood into the earth.

"Ctonie," Cristóbal whispered with reverence.

"Ctonie," Sebastiano repeated.

Then they both began to push against the rock.

The Domina rose indolently from the sacred pool, a kiss of salt permeating her rosebud mouth.

She stretched her neck backward, causing her long raven hair to dip into the water around her hips. The fluid clung to her naked body like golden snakes in the amber torchlight, giving her ivory skin a subtle incandescence. The air was heavy with the scent of damp earth, and vaporous mastic veiled the pungent odor of decay.

The female companions of the Domina moved about her with elegance and fluidity. They knew her body like the rhythm of a song. Artemide gathered the honey-scented hair and twisted it around the nape of the Domina's neck as Kora anointed her back with drops of melted myrrh. When the Domina's body was dry, the two attendants held out the ceremonial garment, an ancient dress of white silk and rubies, threaded throughout with fine-spun gold.

The three women were in the catacombs under the Doric temple of Concordia, the subterranean necropolis of the city of Agrigento. A series of chambers, each connected by decaying wooden doors, separated the ancient dead from the living.

"It infuriates me," the Domina whispered, her husky voice soft despite her irritation, "the way that fool, that cavalier archaeologist, misnamed the temple."

Concordia was the erroneous name that foreigners had ascribed to the sanctuary above the catacombs. But the inhabitants of the ancient city of Agrigento had always known that the temple belonged to Hecate, the triple goddess, the immortal mistress of witchcraft.

The Domina stepped into her garment, and her attendants laced the bodice tightly around her ribs. Kora rubbed amber-scented oil across the Domina's décolletage as Artemide placed emerald jewels upon her bust and fastened them around her neck. The necklace was a Hellenistic replica of the Jewels of Harmonia; the original piece had been lost to time and obscured by mythology.

When their preparations were complete, the two women knelt before the Domina and averted their gazes. She was a pre-Raphaelite beauty, with her jet-black hair and ethereal eyes. Languidly, she walked to the altar, the silk fluttering about her legs in a shimmer of ivory and gold. She reached for the braided basket that had been placed between the ignited mastic and a terra-cotta amphora. The basket was overflowing with barley grains. She plunged her hand into it and retrieved a small golden dagger with a large cerise crystal in its handle. The blade was thin and triangular, and it caught the reflection of her emerald eyes. She smiled faintly as she twisted the point against her finger, her rosebud lips revealing her sharp white teeth.

"Let them in," she announced.

Artemide and Kora hurried to release the chamber door. The worshippers—thirteen men—stood around the entrance, their faces solemn and cadaverous in the torchlight. They were dressed identically, cloaked in black habits that covered their heads and draped down around their feet. Eleven of the men proceeded into the catacomb and formed a triangle around the altar.

The last two—Cristóbal and Sebastiano—carried a pine coffin into the chamber. It was blackened with earth, and they labored under its weight. They set it down in front of the altar and took their places in the triangle. The men were utterly silent, bewitched by the luminous presence of the three women.

The Domina seemed oblivious to their entrance. She stood in the center of the triangle, her eyes unopened and her body inanimate. She could feel the anxiety emanating from the worshippers like a pheromone subconsciously leaked into the air. She was silent for a long while, as were the two attendants by her side, their three bodies locked in soundless preparation for the ritual.

Finally, the Domina opened her eyes and began to speak.

"Not all of you will survive tonight." Her voice slipped through her mouth like a silken caress, her crimson lips in brilliant contrast to her ivory skin. The words had a palpable effect on the men, who stirred within their skins. She stretched out her arms to the worshippers, her eyes lighting up with a brilliant fury, color violently flooding into her features. "But if you have the blood of a god in you, then"—she paused, the corner of her mouth curling into a partial smile—"you will become IMMORTAL!"

The men became frenzied at the sound of the word. Wild screams ricocheted off the catacomb walls, and the stomping of feet sounded like bestial hooves against the ground. Sebastiano, the youngest of the worshippers, tore at his hair in the confusion, his face contorted with alarm. In the mania of that moment, against the dimly lit subterranean walls, the men appeared inhuman, their primal, animalistic selves scratching through.

The Domina laughed briefly, a throaty, almost groaning sound escaping her lips. But her eyes remained empty and hard.

"Enough," she whispered softly, and the men seemed paralyzed at her command. They quickly resumed their solemnity.

"*Il giorno della morte*—the day of the dead. The only day I can raise the shades from Hades." She collapsed to her knees, and her two female companions removed the pine lid from the coffin, revealing the corpse of a man within. The overpowering stench of putrefaction invaded the air, but it had no effect on the Domina. She removed the votive items that had been laid upon his chest—an ornate lighter and a hunting knife—and pressed her palm against his heart.

"You've not been gone from this world for long, follower," she whispered to the corpse, and then she lightly pressed her lips to his.

Sebastiano trembled beneath his gown. The material suddenly became suffocating, and he pulled at the collar around his neck. He watched as the Domina breathed a shallow breath into the lips of the corpse. He felt profoundly disturbed at the tableau and slightly jealous at seeing her engaged in an intensely intimate moment with the dead man.

Sucking in a raspy breath, the Domina struggled to push herself away from the corpse, weakened by the ritual. She resumed her kneeling position over the body. Her features had been drained of color, and her mouth was bloodless, her lower lip almost lavender.

Her hands felt around the dusty floor for the knife, which she had dropped under the coffin. She clasped it in both hands, and summoning her strength, she raised it high above her head. Her lips moved in a pulsation of inaudible words, not breaking the silence of the catacomb. The two female attendants moved quietly behind her and approached the altar, seizing the amphora in their hands.

The Domina's fingers grasped the knife so tightly they turned white from the pressure. She cast her eyes toward the earth and uttered a faint, bestial cry.

Then she plunged the knife deep into the dead man's chest.

The black blood welled up from his heart and met the cerise crystal of the blade. At that same instant, just as the knife connected with his flesh, the attendants smashed the amphora into the earth. The terra-cotta disintegrated with a horrific sound, echoing through the subterranean chamber like an explosion. Black snakes, their bodies smooth and flawless, slithered from the remains of the vase like a shadowy liquid. Some of the followers gasped in terror at the sight.

Artemide hurried to collect the dead man's blood in a bronze chalice, the wine-dark fluid spilling over the rim of the cup in her haste.

She gave the vessel to the Domina, who drank the burgundy liquid, a sliver of blood snaking down the corner of her mouth. She held the chalice out toward the worshippers, their bare feet surrounded by serpents and terra-cotta fragments.

"This is the poisoned blood of Romanos!" She held the cup above her head as the men observed in silent fixation. "A man with no living descendants. On this day, the day of the dead, by the magic of the triple goddess, I offer his blood as a conduit to the chthonic gods!" She poured a few drops of blood onto the earth as a macabre libation.

The two attendants joined the Domina at her side, and then each took a turn at sipping from the chalice.

Leaning forward, the Domina pressed her lips to the corpse again. This time the blood seeped from her mouth as she breathed into his sunken lips. Then she stood and wiped the blood from her face, her eyes never leaving the dead Romanos.

The worshippers stared on, their features painted with morbid captivation.

After a long moment, the silence of the catacomb was shattered by the inadvertent cries from the men.

The jaw of the corpse trembled slightly. A groaning sound rumbled from deep within his throat.

"It's working," the Domina whispered.

Artemide quickly collected the chalice and forced it into Sebastiano's hands, her large violet eyes imploring and hypnotic. "Drink!" she instructed. "While the corpse is still animated."

Sebastiano gulped the viscous blood and felt a tremble of disgust at the back of his throat. His abdomen cramped violently, and he feared he would vomit. He sucked a breath through his nose and forced his lips tightly shut, not daring to contaminate the ritual. He passed the vessel to the worshipper at his side.

The chalice made its way around the triangle of men. Each one took a turn at sipping the poisoned blood.

When the cup was empty, Kora returned it to the altar and then stooped to catch a serpent in her hands. The thick black snake entwined itself around her fingers, and she stroked it affectionately, as she would a child.

The men stood in absolute silence, their faces washed with fear and bathed in sweat. Their eyes seemed to twitch with wild anticipation as they surveyed each other for signs of a response.

Sebastiano was the first to react. His body started to heave, to jerk in spasms. A loud, raspy sound came from his lungs, and he began to scratch at his face feverishly, tearing the skin from his cheeks. His muscles contracted so sharply the bones in his back made a hideous cracking sound, and his head arched backward toward his feet. He fell to the ground, writhing in pain, until the last of his breath escaped his lips and his chest rose no longer.

Some of the men began to scream in terror. They ran toward the doors, but the attendants had already tied them tightly shut with ropes.

In his delirium, Cristóbal tried to untangle the knots, but his vision was so hideously blurred that he could not connect his hands with the door. His left eyeball turned violently in on itself, and only the white of his eye was visible.

One by one, the men dropped to the ground in agony.

They lay piled up against each other, a tangle of limbs and contorted body parts. The air stunk of urine and excrement.

The Domina looked upon them in disgust. "They're all mortals," she uttered, her voice laced with revulsion. "Not a god among them!"

This story appears in *Grave Robbers*, edited by James Ward Kirk.

24 THE BUTCHER OF BARCELONA

elcome, Miss Montblanc. Come in, please." He gestured for me to enter his rustic cottage, shaking his plump, white arm as he did so. The heat from the fireplace cut against the cold mountain air, and as I entered, I was greeted with the delicious smell of freshly roasted meat.

"Thank you. Please, call me Laura." My Spanish was sparse, but he nodded approvingly, understanding my awkwardly composed reply. He extended a fleshy, calloused hand, and I instinctively reciprocated the gesture. I tried not to stare at his jowls as they wobbled from the force of his handshake.

I stepped into the dining area of his home, the ancient stone floor, worn with time, crunching beneath my boots. There was a large collection of female shoes lined up next to the fireplace, and the display struck me as odd. There were at least twenty pairs, in a mixture of colors and types. Stiletto heels stood alongside plastic-looking ballet flats and glittery wedges—not the type of shoes I would expect to see on a pig farm.

"My wife…" He gestured helplessly to the collection. "The woman loves her shoes!"

I smiled understandingly and did not think much of it.

If only I had paid more attention.

Unlacing my boots, I swiftly removed my shoes, and they joined the innocuous collection.

"So, where should we do this?" I asked, my eyes surveying his cottage for an appropriate spot to interview him.

"Right here, at the table. I was just sitting down to lunch." He ushered me into his tiny kitchen, his sweaty hand invading the small of my back. There was something domineering about the way he insisted that I sit facing the fireplace. It gave me an uninterrupted view of the pink flesh slowly roasting on the spit.

I could see my reflection in a large mirror above the hearth, and I looked gaunt and skeletal next to Agustín Grose. He was a head shorter than I, with a toilet seat patch of white hair around his fleshy scalp. The tiny glasses that were squeezed onto his snub nose amplified his small black eyes, accentuating every glance.

I placed a tape recorder on the table and began the interview.

"Your *jamon* has won first place at the Cologne Food Fair again this year. Tell me, Senor Grose, what is your secret?" I tried to sound interested, but my voice came out flat and impassive.

"We've been curing meat for generations—hundreds of years." He fiddled with a mixture of red-and-black spices, tossing them across the spit-impaled meat. The granules that hit the fire seemed to aggravate the flames, causing them to leap and hiss at the raw flesh. "My father owned a *charcuterie* in west Barcelona, as did his father before him, and so on, all the way back to Roman times. I moved out here, to the country, about a decade ago. I enjoy the…privacy."

"How fascinating," I mumbled, unimpressed. I was exhausted from the three-hour drive across the rugged mountains, and hunger was making me irritable. The scent of his roasting lunch was intensely distracting.

"The meat smells delicious," I diverged, pressing my lips together in an effort to keep from salivating. My stomach made an embarrassingly loud rumble.

He continued to marinate the roast as the flames danced around it.

"Is it pork?"

"Yes." He smiled oddly at me, his thin, pink mouth stretching across his face. "Pork cheeks, the most delicious part of the animal."

The smell of cooked pork generally turned me off my food, but there was something tantalizing about Grose's spit roast that drew my hunger to the surface. The pink flesh had now turned a buttery shade of gold, and the fat dripped across the meat as it rotated through the flames.

He sliced a thin strip of the jowl from the spit and threw it into his mouth, chewing the meat noisily; I could hear his saliva mixing with the crackling skin.

Cleaning the large carving knife across his thigh, he glanced at me over his shoulder, the sweat slowly snaking down his forehead.

"Would you like a slice?" The words were unnerving from his small, tight lips, as though he were trying to seduce me with food. At that instant, a large drop of melted fat splashed into the fire, causing the flames to flare up and sizzle. The burst of light illuminated Grose's face so that his nose and eye sockets cast dark shadows across his skin, making him appear demonic, inhuman.

I should have noticed the sinister look in his tiny, pig-like eyes, but my hunger clouded my mind and funneled my thoughts. All I wanted was the pink-gold meat that he dangled before me.

"Yes, please," I replied in a meek voice.

He slashed a large portion off the roast, deftly maneuvering the blade. Removing the flesh from the spit, he placed it on a ceramic plate and set it down before me.

A thin plume of steam rose from the meat, and I remember thinking how ghostly the cloud looked, the translucent spirit of the pig haunting me for eating its flesh. I inhaled the scent deeply, enjoying the warm tickle of the smoke in my throat and lungs.

I cut the flesh clumsily, ravenous with hunger, and stuffed a large piece of the juicy meat into my mouth. It was like nothing I had ever tasted before. The succulent flesh dissolved on my tongue; the crackling skin and spiced liquids warmed my cold body as they slowly slid down my insides.

Grose stared at me eagerly, a maniacal grin contorting his face as he bit on his lower lip. An odd noise rose in his throat, like a pleasurable groan mixed with a guttural sigh. There was an intense look of carnality on his features, and I wondered if he was some kind of sexual deviant, taking pleasure in watching me stuff my face with food.

"This is amazing, so tender." The words awkwardly spilled from my mouth as I took another hearty bite. The meat was rawer than I had ever eaten before—the center of the jowl still oozed dark-red blood—but I was so famished that it didn't bother me.

Grose poured me a glass of inky, viscous wine, and I threw it back greedily. It, too, was delicious, with a distinctive coppery aftertaste.

"I'm glad you find it pleasing." He seemed to hiss out his words like a snake, his tongue tracing over his lower teeth. "I'm going to get you some cheese from the *fromagerie*," he continued, wiping his fat, greasy fingers across his shirt. "Please excuse my absence and enjoy the food."

He opened the back door to the cottage and briskly walked outside. The smell of the pig farm was overwhelming, like excrement mixed with rot, and it spoiled the scent of the spiced meat.

Suddenly, an intense wave of nausea rattled my insides. My stomach seemed to battle with its contents, churning and whining in protest. Acidic vomit shot up my throat. I rinsed my mouth with another glass of wine, and it made me feel better, even slightly hungry again.

There was a single slice of meat left on the spit, and I decided to help myself to it. Grose was taking his time and his plate was still full, so I didn't think it would bother him.

Avidly, I liberated the impaled flesh from the spit and heaped it onto my plate, my mouth salivating at the thought of another helping.

I sat down and began to enjoy the large piece of meat, but I found this particular cut much more difficult to chew than the last. Pulling a partially gnawed piece out of my mouth, I returned it to my plate and examined it. The tough flesh was much more yellow than the rest of the roast, and it was rubbery, almost gummy, in texture. It appeared to be cartilage.

At first I thought it was a piece of pig ear, but the shape was completely wrong—it was rounded, not pointy, and there was an odd striation at the bottom of the lobe.

Something glimmered in the corner of my eye, and it distracted my vision. One of the shoes was covered in glitter, and it caught the afternoon sun. That particular pair had struck me as being out of place when I first entered the cottage, and as I narrowed my eyes to examine the shoes again, I realized that they were much larger than the others.

In fact, none of the shoes seemed to be the same size—they were all different lengths and widths. There was no way they could all belong to the same woman.

The hairs prickled on the back of my neck. Wildly, my eyes darted around the small room, and I began to doubt if Grose even had a wife—there was not a single item in his cottage to indicate the presence of a female.

The breath caught in my lungs. Frantically, I pierced the piece of cartilage on my plate and examined the striation closely.

Of course. I had known it looked familiar. It was a double piercing, the type that was so popular with the young city girls of nearby San Sebastián.

I had been chewing on a *human* ear.

My throat constricted. I couldn't suppress the bile as it burned in my mouth and spilled onto the table before me. Gathering my wits, I scrambled to get out of the cottage.

But I was too slow. My limbs didn't want to cooperate with my mind; they felt heavy and unresponsive, as though I were walking through wet concrete. Involuntarily, my hand knocked over the bottle of wine. The bloodlike liquid splashed across my lap, and I wondered if the odd color was due to some kind of drug, a paralytic agent hidden in the fluid.

My head rolled to one side, sinking onto my shoulder, and I tried desperately to straighten my neck, but it would not comply.

To my horror, in the hazy reflection of the mirror, I saw Grose as he crept up behind me, the shiny meat cleaver gripped in his chubby hand.

He gestured to the remains on my plate.

"I see you've met my wife."

This story appears in *Long Pig*, edited by Dorothy Davies.

25 MISTRESS

er jasmine scent lingers in the empty room. It's her afterthought, someone she used to be but isn't anymore. Her languid lips were soft pulsations against my skin. So out of time with my blood. So out of form with my body.

When it was done, she lay on the bed, her body a silhouette of hills and valleys. She scratched the lipstick across her lips and said she would never be mine. She was not a cigarette to be passed around, a puff of smoke to be forgotten.

I've loved you since we first met—but you are my brother's wife, forbidden and delicious. But my words were absent. She had that effect on me, and I was breathless around her.

She looked at me from under her lashes, and her features were masked by something I could not interpret. She was all things good girls are not, with a cascade of raven hair and eyes like sapphire crystals.

The phantom of my mind had known her many times, but the flesh of my lips only that once. She had cracked monogamy with each kiss, exhaled her claustrophobic marriage with each breath.

Her gold hoop earrings caught the inconstant candlelight, jolting me out of my lethargy. The *nazar* tattoo, just above her breast, followed me around the room, stalking me like a ravenous beast.

"We have an understanding?" Her lips moved in a rhythm of apathy, the air a vicious drop of silence between us. She had burned a part of herself into my being, like a honeybee that stings its prey and dies in the process.

She stood and laced her boots to leave.

Yes, I thought. *We understand each other.*

I am the insect; you are liquid amber.

She abandoned the room, leaving her scent

behind.

I stare into my bourbon, a tawny whirlpool in my glass, and I throw it back like acid in my throat.

———◆◦•◦◗◆◖◦•◦◗◆———

Ava heard the crunch of flowers under her feet. Petals had blown away from a white marble grave. Reds and pinks glistened against the sharp sunlight, littering the headstone. A young girl, perhaps sixteen, stared back at her from a faded photo, as though the color had drained from the picture and seeped into the flowers. She had a mischievous grin, and her black eyes sparkled. A prayer etched in Cyrillic script adorned the headstone, making it seem otherworldly or as though it belonged to a different age.

It broke Ava's heart to see a grave for someone so young, just a few years younger than herself. She picked up a white rose that had blown away and pressed it to her lips, inhaling the perfume of the petals.

Are you with my mother? she thought, her chest heavy with emotion for the deceased girl. *She would love you as if you were her own. She would love you as though you were me.*

She stared out into the cemetery, a sea of

marble and gravel. Some of the headstones were decayed, darkened with age, green with moss. The words on these graves were hand-etched, the letters arched like Gothic steeples. She wondered if there was anyone left to mourn their inhabitants. In the Old Country, the dead were buried in the family sepulcher, descendants and ancestors all piled in together, sharing their final resting place.

She kissed the white rose that had blown away and returned it to the young girl's headstone. She buried the flower deep within the center of a peach-and-violet wreath, scraping her finger on a thorn.

"Ouch!" she whispered inadvertently. A drop of blood had escaped from her fingertip, catching the white rose. It was enough to streak a single petal, the crimson exquisite against the colorless flower. She pressed her finger to her lips and gently sucked the wound until it no longer bled, the taste of copper making her dizzy and slightly ill.

She continued along the cemetery pathway, distracted by the faint thought that her mother was somewhere out there, somewhere between the forgotten headstones and the dead adolescent.

It felt as though she had been walking for hours when her eyes finally fell upon the familiar tomb, its black marble flecked with gold. Her chest slackened with grief, and she felt tears burn behind her eyes.

She approached slowly, biting back emotion at the sight of her mother's picture. Ava had loved that photo of her mother, her features exquisitely angular, the chin and corners of the jawbone feminine despite their sharpness. Her nose was delicate, centered between high cheekbones. She appeared distinctly Russian, a replica of some Slavic ancestress, with jet-black hair and deep-set liquid eyes—beautiful, haunting eyes. The young Katia was dressed in white silk and lace.

Ava touched the corner of the tomb and pursed her mouth as though to speak, but the words died on her lips. Despite the spring heat, the black marble was cool, the gold veins like thin snakes winding across the stone. The center of the grave had been hollowed out and filled with sacred pebbles blessed by village elders from the Old Country.

Fumbling in her purse, she found the small vial of jasmine-scented oil, its lid etched with florid letters. A memory echoed through Ava's mind of Katia teaching her to place a small drop of the perfumed oil on the tip of her finger and press it to her pulse points, then the corners of her neck. "Gently," she had whispered, "don't damage the scent."

As she carefully unscrewed the metal lid from the vial, jasmine escaped into the air.

"You can sleep now, *Majka*," she whispered in the Old Language. The grave did not answer. She became aware of just how bottomless the silence was. The vacant eyes of her mother stared out at her from behind their blackness. She suddenly felt ashamed, as though she had been disrespectful. She lowered her eyes and continued speaking.

"I married the one who murdered you." Her voice was shaking with emotion, the words barely above a whisper. "He's dead now—his brother too. All their land belongs to our family. Your curse is fulfilled. They are wiped out. They will be forgotten."

She tipped the contents of the small vial over the sacred stones. The scented oil glistened on the pebbles and soaked into the earth. She imagined the oil seeping down into the soil, penetrating the coffin and dripping into her mother's bones, carrying the message of revenge with it.

She toyed with the elaborate ring on her finger, inadvertently releasing the clasp to reveal the hidden inner chamber. The smell of bitter almonds permeated the air, mixing with the jasmine in perfect cadence with the scent. There was still a drop of cyanide in the ring, and the tawny liquid seeped onto her knuckles.

That beautiful crimson-amber liquid, the perfect color to blend with bourbon.

This story appears in *Bones*, edited by James Ward Kirk.

26 HAUNTING BEAUTY

he affair ended badly for all involved. Although I loved them both, no one was spared when the secrets came to light. Our shameful little secrets.

I still feel the slight tremble of unease, of fear, when the image of her aureate hair flickers in my mind.

But I had wanted it all so badly, more than it scared me, more than it broke my heart. We may have gotten away with it all, worked it all out, but she showed me what was inside that little mahogany box. Her secret. Her shame. It ruined us all.

——————◆◦•◦)◆(◦•◦————

I visited my brother and his wife a week before she died. "Died" is somewhat of a euphemism. Killed herself would be more accurate.

I remember her sitting in the wicker chaise on the deck of their beach house, a loose chamomile-colored shawl draped over her shoulders, concealing the swell in her stomach. She was five months pregnant at the time. The wooden deck of their holiday home spilled onto the bay before us. We sat in silence, watching the flawless azure sky bleed into the never-ending ocean.

She was unaware of how I watched her, how painfully I still longed for her, even though we hadn't been lovers for quite some time by then. She was oblivious to my suffering because she was consumed with her own, but I didn't know this at the time. I should have seen it in her eyes, those vacant orbs that stared at the sapphire sea, two flashes of emerald suspended in gelatinous crystal.

Eventually, she broke the silence.

"I'm not going to let myself feel anything until a week after the baby is born." Her lips moved in a soft pulsation of indifference that matched the glazed, faraway stare in her eyes. Her buttery voice hadn't yet lost the Sicilian accent of our homeland, even though we had left it all behind so long ago.

She discussed her pregnancy with almost total apathy, disconnection, as she absently petted the small Pomeranian on her lap. He twisted across her open palm, settling on his back as a small child would.

The image was somehow disturbing, as though her hands longed for an infant, but her mind and emotions were divorced from her body. The way she cradled and stroked the puppy was almost instinctual, maternal, but her eyes, the tone in her voice, they were so distant.

I shuddered and inhaled a quivering breath, shaking the thought from my mind. She didn't notice.

"It won't be like the first time. I won't fall in love with this one, not until it's born. Not until I know it's going to live." This was her second pregnancy, or at least the second of which I was aware. The first had ended during her sixteenth week, when the fetus was old enough to suck on its tiny thumb and cry silently within her. It had broken her, to lose that child. She was irrevocably changed.

We first became lovers in those dark days following her miscarriage. She thought the sun would never rise again. I was the perfect distraction, something forbidden, something to help her forget, an escape from the pain. By then, I had wanted her for so long, fantasized about her, about some accident befalling my brother so that I could take his place. In a haze of neediness, I had confessed it all to her, how I had wanted her since we had made the long journey across the Mediterranean and the Atlantic. In the claustrophobic confines of the ship, she had been a visual narcotic. Long limbed and iridescent skinned, she was a haunting beauty against the rancid air and moldy walls of the hull, a phantasm of lingering desire. She was forbidden, preying on me in the privacy of my own mind.

But she was my brother's possession, and she had fallen pregnant shortly before they were married. He had that way with women, a kind of brutish attractiveness that stirred their sexual appetite. I had tormented myself on the night of their wedding, listening to them make love through the thin walls of our flat. Imagining them together, the kissing, licking, sucking, and all the pleasure that went along with it.

During the first pregnancy, her body had blossomed. Everything seemed fuller, her lips like plump rosebuds and her cheeks dewy, accentuating her milk-and-honey complexion. An enigmatic scent emanated from her skin, like sugared water and jasmine. Something about that smell was intensely erotic, as though she were a crisp, ripe fruit, ready to be plucked from an orchard and eaten. But it didn't last.

In the days before her miscarriage, I had known instinctively that something was very wrong with her. Pale-blue veins had traced her limbs like phantom fingers, and her skin turned oddly translucent. When I saw the aubergine crescents under her eyes, I knew there was no longer a child to celebrate. Something within me had understood, even before I saw her crimson-streaked thighs and the splash of blood on the bed sheets.

She suffered alone through the miscarriage, even though I had been there to comfort her. My brother, the handsome young brute, entertained himself with whores and drinking and rarely came home before dawn. It was she and I in our own private world of pain. His absence was an unspoken shame between us. I felt that he blamed her, in his own ignorant, petty sort of way, and she fluttered into my arms like an injured butterfly because of this. I loved her. For all her fragile beauty and self-deprecation, I loved her.

I had taken her out on his boat the week after she lost the child, and we threw a gallon of pig's blood into the ocean to watch the sharks become crazed with bloodlust. I made love to her for the first time out there, on the floor of the old boat, the drops of pig's blood trickling around us and surrounding us in the ocean, as though we were at the center of a pulpy, pulsating heart. She lay there and let me take her, never resisting, never hesitating. When it was over, she smeared some of the blood across my lips and closed her eyes, whispering that she and I would make a family together.

But we hadn't been lovers for more than a year now. A void of apathy had formed between us.

A bird cutting the water wrenched me from my memories. It sliced a fish in half with its beak, the entrails kissing the surface of the ocean in a gory mess.

I glanced at her, wrapped in her silk-and-honey shawl, her lips drawn in a hard line of contemplation. For an instant, I thought she had digressed with me, followed me into that whirlpool of emotion and memory. How self-indulgent to think such a thing, as though thoughts of our past were the only thing on her mind.

"Do you still know how to love?" My words came out colder than I had anticipated. They were laced with my own selfish pain. Even after all this time, her rejection still bit at my insides, gnawing at me until I couldn't control myself.

For a second, she flicked her gaze at me. A ghost of emotion pulsed through those emerald orbs and then dissolved. Her eyes were paradise, and I was locked inside.

I reached over and took her hand, pulling it to my lips and kissing her palm. Despite the heat, her flesh was streaked with lavender, and I feared that this pregnancy would also end in misery.

"Stop it!" she spat, snatching her hand back as though I'd bitten it. The pup on her lap stirred and yelped with irritation as he jumped to the floor.

"He's already so angry with me," she paused, her brows drawing together ever so slightly, betraying the coolness of her tone. "They made a mistake, at the clinic. We thought we were having a boy again. But they were wrong. It's actually a girl. Your brother can't stand to look at me."

In that instant, I understood what she was thinking. *I lost the one who mattered. I lost the male child.* The old, ignorant village standards were still burned into our minds. Even though we lived half a world away now, we still carried the old traditions and the prejudices that went along with them.

I took her hand again, and this time she didn't resist. But she refused to look at me. Her eyes wouldn't meet mine. She was every fantasy I had ever wanted. Every desire, every forbidden, shameful impulse I ever hid in my mind. My lips traveled up her forearm, and I pulled her to her feet. She relented, scratched at my hair as she bit my lip, her tongue licking at my mouth and her hands moving over my breasts.

She forced me down onto the chaise with her, the butter-colored shawl dropping to the ground in a flutter of silk and cream. The pregnancy had swollen her breasts and darkened her nipples. I kissed at her skin hungrily as she pulled at my skirt and then my panties, our sweet scents mixing in the salty kiss of sea air.

A week later she was dead. Alone, she took the boat out into the bay and threw blood into the ocean. She dived into the center of that burgundy pool. I imagined her sinking, descending into that throbbing, liquid heart that she had created in the isolated sea.

Only the top half of her torso was found when she eventually washed onto the shore. They said she had water in her lungs, that she had drowned before the sharks got to her.

But I'm not so sure.

When it was over, we lay tangled with one another, limb upon limb, and my fingertips traced the curve of her thigh, tickled by the nest of her curls surrounding her private chasm.

My hand came to rest on her swollen abdomen, and for a second, my breath choked in my throat.

I imagined the tiny fetus in her womb, a translucent creature with black eyes pulsing in rhythm with her heart. Black eyes, the eyes of my brother.

My brother. Then I knew. Then I understood. I realized why she had miscarried and why she would lose this child as well.

"My brother is sick, isn't he?"

My question hung heavy in the air. She met my gaze then, finally, and I saw the recognition in her eyes, as though she had been waiting for me to figure it out all along.

"Come," she whispered, her voice like melted butter. "I want to show you something."

She took my hand in hers and led me into the beach house. She didn't bother to dress or conceal her body.

I followed the crease of her buttocks with my eyes, the way her hip sashayed as she softly padded through the house. She glanced back at me, warmth and sadness intertwined in her eyes.

We took the wooden stairs down to the basement that my brother had converted into a studio for her. Candles lined the stairs, as the electricity had been disconnected during the renovations. A strange smell hung in the damp air. Familiar, sickly sweet, like rotten fruit.

Rot. It was the smell of putrefaction.

"Apollonia—" I started, but she had already let go of my hand. She was walking into the shadow-drenched corner of her studio. My heart began to thud in my chest, and I felt the prickle of anxiety in my gut. There was no mistaking it now. The smell grew intense, overwhelming my senses and clouding my mind.

She was no longer visible, swallowed whole by the darkness.

Then she emerged, like a sea nymph from the water; she walked out of the shadows into the soft, pulsating candle glow. Her hair, like fine-spun gold, snaked around the nape of her neck, trickling onto her breasts. Her skin was unnaturally pale in the candlelight, flawless, as though carved from marble. Her emerald eyes throbbed in time with the candles, with the walls, with the soft thudding of my heart.

In her hands, she held the small mahogany box.

"I brought this with me from Sicily. The only treasure I ever possessed." Her eyes had that faraway look again. She traced a finger over the ornate carvings on the lid. The side that faced me had a detailed illustration of the volcano, Etna, our home. Lava and smoke spewed from the wooden picture, and as my eyes fumbled their way down the fiery path, I saw the depiction of the old Doric temple from our village.

"You asked me if he is sick. Of course he is! He is infested with diseases from his whores!" Venom drenched her voice as she spat the words. She was absently walking toward me, the stench intensified with every step. Instinctively, a hand flew to my mouth to suppress a gag. "His sickness is the reason I miscarried. It is why I could never have a family!" Her face was contorted with fury, possessed by a foul mask of emotion that I couldn't fully interpret.

A mixture of rage and grief clawed at her features, and there was a shimmer of something else in her eyes, a quality I could only recognize as a reflection of myself. Some kind of bestial, primitive self, scratching through the layers of civility and emotional repression.

She was only inches from me, her eyes flashing and her fingers clutching the box so tightly that her knuckles were like pearls against the mahogany.

"He's the reason I lost the boy, why I lost my son." Emotion cracked her voice, and her eyes fell to the box in her hands. Then I understood exactly what was inside, why she had needed to show me the source of her misery.

I opened my mouth to speak, to beg her to stop, not to show me the contents of the box. But the air caught in my lungs, and a choked, raspy breath escaped my lips instead.

She lifted the wooden latch on the lid. The stench became unbearable. Rotten meat and sulfur.

"My son," she whispered, the anger draining from her face. She pulled back the mahogany lid to reveal a pulpy, bloody mess inside.

I tried not to look, tried not to see the small black eyes. Those tiny, misshapen orbs covered in a milky-blue film of decomposition.

Those eyes, like drops of onyx, which never saw the light of day.

This story appears in *What Lies Beneath*, edited by Dorothy Davies.

27 KISS OF DEATH

he awoke with a faint sense of disgust in the pit of her stomach. Her mind was not yet lucid, still laced with disorientation from the brief, fitful sleep that had possessed her during the early hours of the morning. Her limbs ached with heaviness. Her mouth was painfully dry, and her lips felt cracked at the corners. She swallowed bitterly, with difficulty, as though she were trying to force a rock down her throat. Her hand fumbled across the items on her bedside table in search of the glass of

water she had placed there the night before. The haziness of sleep hadn't yet left her vision, and she couldn't distinguish her surroundings, only large, blurry patches of light and dark. Her fingers brushed against the coolness of the glass, and she brought the water to her lips.

She had almost swallowed her second gulp when she realized something was wrong. The liquid was too thick; it was viscous and tasted of salt and metal. Something twitched inside her mouth, and instinctively, she spat the fluid on the floor. The glass slipped from her fingers and smashed on the tiles, causing her muscles to violently clench at the sound.

Apprehensively, she switched on her bedside lamp and examined the mess on the floor. As she realized what she had drunk, her throat constricted in disgust, and a spasm of nausea shocked her insides.

The glass had been filled with rotted blood. Viscous, black blood was slowly seeping across the white tiles where the glass had shattered. Maggots, their bodies bloated from feeding on the rancid fluid, were crawling toward her, slithering up her slender legs. In the dim lamplight, their translucent skin was a foul, hepatic shade, mixed with black clots of undigested blood.

Clumsily, she fell from the bed and ran toward the adjoining en suite, not caring if she stepped on shattered glass and cut herself in the process. The maggots squished under her feet and felt pulpy as their remains wedged between her toes. Her lungs were on fire, and the breath was constricted in her throat. The acid shot up her chest, and vomit bubbled at the back of her throat.

In her haste, she crashed against the opened door of her armoire, causing the full-length mirror attached to the door to shake in its frame. For an instant, she froze, fear prickling down her spine.

In the reflection, she saw a man. He stood behind her, watching her, his lips curled in a brutal smile.

He was little more than an outline, a hazy silhouette against the dimly lit room. He wore a black hat tipped at the side, the brim partially obscuring his features. But she could see enough to recognize the look on his face, the anger burning behind his eyes as he stared at her. He traced his tongue across his bottom lip and reached out his hand to grab her by the nape of her neck. She blinked. The mirror swung open and shut, and he disappeared.

Terrified, she staggered into the bathroom and fumbled with the tap, frantically rinsing her mouth. Her hands shook uncontrollably, and the water slipped through her fingers. She splashed some water on her face but couldn't wash away the thick drizzle of blood that had stained her bottom lip and run down her chin. Anxiously, she scratched at her face until her skin was raw and the blood was no longer visible.

She leaned over the small basin, breathing heavily, her hands clutching the porcelain edges tighter than she realized, so hard that her knuckles looked like giant white beads and her fingers went numb. The cool white tiles of the bathroom suddenly felt like the satin lining of a coffin, the walls tightening around her, smothering her. Staring at her reflection, she didn't recognize the girl in the mirror, the disheveled teenager with pallid skin and a badly scratched face. Wild, crazed eyes stared back her, with bloodstained lips quivering behind a veil of matted black hair.

I can't go on like this.

She contemplated telling her father that the visions had returned. That would mean another trip to San Sebastián, back to the institution. She tensed at the idea of being confined to the hospital again. The therapy, the shock treatments, the entire process would drag on for months until she was so worn down that violent images no longer scared her. Even the humiliation of being stripped naked and searched for self-inflicted cuts wore away after a few weeks. She had learned to hide those tiny slivers of pleasure where even the nurse couldn't find them—on the delicate fold of skin between her inner thigh and her sex.

The electroshock therapy seemed to work for a brief time, to fry her mind into submission. But it came with a price—it killed a small part of her with it. Every time she returned home from the hospital, her body was thin and frail, pumped full of antipsychotics. She felt misplaced, a foreigner in her own skin. A part of her had evaporated, dissolved by the drugs. She didn't have the energy, the strength, to endure another stay in that little piece of hell.

But she needed help, and there was only one way she could think to help herself.

Feverishly, she rifled through the bathroom drawers until she found the little white bottle of pills that she had hidden there two years ago—her safety net if things ever got too dark. "Temazanine," she whispered, reading the clinical blue letters on the bottle. "For the relief of insomnia. Do not exceed the recommended dose."

One hundred sleeping pills. One hundred tiny kisses of death. A brief thrill of excitement danced in her stomach as she rattled the bottle, causing the pills to chime against each other. She ripped off the lid and placed one in her mouth, swallowing it dryly. It was like a candied breath upon her lips, sweet and filled with the promise of rest.

But a sobering thought flooded her mind. She had to make it look like an accident somehow, or her father would feel responsible, as though he had failed her. She couldn't do that to him, not after what he had gone through with her mother's suicide. No, she would not be so cruel.

There were also scissors in her drawer. She could cut her thigh with them, as though they had dropped from her hands accidentally. Or perhaps if she bashed her head against the side of the bathtub, he would think she had slipped. She could throw water on the floor, make it look like she had been clumsy while climbing out of the shower.

Suicide. The word echoed in her ears. No, she would make it a clever accident. She would even fool herself into believing it was unintentional, just a tragic mishap that resulted in her death.

"Dolores."

Her head whipped up, and her muscles tensed as she saw the reflection in the mirror.

The man had returned. He was standing directly behind her, whispering in her ear.

His tongue slowly traced his bottom lip, revealing his teeth, a rotted collection of yellow bones in his mouth.

She tried to scream, but his hand clamped violently against her lips.

"Hush," he mouthed, his breath hot and foul against her skin. "There'll be plenty time for screaming when I'm done."

He's not real! He's not real!

But she could *feel* his nails cutting against her skin, the hot breath blowing on her neck. It was tactile; she was lucid.

This wasn't a vision.

She writhed against him and tried to reach for the scissors.

Too late.

He brought the blades to her abdomen and stabbed them violently between her ribs. Her white nightgown instantly soaked red with blood.

He forced the blades down until he had split her open to her groin. The cut was jagged and thick, and she stared helplessly as bone-white intestines spilled into the sink before her.

He laughed, a bitter, half-crazed cackle, and he ran his tongue across her neck, lapping at the sweat that had pooled at her shoulder. He pulled her head back and locked his rotted mouth upon her lips.

"Just like your mother," he whispered.

This story appears in *Blood and Guts*, edited by Briana Stoddard.

28 ARA'S MARK

Rest didn't come easily to Ara that night. She lay in the dark for hours, her mind liquid and entwined with thoughts that were not her own. Try as she might, she couldn't rid herself of the terror that was seeping into her body. She was feeling *it*, experiencing *it*, over and over again. She opened her mouth to breathe, but icy water rushed into her lungs. She was choking, coughing for air, struggling to scream and tear the hands away from her body. So many hands—holding her down, forcing her to swallow bitter mouthfuls of viscous black fluid.

Then the vision dissolved, and she was alone in her bed, her body violently shivering against the sweat-drenched sheets.

Hours passed. She kept her eyes squeezed shut, fearful of what she would see if she opened them. The silence was rigid, veiling her in its noiseless infinity, accentuating the chattering voices in her mind.

Frustrated with her nervous energy, she struggled to summon enough courage to get out of bed. She sat up, feeling lost and enveloped by the jewel-black darkness that surrounded her.

Ever since childhood, Ara had been able to see exceptionally well in the dark. Her vision slowly adjusted to the absence of light until, eventually, the silhouette of her bookcase became visible. The night was transformed into a graphite perfume, a soft-gray ether drowning her bedroom. Her Burmese cat stirred quietly at the side of her bed, groaning in her sleep before she resumed her silent breathing.

Ara's hands fumbled across her nightstand, her fingers clumsy and eager. She was searching for the little vial of pills that would soften her thoughts and hush the screaming silence that bit at her ears. Insomnia was a common companion for Ara. Her mind was claustrophobic; too many thoughts were fighting for her attention. The sleeplessness sometimes wore her down to the point of delirium, where she could no longer function normally, where every stranger became a hollow-faced corpse and every smell sickened her, as though the world about her were rotting from the inside out.

After a liaison with her candied pearls, she could sleep for sixteen hours unbroken. Then the cycle would start again. The little sweets caused rebound insomnia, and she would find herself reliving the restlessness, chained to her bed, too exhausted to move and too wired to sleep.

Her fingers knocked against the pill bottle, and a brief thrill of anticipation fluttered in her stomach. She loved the pop of the vial's lid, the sound resonating against the silence, causing her mouth to salivate slightly. She kissed the bottle against her lips and threw it back like a shot of whiskey.

Empty.

She groaned heavily into the vacant air and threw the vial across the room.

Dejected, she hugged her arms against her body, the cool night air painting her skin with seeds as she emerged from the bed. Her satin slip offered no warmth as it hung suggestively around her wide hips and full breasts. She enjoyed the feel of the fabric against her skin. It was sensual, natural. It stirred an instinctive longing, the pang of sexual desire bleeding with her fear. She wanted a body in her bed, soft hands playing with the lace trim of her slip, its crimson color like blood against her skin.

Absently, she traced a finger over the birthmark on her wrist, just as Yasmina had many times in the past after a long night of sweat and bedroom violence.

But she hadn't been with Yasmina in over a year.

She tiptoed lightly toward the window of her bedroom. A crescent moon watched her from behind lace curtains and frost-bitten glass. The patterns in the lace created luminous figures who danced upon the bedroom floor and across Ara's toes. She paused briefly, staring back at the bone-colored sliver of the moon, asking it silent questions and deriving some comfort in its absent replies. At least one thing was constant.

"You match my birthmark tonight," she said, holding her wrist up to the velvet sky. A wispy cloud stretched across the crescent, its gray, skeletal fingers lacerating the moonlight. Ara found the tableau intensely disturbing, and she snatched back her arm, hiding the mark defensively against her chest.

The bottom of her bookshelf was lined with her favorite novels. She ran her finger over the well-worn spines of the books, recognizing the titles by their thickness. No particular narrative called out to her through the darkness. Not a single novel seemed to speak her language that night. She toyed playfully with *The Count of Monte Cristo*; she found Haidée intensely erotic. Then her fingers felt something thicker, a rough, stiff cover she didn't recognize. She slid the book out from its tight fit on the shelf.

Definitely not mine. Where on earth did this come from?

She couldn't make out the title in the dark. Ara slinked back to her bed and pulled the sheets about her. She flicked on the bedside lamp and gazed in astonishment at the beautifully bound leather cover. It was a deep shade of burgundy, with strings of gold thread woven down the spine, the ends of the pages colored in the same deep-aureate tone. The title was etched in a beautiful, florid script.

Umbra.

No author.

Her Latin was rusty, but she recognized the word.

"Shadow," she whispered, her voice dissolving into the silence like smoke.

She pried the cover open with difficulty. The book was stiff and very old. The pages were the color of café au lait, and some were illustrated with elaborate pictures, hand-drawn in a dark-violet ink. She paused at an intensely disturbing image: an ethereal young girl, her hair and eyelashes exceptionally thick, standing in a body of water so that only her large, liquid eyes and forehead were visible.

What haunting eyes, Ara thought.

Eyes that could draw you into their sadness, the emotion painted upon them so vividly. Eyes that could drown you in the lagoon the young girl was standing in. The tips of her lower-lid eyelashes gently kissed the water; her tears slipped softly into the surrounding liquid. She wore petals in her hair, and a few had become dislodged, floating about her as her tresses and the water blended into a single, violet fluid.

Ara turned the pages slowly and inadvertently gasped when she saw the next sketch. It was the same young girl, violet curls and flower petals, but this time she was floating on her back, upon a roughly made wooden raft. Her eyes were closed, covered with two small coins. Her arms had been crossed over her chest, but one hand had fallen by her side so that her fingers hung limply against her body. She was draped in a thin dress, the fabric almost translucent, causing the curves of her flesh to show through. Her rose petal nipples were like lipstick stains upon her chest, a chest that no longer heaved with breath. It was sunken with mortality.

There was a small script beneath the picture. Ara struggled to translate the words in her mind.

"...in punishment for her ancestor the witch was drowned and then placed upon the fluid altar of Lythy, as an offering to Artemis Limnatis, the goddess of the Lake. Place of capture: Bibinje, 1689."

"How horrible!" Ara whispered, her heart breaking for the childlike beauty who had been drowned. She struggled to read the surrounding page in the dim lamplight.

"...the maiden, who was in possession of beauty so bewitching that her eyes alone could seduce any man, woman, or beast, was with child when the villagers of Bibinje drowned her. She was unwed, having already borne a female progeny—the union was determined to be with the pre-Christian god Apollo

Pythius. The worshippers of the sect of Pandora were able to recover her corpse from the Christians and anoint her in the ancient custom, with the hope that the witch would be revived by tasting the blood of her descendants."

Ara squinted to see the sketched picture more closely. There was definitely something—a mark of some sort—on the witch's wrist, black against the wispy sleeve and lavender petals.

Frantically, she fumbled through the contents of her bedside table, searching for the antique magnifying glass she had hidden in one of the drawers. The emerald in the center of its handle glistened in the dim lighting of her room, signaling its location.

She pressed the glass to her eye and focused on the small marking, a brief thrill of terror bursting through her spine as she realized what it was.

A crescent-shaped birthmark—identical to Ara's mark—the waxing moon, just below the Mount of Luna on her left wrist.

Ara's eyes frantically worked over the text on the adjoining page. She struggled to string the words together, looking for anything that would hint at the significance of the birthmark.

Nothing.

She couldn't identify a single word in relation to the markings on the witch's wrist—on her *own* wrist.

Blinded by frustration, she shut the book heavily and stalked back to her bookcase. She pulled out her Latin dictionary and settled back into her bed, determined to translate the book from cover to cover.

She was lost somewhere around the twentieth page of her translation when she felt the tingle on her thigh. Fingertips, gentle pinpricks, tickling the flesh where the lace of her slip met her skin.

She didn't immediately see the hand that touched her, but oddly, it didn't alarm her. The long, slender hand of a woman, with beautiful fingers that delivered delicious strokes across her thigh and gently moved up toward her pulsating sex. Ara's eyes traveled up the arm to the woman's naked bust. Ivory breasts, decorated with violet curls and a delicate collarbone.

Inexplicably, the dull lamplight had faded, and the woman was a silhouette against the darkness, a faint shadow against the night. She lay on her side, her head resting on her tilted arm, with her eyes adoring Ara, her lips in a provocative state of anticipation. Her fingers traveled across Ara's sex, drawing the sweet juices from their hiding spot and painting them across her inner lips. Ara felt a strong, constant pulsation in her clitoris, in perfect cadence with the finger strokes of her stranger.

A crescendo started to rise in her blood, a steady hammering dancing through her veins. She let her eyes fall shut, her eyelids like two erotic bodies pressed together.

The stranger's mouth was upon her breasts. Firm lips, with sharp teeth biting into her flesh until a drizzle of hot blood spilled down her erect nipples. The teeth scratched at her in the darkness, the biting growing harder with each frenzied stroke between her thighs.

Ara was on the verge of tipping over, of swimming in the showering orgasm, when the stranger stopped, the lyrical stroking coming to an abrupt end.

Something hard and sharp drove into Ara, stabbing deep into her chasm, painful and perfectly satisfying. She moaned with agony, with pleasure, her hands gripping the body that was upon her. She drove her hips to the rhythm of the stranger. Ara bit deep into the shoulder that smothered her face, expecting to taste salt and skin, but the stranger was like a candied breath upon her tongue. She arched her back beneath the shadow, writhing and moaning in rapture. The long, thick strokes drove her to orgasm, and she rode the hot waves until the tingle passed all through her body. Her flesh was wet with perspiration, but she felt the hot juice of the stranger against her thigh.

She had sunk into her bed, panting for breath, when she noticed a subtle noise in the air. It parodied the crescendo of her blood, rising gently until it surrounded her, a terrifying cacophony. She didn't recognize the sound at first, it had been so delicate, but now it was everywhere, the overwhelming cackle, the guttural laughter. The silhouette with adoring eyes was dissolving, dissipating before her vision.

The stranger had vanished. She had faded like an erotic memory. The night air hung heavy with the taunting echo of the laughter—a horrible, mocking, victorious sound. The cat had been hissing viciously, the hair on her spine raised with anger, but Ara had not heard the creature; she had been locked within the vision. The cat stalked her bed, ready to attack.

The book lay open against her thigh. The inside cover, previously blank, was now wet with writing—rough letters, scratched upon the paper with the faint blood that had drizzled from the bite on Ara's breast, written in the same florid script as the title.

Now I've tasted the witch.

This story appears in *Magically Delicious*, edited by Brianna Stoddard.

29 SACRÈ COEUR

ardens of light die away
Lovers' love begins to stray
Kingdoms crumble and
rulers flee
But still my heart belongs to
thee

ABOUT THE AUTHOR

Marija grew up in a delicatessen, with a multiethnic family, where pickling cabbage and knife throwing were taught at an early age. She would scribble stories on butcher's paper, which would then be passed on to unsuspecting customers when they received their groceries.

She lives in Sydney with her husband (*el carnicero*), her daughter, and a bunch of pirate pets.

www.marijaelektrarodriguez.com

ALSO BY MARIJA ELEKTRA RODRIGUEZ

The Remains of Beauty & Other Stories

The Anatomy of Insomnia & Other Stories

Through a Glass Darkly & Other Stories

Lazaretto & Other Stories

The Cult of Persephone & Other Stories

The House of Atreus & Other Stories

Violet & Other Stories

Children of the Dark & Other Stories

Notre Dame & Other Stories

Haunting Beauty & Other Stories

In Love with Drowning & Other Stories